Trust No Man 3

**Lock Down Publications
Presents
Trust No Man 3
A Novel by
*Ca$h***

Lock Down Publications
P.O. Box 1482
Pine Lake, Ga 30072-1482

Visit our website at **www.lockdownpublications.com**

First Edition 2009
Printed in the United States of America
This is a work of fiction. Names, characters, places, and incidents either are products of the author's imagination or are used fictitiously. Any similarity to actual events or locales or persons, living or dead, is entirely coincidental.

Cover design and layout by: Marion's Design
Book interior design by: Shawn Walker
Edited by: Shawn Walker

Stay Connected with Us!

Text **LOCKDOWN** to 22828 to stay up-to-date with new releases, sneak peaks, contests and more…

Submission Guideline.

Submit the first three chapters of your completed manuscript to ldpsubmissions@gmail.com, subject line: Your book's title. The manuscript must be in a .doc file and sent as an attachment. Document should be in Times New Roman, double spaced and in size 12 font. Also, provide your synopsis and full contact information. If sending multiple submissions, they must each be in a separate email.

Have a story but no way to send it electronically? You can still submit to LDP/Ca$h Presents. Send in the first three chapters, written or typed, of your completed manuscript to:

LDP: Submissions Dept
Po Box 1482
Pine Lake, Ga 30072

DO NOT send original manuscript. Must be a duplicate.

Provide your synopsis and a cover letter containing your full contact information.

Thanks for considering LDP and Ca$h Presents.

Ca$h

PROLOGUE
The Execution of a Street Legend
March 3, 2003

Four guards and the warden led Youngblood into the state's death room at the Diagnostic Center in Jackson, Georgia. With respect to his culture, no chaplain accompanied him. Youngblood did not need a figurative crutch. He was ready to face his execution the same way he lived: *With no fear.* He had, by stopping his appeal, told the state to bring it on. Well, tonight, they were bringing it.

Juanita, Poochie and Swag were present as witnesses, per Youngblood's request. His mother, Ann, had declined to attend the legalized murder of her child. She wanted to be there to say goodbye to him, but she knew they would have had to kill her, too, because as soon as they strapped her baby to that gurney, she would've acted a fool.

Three witnesses for the state were also present. They sat outside of the viewing window along with Youngblood's family and friends.

Juanita and Poochie held hands, giving one another strength. Swag put a hand on top of theirs.

"Try to stay strong," he whispered.

Youngblood saw their faces through the viewing window. He flashed them a strong smile and tapped his heart with his fist. Then they restrained his hands and there was no resistance from him when he was strapped down on the gurney.

"Do you have any final words?" asked the warden, a black puppet.

Youngblood turned his head to the side so he could see his people. The death room had a PA system so his voice could be heard clearly.

"Tell my Ma Dukes that I love her, and that my choices were my own. They, in no way, reflected on her. Tell all my seeds that I leave here at peace because I trust that they'll be all right. Tell 'em I love 'em. Poochie, thanks for being here. I love you."

"I love you, too," mouthed Poochie.

"Swag, you held me down, fam'. Stay thorough and you'll rape the rap game. Juanita, baby, no words can suffice. So I'll just say you represent my legacy. You and my tribe. I love you, Queen. Knowledge, knowledge," he concluded, which meant *peace* in their culture.

"Peace, god, I love you," Juanita said aloud.

"Hold Inez down," added Youngblood.

Juanita nodded, wiping away tears that poured down despite the strength she was trying hard to maintain.

Youngblood smiled his understanding and blew her a kiss. "Swag," he stated, "tell the streets I said: *disloyalty is unforgivable and Trust No Man.*"

Youngblood then turned his head toward the warden. "Bring it on," he said with a brave heart.

When the death fluid was pumped into his arms, Youngblood did not flinch. He locked eyes with Juanita and relinquished his life, dying with his eyes open, smiling at his queen.

"I love you, always, baby," Juanita whispered through her tears, as she realized Youngblood was gone.

Poochie stood up from her seat in the viewing room, clutching her Bible so tightly that her knuckles were white. She glanced in the window one last time and saw that Youngblood's head had fallen slack in death, but his eyes remained fixed on them as if he were observing their reaction. Briefly, Poochie was afraid to move, unsure if her step would be steady enough to support her trembling legs.

"Lord, you promised not to put more burdens on me than I can bear so I'm trusting in you," she said silently. She knew His power. What she didn't know was how she was going to be able to help stem the immense anger that Youngblood's execution would breed in Lil' T, Youngblood's son by her daughter, Shan. "I'm giving it all to you, Lord," Poochie said, as she felt Swag holding her up on one side and Juanita supporting her on the other.

They exited the room with heavy hearts. Swag was bristling inside. His nigga was gone. He knew Youngblood's legend would live on because street niggas in the A would forever recall how Youngblood had put his robbery and murder game down and then stared death in the face, telling those crackers to bring it on. Swag planned to glorify that in his music. There was no way he wouldn't tell the streets how his fam' went out like the gangsta that he had been in life.

"And I'ma hold your fam' down, my nigga," Swag vowed.

He looked at Juanita to see how she was holding up as they made their way down the long hall that led to the entrance. He saw Juanita release Poochie's arm and then cover her face with both hands and began to sob. Swag let go of Poochie's other arm and reached out for Juanita.

She fainted into his arms.

Painful Reactions...
Kentucky Correctional Institution for Women

Three years into a seven-year bid for her role in a murder committed by Youngblood, but unrelated to the murders for which he was executed, Youngblood's ride or die chick, Inez, was heartbroken by the news that her boo had been put to death.

"Nooooo!" cried out Inez, sinking to her knees on the cold bare floor of her cell.

Her cellmate turned off the radio to spare Inez more grief from the sad news. Tears streamed down Inez' face in rivers.

"Baby—baby—baby." She sobbed as she made it up and onto her knees, laying her head on a pile of letters she received from Youngblood from death row.

She looked up to search through the pile for the very last letter he had written her. It had arrived yesterday. Finding it, she read the words once more.

Hello Beautiful,
The time is nearing when I'll depart this earth in the physical but I know I'll forever be alive in your heart. Real talk, shawdy, I've never known a woman who was a rider like you. You didn't just ride until the wheels came off, you rode on an axle and hope. When those crackers pressured you to flip, you gave 'em the finger. That's the same toughness I expect you to show when I close my eyes for the last time. If muthafuckas think you'll fold when I'm gone, they don't know the boss female I loved and respected to the utmost. Baby girl, a nigga's love for you can't be expressed with words, it's too deep. Just know that as I count down my final hours, I'll be reminiscing about you, wishing I

could hold you just one more time and whisper these three words in your ear: I Love You.

Inez could read no further because her tears blinded her. It felt like his soft lips were pressed against her ear and his strong arms were wrapped around her. But she knew that neither could ever happen again. He was dead.

She picked up a picture of him that she had cut out of Don Diva. "I'm going to miss you so much!" She turned the radio back on to hear what else was being broadcasted about her baby's daddy.

In tribute of Youngblood, the station was blasting *Missing You* by *Puff Daddy*, featuring *Faith* and *112*.

Life ain't always what it seems to be/ words can't express what you mean to me/ even though you're gone we're still a team...

Inez' sobs echoed throughout the cellblock.

"I know it hurts, chick," her cellie, Brandi, said, wrapping a motherly arm around Inez.

"Yes, it does," Inez said as she wept.

For the past three years as Youngblood sat on Georgia's death row awaiting an execution date, Inez had known that this day would eventually come, but knowing it hadn't made it any easier on her heart. The ache in her chest doubled her over. Inez buried her face in Brandi's lap and sobbed.

"Hold on to the fond memories and let go of everything else," said Brandi. But even to her own ears that sounded impossible. From the many long talks that they had shared, Brandi knew that Inez' love for Youngblood was epic, and so would be her pain.

"What a life to take/ what a bond to break...I'll be missing you." Inez tried to sing along with the song on the radio.

There was no melody to her tone, just pure heartache. She wept for his children, his mother and herself as memories of Youngblood flashed through her mind and the pain rose up to choke off the next verse of the song before it could come out of her mouth.

"I'll never stop loving him," she vowed once the sobs calmed down a bit.

"I know, baby. I know." Brandi's voice was consoling.

"Even his death won't break our bond."

***

No bond is stronger than the bond between mother and child. Ann was at home praying that the phone call she awaited from Poochie would bring news that there had been a stay of execution.

"My Father in Heaven, blessed be they name. I know that my son has forsaken you. But, oh Lord, I have served you faithfully even when you took Toi away and I wanted to give up. But I trusted in you, Lord. I don't ask you for much, so please hear this prayer. He's my first born. Please don't take him away from me. Touch his heart and may he preach your word from inside the prison. Give ear to my words, oh Lord. Consider my meditation. Give heed to the voice of my cry, my King and God, to you I pray."

The shrill ringing of the telephone interrupted her prayer. She jumped as if she were frightened by the sound.

"I'll answer it," her husband said. He had been at prayer, by her side.

They rose up together. "Lord, if you must, take my life and spare my child's," she prayed.

Her husband reached for the cordless phone on the nightstand. "Hello?" He listened to the caller without saying a word. Finally, he replied, "Thank you." Behind him, Ann's body shook with nervousness. She tried to read the expression on his face once he turned. A pregnant silence quickened her heartbeat. "I'm sorry. He's gone," he finally said.

Ann fainted across his arms.

***

Meanwhile, up in the A, another one of Youngblood's baby mama's hadn't kept it thorough at all while Youngblood was alive, and now that he had just been killed by the state, the guilt of her shady acts had her by the throat. Cheryl's arm went around her daughters as they listened to the television reporter announce that Youngblood's execution was successfully carried out.

"What is executed, Mama?" asked eight-year-old Eryka.

"Yeah mama, what's exemacuted?" chimed her sister who was only eleven months younger.

Cheryl didn't know what to tell them. They both loved their daddy so much it was heartbreaking. They had been toddlers when she ran off with them and Youngblood's million-dollar stash.

That was so lowdown, she admonished herself now. Because even though Youngblood had emotionally abused her, he had been very loving to his children.

Cheryl had thought that without money Youngblood wouldn't be so arrogant, and that a cold taste of karma would make him nicer. Obviously, she had been wrong. Her thievery had brought out the beast in him. But she also knew his more gentle side. Memories of him giving her a piggy back ride and playing hide and seek with the girls came rushing back in still photos in her mind. Yes, he'd been a killer, but he'd also been her dude and her first love.

I'm sorry for what I did to you, she thought. Cheryl's shoulders rocked as guilt welled up inside of her.

"Mama, what's wrong?" asked Eryka, hugging her while Chante tried to wipe away her tears.

"I'm okay." Cheryl sniffled.

Somehow, she found the words to explain to her daughters what *executed* meant. Their cries wounded her heart and when Youngblood's mug shot flashed on the television screen again, Chante ran up to the flat screen and kissed her daddy's face, announcing, "Nope, Mama, my daddy ain't dead."

Cherly, hearing this, began to weep harder.

Later, after she had sent them off to bed and looked in on her five and four-year old sons, she passed her mother on the way to the bathroom.

"They killed Youngblood tonight," she reported somberly.

"Humph!"

"Dag, you could show some sympathy."

Her mother turned to face her and blared, "Did he have any sympathy for me when he kicked in my door and attacked me? What about all those people he killed? Did he have any sympathy for them? You know, the good Lord said *an eye for an eye*." With that, she continued into the bedroom, leaving Cheryl's mouth agape.

It took every ounce of strength in Cheryl's body not to react. *He is still your granddaughters' father!* She kept her rants to herself as she went into the bathroom and closed the door behind her.

She ran a tub of hot water and undressed. Memories flooded her brain, causing tears to fall again.

I shouldn't have allowed myself to get fat. I knew he wanted a showpiece. That was my fault. It was dead ass wrong for me to steal his money from him, knowing he'd give me the world. And to take his kids? Who was I hurting? My girls that's who. That's probably what gave me that "fuck the world" attitude.

Then there were the things that Youngblood had never found out about. After Cheryl had gained weight and lost Youngblood's interest, his indifference toward her had crushed her. To get even, Cheryl had fucked damn near every nigga in the apartment complex where she, Youngblood and the kids lived. She thought that would make her feel better, but it had made her feel worse. *I'm a ho. Worse. A fat ass ho.*

She couldn't blame him for no longer desiring her. She knew no man wanted a fat bitch who couldn't keep her legs closed.

He hadn't let her down. It was she who had failed to measure up to what he needed. It destroyed her to know he died without ever forgiving her. Her torrent of tears dripped into the bath water as she reached for the Gillette razor on the side counter. I sold him out just as badly as his partner did. She shivered as she thought of her betrayal.

There was only one thing she could do to atone. She swiped her wrist with the razor and was surprised not to feel any pain. The razor made a thin but deep cut across her wrist. Closing her eyes, she cut deeper.

As the blood dripped from Cheryl's wrist down into the water, across town the one who had betrayed Youngblood the worst was feeling no guilt at all.

***

The CO unlocked the cell door and six hardened convicts stepped inside. Every one of them were strapped with long sharp metal shanks.

"You snitch muthafucka! Your testimony got a thorough nigga the needle, and now your ass gonna die an even slower death," threatened the biggest one in the bunch.

Lonnie wore the look of a snitch who knew his reckoning day had arrived. He slowly backed into a corner and began to plead, "Man, I ain't have no choice. Those white folks were gonna give me and Delina life without parole."

"Stupid nigga, you ended up with life without anyway!"

"But I freed my girl."

"If ya bitch couldn't do a bid, you should've never taken her on the lick. Snitchin' is inexcusable. Because of rat muthafuckas like you, a lot of good niggas have fallen." His mammoth fist crashed into Lonnie's mouth, causing his head to slam into the wall behind him.

When Lonnie tried to fight back, the others attacked.

"CO! CO! Help me, please!" he yelled like the bitch nigga he'd turned out to be.

"I'm not saving you!" the young CO, who stood nearby, yelled back.

The sharp tip of a shank pressed against Lonnie's throat. "You'sa real pussy, and pussies get fucked!"

They threw him down and pinned him to the floor on his stomach, ripped off his pants and gripped his ass. Sweat poured down his face and he began to shake all over. Fear gripped him tighter than his assailers hands.

"Man, please don't do a nigga like this. Anything but my asshole," he pleaded to no avail.

"You fucked one of the trillest niggas the A has ever bred. Now I'ma fuck you, literally, you rat bastard!"

As his attacker began his penetration, Lonnie screamed and bolted up from the nightmare he was having. He swung his long legs over the side of the bunk and thanked God it had only been a dream. He allowed his muscles surrounding his ass to relax.

"CO!" he called out from his cell in the protective custody housing unit. "I need some Tylenol."

14

A young-looking CO came to the door. "They executed ya mans a few hours ago. It should've been you!" he snarled and threw two Tylenol pills through the tray hole. The pills rolled across the floor. "You're more pitiful than his baby mother that helped sink him," the CO spat over his shoulder as he returned to his post.

***

To those in her circle, Shan was pitiful.

One of the trap boys at the house where she was getting high looked at her with disgust. "This dusty ass bitch over there sucking a glass dick and those pussy ass crackers just murked her baby's daddy."

From the small table in the kitchen, where she sat getting geeked up, Shan overheard him. She didn't give a fuck what he thought of her. If anyone expected her to shed a tear, they needed not to hold their fuckin' breath.

So what, they killed the nigga, she said to herself. *He thought his shit didn't stink. Kept dissing me like I was a punk bitch. Who's the punk bitch now?* She chuckled as she continued smoking the pungent crack rock.

Did they understand she dropped a dime on him because she would have rather seen him in prison for life than riding around with the next trick in his passenger seat? She knew they would never understand that, but she also didn't expect him to be sentenced to death. *It is what it is,* she said to herself.

"A fiend will sell out their own mama," Shan heard a second boy intone. "I don't ride no nigga's dick, but she brought a real nigga down! Trife ass ho!"

Shan drew back as he walked over to the table and snatched her up by her ponytail. Her dry, brittle hair threatened to break off at the constant pressure. "Your money ain't no good in here no more." He gritted, dragging her by the hair and throwing her outside.

"Get your goddamn hands off me! I'ma call the police and tell 'em y'all selling drugs up in here." She spazzed.

Clacka!

The boy pulled a strap from his waist, locked and loaded it, and put it to her head. "Bitch, if you ever threaten to snitch on me again, I'ma do to your grimy ass what Youngblood didn't get a chance to do." He knocked her to the ground and spat on her.

Shan stumbled to her feet and headed around the corner to her apartment, hurling obscenities over her shoulder. "I'll get my son to come around this muthafucka and kill all y'all."

She knew that Lil T was a young beast, and that none of those niggas could outgun him, but she wasn't sure if he would defend her honor.

In fact, Shan wasn't even sure she had any honor left for him to defend.

***

Lil T wanted to kill somebody.

His pop had been his idol and now he was dead. Angry tears stung his cheeks as he turned up the volume on his stereo.

A fat cockroach crawled across the console. He knocked it to the floor and squished it with the bottom of his new Forces.

"You thought shit was a game? I'm a muthafuckin' killa!" He taunted the dead bug.

Exasperated, he sat down on the worn couch and stared at the digital clock on the coffee table. It read 4:03 a.m., and it had been four hours since his pops was executed.

It felt like a pair of strong hands was squeezing his heart. He vowed that these were the last tears he would ever shed in his life.

He was the thirteen-year-old son of the realest nigga the streets had ever seen.

Ain't no bitch in me. My pop might be gone, but I'ma show niggas that he lives in me.

He retrieved his .380 from under the couch cushion. While wrapping his finger around the trigger, he thought about all the good times he had with his pops.

16

Youngblood's voice boomed from the speaker on the stereo. He was spitting a verse on Swag's latest CD, a verse that he'd recorded over the prison phone a month ago.

When I die the whole world gon' remember me/ let 'em ride in memory of a fallen G/ nigga's try but there will never be another me/ I'm only humbled by the cries of my moms and my five seeds/ on death row because a coward showed disloyalty/ that just show that my bitch had more loyalty/ when I go/ make sho' my bitch get my royalties/ I'm a G' til I die/ bury me if I can't fly/ and let that be my eulogy

A sound at the front door jerked Lil T's head around. He sprung up off of the couch with the .380 ready to spit. If a fool was on some kick in the door shit, he was gonna dress 'em in black.

"Boy, where the hell you get a gun from?" Shan asked Lil T as she stumbled in the door. Lil T ignored her as he'd done so many times in the past.

Shan blasted him with her words. "Don't be bringing no guns into this fucking house! You gonna end up where yo black ass daddy at."

Lil T's nose flared. He noticed that his mother's hair was all over her head, her nose was running and her clothes were torn, but he didn't bother asking what happened. "Yo, my pops was executed tonight," he grumbled.

Instead of sympathy, he was met with a round of applause. "Yaay." His mother clapped.

"What did you say?" he snapped, appalled by his mother's response.

"I said muthafucking yaay!" she repeated, clapping louder.

Lil T pointed the gun at her. "If it wasn't for you, my pop would've never got caught. Now you want to stand there and say some dirty shit like that?"

"You little ugly bastard, don't you ever talk slick to me! Either show me some respect or get ya lil' grown ass out of my house!" She jumped in his face, ignoring the gun in his hand.

"You don't respect yourself." He hurled her words back at her.

"I may not! But I don't care what you see me do, I'm still your mama and you're gonna respect me!" She pushed him in the chest.

Lil T was tempted to push her wig back, but something stopped him. Still, he was hot. "You sold out my pops. I ain't got no respect for you!" he spat.

"Get out!" She pointed to the door. "Let's see if you're man enough to make it on your own."

Lil T didn't bother responding, he just grabbed a few things, including his pop's CD, and stuffed them in a duffel bag. He slung the bag over his shoulder and went into his little sister's bedroom to awaken her and say goodbye. They had different fathers, but Lil T loved her, nonetheless.

"Wake up, lil' sis," he whispered softly while gently shaking her. Eight-year-old Laquanda stirred awake. She wiped sleep from her eyes and sat up in bed. "Quanda, I'm leaving," Lil T said, choking back his emotions. "Shan is putting me out, but it's all good. I don't wanna be in the same house with her no more anyway. I just want you to know that I love you and I'll be coming to check on you often."

"No, I don't want you to leave. You know Mama just be talking," she said, pleading with her eyes for him to stay.

"It don't even matter. This was something that's been coming ever since she helped send my pop to death row. You know they killed him tonight. And the way I see it her hand was on that needle, too."

Laquanda didn't know how to respond. All she could think of to say came out in one gulp of emotion. "I love you bruh-bruh." She bawled, wrapping her arms around him.

"I love you more." He held her tightly. When it was time for him to go, he had to pry her arms from around him.

Lil T held in his own tears as he kissed his sister goodbye and walked out of the bedroom. He went into his own bedroom and gathered up an arm full of gear. That was all that he needed. He planned to get the rest just like his pop had gotten it—the ski mask way.

On the way out of the door, he grilled Shan. "I got the blood of a street legend pumping through my veins. I'ma be all right!" He snarled as he stepped into the mean streets of Fulton County as a thirteen-year-old man-child.

Outside, the hood was in flames. Street niggas were rioting, looting and busting their guns in reaction to the execution of Lil T's pop.

Youngblood had been a hood icon, and now his son was turned loosed on the streets of the A about to carry on his father's legacy.

Ca$h

CHAPTER 1
The Present
Six Years Later

After just three days of watching constant traffic going in and out of the record store in East Point, Lil T knew the spot did big numbers. Now it was time to make the niggas who ran the spot pay taxes because they were selling more than CDs.

Last week, he had observed a sexy ass chick catch a flat right in front of the house. She stepped out of her peach cobbler colored Ford Freestyle in denim booty shorts, a beige wife beater, that provided a hint of her dark nipples, and high heeled open toe Steve Madden sandals. In no time at all, her flat tire was being repaired by four trap boys who'd been admiring her from the window.

The chick focused her attention on Saadiq, the one that she knew was the shot caller. His high yellow complexion, long, sandy brown locks, pretty boy features and athletic build easily stood out from his clique. He was checking her out, too. She stood about 5'7", although at least three of those inches could be attributed to her heels. He loved the way she stood back on her legs— that shit was a turn on to him.

Saadiq's eyes traveled up her body. Her waist was small and her hips were wide. Her titties set her wife beater the fuck off. They were just a bit more than a handful and they pointed at him. Saadiq ran his tongue around the inside of his mouth. *Ooo la la,* he thought.

Her hair flowed down past her shoulders. A Chinese bang added flavor to her style. Saadiq couldn't quite guess the color of her eyes, but they were just as beautiful as the rest of her. He wanted to tell her that she resembled the model Amber Easton, but that wouldn't have done her justice because shorty was one of a kind.

By the way the boy stood speechless, Lil T knew she had the nigga at hello.

While his boys changed her tire, Saadiq spat his mack game hard for her. She listened with a dimpled smile and when the tire was repaired he gave her his number.

"Hit me up," he said.

"I will, boo," she said, eyeing him like candy.

The next day she called him and asked if she could come through and take him out to the ESPN Zone sports bar for a light meal and a few drinks. Saadiq was with that and he hoped she would get a little tipsy and come off of that booty.

He dressed in his beige linen short set, ready to show her how his dress game stayed on point. He slid into his orange and beige Prada sneakers before splashing on a little Jean Paul Gautier cologne on his way out of his grandmother's door.

As soon as he stepped onto the block where he hustled, the girl pulled up in her truck and scooped him up.

"Sup, baby girl?" spoke Saadiq as he slid into the passenger seat and closed the door.

"You, Daddy. Mmm you smell so good."

"Not as good as you look. 'Cause for real, you're gettin' your pretty on something serious," he said, rubbing her thigh.

"Aww, thank you," she cooed, pulling away from the curb.

Saadiq's dick was already jumping inside of his pants. He could hardly wait to get up inside of those thighs. He wasn't going to rush the night, though. Baby girl was a dime that he wanted to bag and keep.

"You'll be thanking me for a lot more before it's all said and done because I'ma make you mine and treat you real good. Real talk, you won't have a worry in the world. Just fuck with me, baby girl," he said.

"Wow!" Her smile told him how impressed she was.

As they headed toward I-75, Saadiq was already formulating in his mind the many places he would take her and profile with her on his arms.

Niggas are gonna be hatin' stupid hard. My trap is pumping, my gear is tight and I'm about to bag this bad ass bitch.

He was so busy stroking his own ego he did not notice that he had been targeted.

Lil T popped up from the floor of the backseat and pressed a banger against Saadiq's head. The hair on the back of Saadiq's neck stood up.

"Y' all niggas eating good, Saadiq. It's time to share the wealth. Now, before you do something stupid, like reach for the strap that's on the right side of your waist, this is just an extortion—don't make me turn it into a homicide."

Saadiq stiffened. "Bruh, who is you?" he inquired.

"I'm the nigga that'll splatter ya noodles all over this windshield if you don't cooperate. Now put ya hands on the dashboard.

Saadiq did as commanded.

Lil T's boo, Kamora, reached over and removed the glock from Saadiq's waist. He shot her a look of death, while trying to avoid his own.

"Dog, I'm just a worker. I don't call no shots," he explained needlessly. Lil T had done his homework.

"I already know who you pump work for, so you're gonna call ya dude and let me holla at 'em. And if you pull out anything besides a cell phone, I'ma give ya loved ones a reason to get all dressed up and sing a slow song."

Kamora bent a corner, and they drove down a quiet residential street as Saadiq pulled out his cell phone and called his mans.

"Put that shit on speaker," barked Lil T.

Saadiq complied just in time for his connect's voice to come out loud and clear. "Sup, fam?" his connect answered.

"Yo a nigga snatched me up and made me call you."

"Say what?"

Saadiq quickly explained his predicament, including Kamora's part in the set up.

"I tried to tell you that sniffin' up behind pussy was gonna get you fucked up. Who is the nigga? I ought to hang up and let him slump your stupid ass!" snapped his supplier.

"My bad, big homie."

Lil T cut in. "Yo, Zeke, this is Lil T. You probably know me by my street name Trouble. And if you recognize my name, then you know how I get down."

Zeke recognized the name immediately. It was ringing loud in the city. Trouble was pressing all of the dope boys, snatching niggas up and leaving them faced down.

But a fish's pussy wasn't waterproof if he was gonna let some teenage baby gangsta extort him, he told himself. "I know who you are, youngin'. But do you know who I am? I've been in the game since the nineties and you tryna press me? You betta check my profile!" Zeke warned.

"Miss me with the *rah-rah* shit. You either kick me ten stacks a week or I shut you down."

"I'm telling you, you're out of your league."

Lil T chuckled. "I feel you. Now you're about to feel me."

The sound of two gunshots reverberated through the phone. Saadiq's head splattered like a busted pumpkin. Blood splashed all over the seat, passenger window and the dashboard.

Kamora didn't even blink. She'd become used to Lil T putting his murder game down, so all she was concerned with was where she'd get her whip detailed.

She picked up Saadiq's cell phone that had fallen between the seats and passed it to her man.

"Buy a bunch of caskets, nigga, if you plan on testing my gangsta. And when you pick out your own, don't put the bitch on layaway."

***

"You know that shit turned me on, don't you?" said Kamora, straddling Lil T's lap on the sofa in their living room an hour later.

"What turned you on about it?" he asked, blowing Kush smoke into her face.

"The way you didn't hesitate to smash Saadiq when his people started talking all of that killa shit."

"You ever known me to hesitate?" Lil T inquired.

Without a second thought, she shook her head and then put her arms around his neck. "You're a G, bae," she gushed.

"And you're my gangsta bitch." He palmed her ass as she looked deeply into his eyes.

She smiled as she always did at his uncanny resemblance to C-Murder. Of course, she would never say to Lil T that he resembled anyone but his pop.

"For life," she purred. Kamora took the blunt from him, hit it and then placed it in the ashtray on the coffee table next to the couch.

Wrapping her arms back around his neck, she covered his mouth with hers and slid her pierced tongue inside of his mouth. He cupped her ass and adjusted her on the bulge in his jeans. "This what you want?"

"Mmm hmm. You already know." She was always hot for him.

"A'ight, let me take a quick shower. I think I got that nigga's blood on me."

"Can I join you?"

"You don't even have to ask," he replied and led her from the living room to the shower.

***

As soon as they were undressed and under the water, he pressed her back against the wall, lifted one of her legs and eased his hardness inside of her. His width spread her open deliciously.

Kamora begged him to fill her up with all of his length. She was anxious to cum all over his dick tonight. She grinded her hips and moaned his name as he went deep. The warm shower water cascaded down on them, intensifying their pleasure. Her grip was like a warm glove.

"Fuck me, bae. This is your pussy. Make it cream for you," she whispered and sucked on his neck.

"A'ight. Damn, shawdy, you got that wet-wet," he moaned, stroking slow and deep.

She clawed at his back. "Gimme that good dick, bae. Fuck your bitch like there's no tomorrow. Oh yes! Just like that. You like how I'm throwin' this pussy back at you?"

"I love it. Tell me you're my bitch for life."

"Don't play—boy, you—know a bitch—will die—for –you!" The orgasm she felt building up nearly left her breathless. "I can't hold it, bae. I gotta cum! Cum with me. I wanna feel all your seeds inside of me!" She panted, on the verge of a climax.

"Okay, I'ma cum with you, shawdy." He quickened his stroke until they both exploded together.

Twenty minutes later, he was stretched across the bed while Kamora lotioned his body. He blew Kush smoke toward the ceiling as she studied the tats that covered his torso. They had gotten together a week after Lil T's seventeenth birthday. Two years later, they were still going strong, so she was not seeing his ink for the first time.

Her fingers traced each letter of the words tatted across his six-pack. *Like Father, Like Son* encircled a scar from a gunshot wound. A ski-mask covered one side of his well-toned chest, a tat of his father's face was on the other side, with *Youngblood* etched underneath it, trailed by *R.I.P.* Lil T's arms were sleeved up, too. But the tat she adored the most, *Trust No Man*, covered his entire back.

Reaching for more lotion on the nightstand, her hand brushed across the German Luger and then Lil T's platinum chain and the icy medallion, which was a five-inch urn that held some of Youngblood's ashes. It was Lil T's most prized possession.

She thought back to the night, a year ago, when a nigga had tried to jack him for the chain.

They were leaving out of the club on their way to the car, when a short dude with an unusually large head, stepped out from a crowd and threw down on them.

"Break ya' self!" he commanded Lil T, who didn't hesitate. Being a jack boy himself, he respected the game.

He gave up his trap without protest, but he studied the robber's face.

"You too, bitch, with ya cute ass. Gimme ya jewelry, too," he demanded of Kamora and she obeyed.

"Let me get that chain, shawdy," he said to Lil' T while keeping the gun leveled at his stomach.

Lil T shook his head. "Nawl man, you gon hafta take my life 'cause that's the only way you'll get this," he stated while regretting leaving his banger in his whip.

"You think it's a game? Nigga, I'll wet ya shirt."

"You're not getting my chain, homie—"

The bullet cut off his words. His stomach felt like a ball of fire as the impact knocked him off of his feet.

Kamora attacked the robber with flailing fists, determined to keep him from shooting Lil T again. She managed to land a half dozen punches before the robber slapped her across the face with the gun and bolted off.

Afterwards, she blamed herself for what happened because Lil T had told her over and over again that he didn't like going any place where he couldn't take his tool. He had only conceded to take her to her cousin's birthday party to stop her from pouting.

"If you would've died that night I don't know what I would've done," she said to him now. He knew exactly what she was referring to.

"Shawdy, let that go. That's a lesson learned. I bet I'll never get caught slippin' again. And sooner or later I'ma run into that nigga and show him that he never should've let me live."

"Okay, bae, I love you."

"Do you?" he teased.

"With all my heart. I'm gonna ride for you like Inez rode for your father. Or like Keisha did."

"Not like that fake bitch, Juanita?"

"Oh no. Never like Miss Thang."

"And definitely not like my fake ass mama."

"I wasn't gonna go there, but since you did— I would rather die than flip like she did."

"I believe you, shawdy. That's why I love ya old ass," he joked.

"Don't clown." She playfully punched him. "I'm only four years older than you."

Their kidding was interrupted by her ringing cell phone. "That's lil mama named Sharena," she said with wide eyes as she read the number on her caller ID.

"Who?"

"The bitch who fucks with Byron?"

Lil T sat up. Byron's mother, Delina, had testified against Youngblood. "Play that bitch right, shawdy. You know how much this means to me."

"I got you, bae. Shhh!"

Ca$h

CHAPTER 2

Lil T drove down Boulevard Street. A mural of his father was painted across the whole side of a liquor store. He knew the owner of the store pumped weed and pills out of there, but he didn't put his press game down on dude because the mural showed that he had much respect for Youngblood's legacy. Other business owners had been pressuring him to do away with the tribute to a deceased thug, but the man refused to buckle under.

As formality, Lil T honked his horn as he passed by the store. Catching a glimpse of his pop's mural out of the corner of his eye, he unconsciously fingered the small urn that hung on the thick chain around his neck.

Making a right at the light, he drove past what used to be the Englewood projects, his pop's old stomping grounds and the hood where he grew up. The projects were demolished now, but the memories were forever.

Kicked out of the house at thirteen, Lil T had grabbed a ski mask and feasted off of this hood.

On Hill Street, he parked in front of a dilapidated house and made a call. "I'm outside."

A few minutes later, a tall teenager came out and handed him a manila envelope. "It's a band short, my nigga," he mumbled.

"Fam, stop testing me!" Lil T warned.

"Nawl, Trouble, I'm not testing you, bruh. Shit been slow. I put that on everything I love."

"That's a new song, right? Nigga, you been singing it every week. Just because I like you, it don't mean I don't want my dough. I cut ya taxes because I fuck with you, but don't try to play me or I'ma get upset. You know my get down. Pay me or the undertaker. Which one?" Out of nowhere, the strap appeared in Lil T's hand and it was aimed to spit dead between the boy's eyes.

"I got you, fam.' Let me go back inside and get it," the boy stammered.

A while later, Lil T drove off with his trap right. He made two other collections without incident and then headed to visit his half-sisters.

As he headed out to their home in Decatur, he shrugged off the animosity he knew he would encounter from their grandmother.

Her face was stone when she answered the door. Lil T brushed it off. "How you doing today?' he asked politely.

"I'm fine," she replied with a stiff upper lip.

"Is Eryka and Chante around?"

"Where else would they be?" She stepped aside and allowed him into her home, taking in his thuggish appearance, sagging jeans and long dreads.

He's just like his daddy, a street thug, she thought.

Like every time before when he visited, Lil T could feel the contempt that she held for him. He didn't sweat it, though, because he hadn't done anything to the bitch beside resemble his pop. If the old bitch had a problem with that, she could eat a dick. He wasn't going to let her attitude keep him away from his sisters.

Fourteen-year-old Eryka came bouncing down the stairs smiling when she heard Lil T call her name.

"Hey, boy," she said and gave him a hug.

"Sup, sis? What you been up to?" he asked.

"Nothing but fighting off the haters."

"Oh, you still Facebook banging?"

"Shut up!" She giggled. "I'm a G like you."

"You not no damn gangsta." He laughed. "Where's Chante?"

"In the den doing an assignment for school. You know how she is, always studying. Me? I don't have time for that. I like to have fun and kick it with my friends," said Eryka as she led him to the back of the house where the den was located.

Following her, Lil T noticed her shape was beginning to blossom. She was thick and red like her mother must've been when his pop bagged her, he thought. Soon, grown ass niggas would be tryna holla, thinking Eryka was legal. He already knew he was going to have to smash some old fool for pushing up on his lil sis. He felt a responsibility to watch out for them ever since Cheryl's suicide.

"Sup, bookworm?" he announced, startling Chante.

"Hi, bruh-bruh. I'm working on a science project. You wanna see?" He looked over her shoulder at the computer screen.

He had bought them the computer six months ago.

Lil T stared at the monitor, but had no idea what he was looking at. Chante burst into laughter at his facial expression. She began explaining what the project was about. Listening to her explain the project, it amazed him how smart she was and how different she and Eryka were, not only in personality but also in appearance. Eryka resembled Cheryl, while Chante's features strongly favored Youngblood.

Both of his sisters were crazy about him. They battled back and forth for his attention, and he enjoyed spending this quality time with them. He kicked back and chopped it up with his sisters, but he couldn't stay long because Kamora was blowing up his phone. He gave Eryka and Chante two hundred dollars apiece and promised to spend more time with them soon.

On the way out, he gave their grandmother five hundred dollars to help with their care. This was something he did on a regular, and although she acted as if she didn't care for Lil T, she gladly accepted the money.

"Thank you," she mumbled as he said goodbye.

Lil T smirked, thinking about what he'd read in Trust No Man 2. The book Youngblood had written:

I rang the doorbell.

"Who is it?" the woman asked.

"Terrence," I answered as clearly as my wired mouth would allow.

I heard the door lock turn, and the door opened just a crack. Lonnie's foot kicked it loose from the security chain and knocked the woman backwards but she didn't fall, nor did she scream. She just stood there, petrified like a deer caught in headlights.

I pointed the gun at Cheryl's mother.

"Tell me where Cheryl is!" My voice was low and demanding.

Lonnie closed the front door, grabbed her by the throat and pushed her toward the stairs, damn near lifting her clear off of her feet. His gloved hand dug into her throat as he forced her up the stairs and into the bathroom. When he released her from his grip, Cheryl's mother coughed violently. As soon as the bitch caught her breath, I nodded to Lonnie. My partner grabbed her by the back of her hair, forced her

over the commode and pushed her face down in the toilet water. I nod-
ded again and he yanked her head up. The bitch was coughing, crying,
and gasping for breath all at the same time.
   "Tell me where Cheryl's at!" I said for the second time.
   "I--don't—know," she cried.
   I nodded to Lonnie and he dunked her head in the toilet again. This
time, for thirty seconds. When he brought her up, she was coughing
profusely, desperate for air. "Where's Cheryl?" I asked again.
   "I swear—I—don't know!"
   I punched her in the eye. "Drown this bitch!" I said to Lonnie.
   Lil T could imagine the scowl that must've been on Youngblood's
face when he said those words and the fear that must've been in the
woman before him now. Yet, she was still testing the gangsta of his
pop's bloodline. "Let me ask you something," he said, stopping in the
doorway.
   "What is it?"
   "Is that the scar under your eye from the time my father punched
you in your shit?"
   She gasped. The look on her face showed that she was appalled by
his obvious sarcasm.
   "I'm just saying. Don't make me go there." Lil T gritted.
   Slowly, he turned and walked out.
   "You little fucker!" She slammed the door behind his back.
   Lil T chuckled to himself and kept stepping.
   Inside of the car, he checked his phone and saw that he had six
missed calls and an urgent text message from Kamora. Something had
to be wrong. He called her back ASAP. "What's poppin', shawdy?"
   "Bae, I was leaving the West End and I noticed a black Pathfinder
get behind me. I made a few turns just to see if I was being followed
and the muthafucka is still behind me."
   "Where you at?"
   "On I-20 East."
   "You strapped?"
   "Always." She patted her Glock .50 on the seat between her legs.
   "Okay, don't panic. If they're on some jack or murder shit, they
won't make a move if there are witnesses around. So just stay on the

interstate. I'm just leaving Decatur. Drive on out this way and get off on the Candler Road exit. Turn into the gas station where I fixed your flat tire that time. Be sure to drive around to the side of the building where the air pump is. I'll be waiting. How many niggas in the truck?"

She checked her rearview. "Two, I think."

"That's all? Those fools gonna wish they had an army of goons wit' em. I got that yoppa in the truck, so when it pops off, stay out the way."

"You're making my kitty cat tingle," she purred, excited about what was about to go down.

"Later for that. Lead those lames to their death. I'ma show 'em what happens when they fuck with my bitch." He was getting crunk by the minute, anticipating smashing two fools who thought they could test his boo.

The gas station was only a mile or so from where he was, so he arrived there in minutes. "Stay on the phone and talk to me until you get here. Just pretend that you haven't noticed them. I hope they're not just a couple of niggas tryna holla at you 'cause if so they 'bout to win the wet T-shirt contest."

Ten minutes passed before he saw her pull into the gas station. The SUV she described turned in behind her, as well. Lil T ended the call without a word. Kamora parked at the air pump and checked her strap, making sure the safety was disengaged.

Lil T crept up on the passenger side of the Pathfinder like a trained assassin. He asked no questions. He just let his AK-47 do the talking.

The front passenger door windows exploded in a spray of glass. The weapon coughed out quick, repetitive annihilation. Then Kamora's Glock joined the party.

When the gunfire ceased, two bodies were left twisted and lifeless. Now came the most dangerous part—getting away from the scene before po-po arrived.

Lil T shouted, "Mash out, shawdy!"

They peeled away from the murder scene at the same time. Kamora took the expressway, while Lil T stuck to the residential streets, which he knew well. His hands were steady on the steering wheel but his pulse quickened. The sudden blaring of police sirens mixed with the whirl of the helicopter had him worried about his shawdy.

CHAPTER 3

Lil T made sure that po-po wasn't on his ass and that the helicopter wasn't following him before he turned onto his grandmother Poochie's street. He whipped into her driveway and hurried up her porch.

Poochie was nursing her evening cup of coffee and trying yet again to persuade Shan to check herself into a drug recovery program. The fruitless conversation was interrupted by loud pounding on the door. She placed the steaming cup of coffee down on the table and rushed to the door with Shan on her heels.

"Hey, Big Ma," Lil T said, but ignored his mother as he came into the house and began turning off all the lights.

"Why are you breathing so hard and turning off the lights? What have you done now?" Poochie worried. She knew that Lil T and trouble were synonymous, but he was her heart.

"He prolly done killed somebody," said Shan.

"Shut the fuck up!" he snapped.

"Boy, don't talk to your mother like that." Poochie scolded him.

"My bad, Big Ma, but she always got something slick to say out her mouth and she know I don't like her."

"I should've flushed his disrespectful ass down the toilet when he was nothing but sperm!" Shan replied, glaring at Lil T with contempt.

Lil T didn't respond. He was busy peeping out of the living room windows. He took his cell phone out of his pocket and tried to reach Kamora.

"C'mon, shawdy, answer yo phone." He pleaded, but received no answer. He dialed her number twice more with the same result.

If po-po had his boo in cuffs, there was sure to be a lot of cop killings in the A real soon.

Just as he headed toward the door, his phone rang, flashing Kamora's name across the screen.

"Sup, shawdy, you okay?"

"I'm good, bae. What about you?"

"I'm Gucci. Where you at?"

"At McDonald's on Gresham Road in the drive thru," she responded matter-of-factly.

"Shawdy, you're too damn gangsta."

"Call me Keisha," she quipped, referring to the thorough chick she'd read about in the novel about his pop.

Keisha had immortalized herself in hood lore by busting her gun at po-po instead of surrendering. Though she'd died in a blaze of police gunfire, her legend was almost as strong as Youngblood's.

I was worried about you, girl, and you're chillin' at Mickey D's. Go to the house. I'll meet you there."

"Okay, but I'ma need you to beat it up tonight. You know gunplay turns a bitch on!"

Shan was still ranting as Lil T got off of the phone. He frowned at her and said, "If it wasn't for Big Ma, I would really hurt your feelings."

"Say it, nigga, with ya ugly ass!"

"Ugly? Look at you!" He looked her up and down.

Shan's hair was dirty and pulled back into a little bitty ponytail. Her lips were chapped so bad, they looked like fish scales and her eyes bulged out of her head. She sprang up off of the couch and swung on him. Lil T swatted her punches away.

"Y'all stop!" Poochie screamed. It pained her heart to see them at each other's throats.

For the past six years, she had tried to mend their broken relationship, but the damage was too severe to repair. No one understood the many demons Shan's drug addiction brought into her better than Poochie, who was a recovered crack addict. She had tried over and over to explain it to her grandson just as she did at that very moment.

"It ain't that, Big Ma. It ain't even got nothing to do with her kicking me out. It's what she did to my pop that's unforgivable," Lil T told Poochie.

She never offered a comeback because there was none, except to pray that he would allow God to change his heart. She knew that he could be stubborn as hell.

"Big Ma, I'ma see you later. You need anything?" Lil T pulled out a stack.

"No, I'm fine. The Lord always makes a way for me."

Shan reached for the money. "I need something," she said.

Lil T grilled her and stuffed the stack back inside of his pants pocket. As he tried to walk out of the door. Shan grabbed the chain around his neck and yanked it. It broke and the urn fell to the floor. Poochie's mouth flew open. She knew what the urn contained, as did Shan.

Lil T bit his lip, fighting back the urge to go off on her. He bent down and scooped the urn up. "You're lucky none of the ashes spilled out," he said.

In one of the last conversations he had with pops, Youngblood had stressed to him, *"Your mother brought you in this world. It's your duty to love and respect her. Promise me you'll always do that."*

Lil T was still a shorty, then, but he had adamantly refused to make his pop that promise. *"Nope, she told on you,"* he replied. And to this day, he believed his pop had understood.

"Nigga, you don't scare me," Shan said.

Lil T looked at the broken chain. He wanted to snap his mother's neck but restrained himself. He glared at her once again and then walked out of the door with his chest heaving.

Driving away from Poochie's house, Lil T pushed the beef with his mother to the back of his mind and tried to recall if he'd even seen the face of the two dudes he and Kamora had murked. The two faces suddenly became crystal clear in his mind. They had been outside the trap house the day Kamora met Saadiq. Zeke had probably sent them to avenge Saadiq's death.

"Niggas think it's a game? I'm 'bout to show 'em why they call me Trouble," he said as he drove on Highway I-85, going home to check on Kamora.

Ca$h

CHAPTER 4
Trouble

Yep, that's exactly what it is, and this is how it's poppin' off— niggas wanna see me? I'm not hard to find! I don't fear no muthafucka! I was born to die anyways, and I've been on a date with death er' since my pops got executed. It's nothing! I'm project born and street raised!

Six years ago, the grimy woman that gave birth to me kicked me out in the cold, thinking that because I was only thirteen at the time, I wouldn't make it.

My grandmother, Poochie, took me in to keep me out of the streets, but I quickly bumped heads with her new husband, The Good Reverend. She wasn't about to choose any man over her grandson, so when the Good Reverend issued an ultimatum, she quickly showed his ass the door.

Eventually, I took to the streets anyway, but Poochie loved me just the same. But as I looked down at my feet, I realized what I had always known: Shan had it twisted about my survival in the streets. I'm nineteen years old now and a young G is still standing. With the blood of the most official nigga ATL has ever bred running through my veins, I'm setting the A on fiyah. And any nigga that's not trained to go, better fall back or I'ma leave 'em leaking.

I slumped my first nigga three months after I got kicked out of Shan's house. He was a trap star and I needed to eat. I snatched the lame up, took his trap and left him in need of some pallbearers. Er' since then, I'd been a dope boy's worst nightmare. I preyed on those marks just like they preyed on fiends.

Pushin' work was their hustle. Robbing niggas and pushing scalps back was mine. *Same toilet, different shit.*

I'm Lil T, the son everyone knew would grow up and walk in his father's footsteps. They don't call me Little Youngblood no more, like they did when I was younger. I deaded that shit because Youngblood was one of a kind. The streets nicknamed me Trouble. That, I don't have to explain. I don't fuck with niggas because they're not to be trusted. Instead, I got my thorough bitch riding shot gun with me as I avenge my pop and put the city under siege.

This is my story and I'ma tell it as gutter as I live it. If you ain't built for this gutter shit, now is the time to bounce because trust, this ain't no story of me tryna get out the streets. Fuck that, I am the streets. And I fully expect to die here. But before I do, I'ma stack bodies so high they'll need to ride an escalator to reach the top of the pile. Follow me while I take you on a journey you'll never forget.

At the crib

Everything was gucci with Kamora. We just chilled for a few days and tried to figure out how those niggas found her. After thinking it over, I realized Zeke had any number of niggas under his thumb who he could send at us.

"We're just riding on anybody on his team," I told Kamora.

"I was thinking the same thing bae," she replied. That's what I loved most about baby girl, she was always ready to ride.

We went inside Chilli's in Riverdale where we were meeting Inez for lunch. Already seated at a table when we got inside, she had the Jada Cheng model-look perfected— the straight brown hair with blonde highlighted streaks, thinly arched eyebrows and a buttery complexion. The soft white cotton pantsuit presented her well. Oversized sunglasses rested atop her head, holding her hair back from her face. In her mid-thirties, Inez was still dimed up.

Pop was gettin' it in. I smiled. "What's poppin'?" I asked as she stood up to hug me.

"Not much at all," responded Inez. "Hi, Kamora. Are you keeping him in check?"

"Hmph. I'm trying," my shawdy said.

The two of them were close, but it had taken a while for Inez to warm up to her. I was glad when she finally did approve of Kamora, because I trusted Inez' opinion like no other. The way she repped for my pop forever earned my respect.

Two years ago, when Inez came home from doing a seven-year bid, she didn't get brand new. She was still as real as ever. She could tell that I was some real shit, too, and she didn't try to preach to a nigga. All she did was remind me to stay on point.

"You read all about how a nigga your father trusted and loved like a brother had flipped on him," she constantly stressed.

In the presence of Kamora, she said, *"It's the one you trust most who'll end up betraying you. No disrespect to your girl, but how can you be sure she's built to last? Built to withstand the pressure if y'all get cased up?"*

I was about to answer when I felt Kamora's hand on my arm. *"Nawl, bae, I can speak for myself."* She looked Inez dead in the eyes. *"Miss, Inez, I've heard all about you, and I know that you're one hundred. I respect you to the utmost, I really do. You chose to do a bid rather than flip on your man— that's what a real woman does. But I'll do you one better, I'll die by my nigga's side."*

Inez wasn't impressed and her bland expression told Kamora so. *"Everybody is a rider until those steel bracelets get put around their wrists."*

"Shawdy, is official," I cut in to defend my boo. *"Remember that nigga who shot my pop? The one that Swag was gonna get, but my daddy told him to let it go?"*

"I recall who you're talking about." Inez nodded. *"The dude had been one of few men who violated my pop and lived to brag about it. Swag had told me the nigga's name, and I tracked him down through a couple of old heads."*

"What about him?" asked Inez.

"Kamora ended his story. She rocked that ass to sleep like Keisha did Rich Kid. But she slumped him all by herself. All I did was point the nigga out to her. Shawdy ain't just a pretty face, she pop them hammers."

"Lonnie was a kill, too, until they put him in cuffs. Then the bitch came out of him."

"I'm not a snitch! And I don't appreciate you mentioning my name in the same sentence with one." Kamora had snapped, and her light brown eyes darkened a bit.

Inez wasn't ruffled. She calmly replied, *"Maybe you're not a snitch. Maybe you're as real as Lil T thinks you are— only time will tell. In the meantime, understand that I love that boy as if he was my own. If you betray him, I promise I'm going back to prison for life. You can write that shit in ink."*

Since that conversation two years ago, Kamora and I had gotten arrested for suspicion of murder in an unrelated case. We remained in jail sixty-three days while the detective tried to build a strong case against us. And when they couldn't come up with enough concrete evidence to take us to trial, they offered to release Kamora if she would testify against me. Shawdy laughed at them and told them to kick rocks.

With scant evidence against us and unable to make Kamora flip, the authorities had no other choice than to release us. The ordeal had earned Kamora Inez' trust, so now Inez spoke freely in front of her.

The waitress took our orders and bounced. I told Inez about the latest two niggas to catch bullets from me and shawdy's guns.

She remarked, "Lil T, you gotta be careful. Those crackers downtown won't ever forget that y' all slipped out of their grasp. If they ever get solid evidence against you, they'll nail you to the cross. They know who your daddy was."

"I want 'em to know."

"That's that same arrogance your father had," she replied with a smile.

"Fuck po-po," I said.

"Lil T, your name is blazing in the streets. You have niggas afraid, and that's dangerous because there's no way to predict what a scared person will do. Maybe you should fall back for a while. I talked to Swag the other day, and he wants you to go on tour with him. His new record label is doing well. He can give you an A&R position."

I laughed.

I'm not an *industry* nigga. I'm a *in da streets* nigga. Tell Swag I'm good."

"Okay, just be careful. You know Tamia would be tore up if something happened to you."

"My lil' sis ain't no lame. She know that any day could be my last day."

"Don't talk like that."

"I'm just keepin' it one hunnid'."

Anyway, niggas don't wanna see me. I go hard in the muthafuckin' paint. But fuck all that." I could talk gutter and not offend Inez. "I got some good news. Byron is about to get touched."

Inez' eyes lit up. "Do you mean Byron as in Delina's son?"

"True,' I muttered as the waitress returned with our food. The aroma of the chicken fingers and pasta made my stomach growl.

Inez was quiet until the waitress walked off again. Then she said, "Make him suffer for what his mother and her weak ass nigga did to my boo. She didn't spare your father, so don't spare her son."

"An eye for an eye." I raked food off of the platter onto my plate.

"What about the other boy? That bitch has two sons," she inquired.

"I can't locate him. The word is that he joined the army."

"I'd give anything to get my hands on Delina. I would wax the floor with that bitch." Inez fumed.

I laughed, imagining Inez throwing fists. She was gangsta, but she looked like a diva. "The bitch's ass you need to kick is Juanita's."

"Hmph! Please don't mention that uppity bitch, or you'll make me fly out to Nevada to mop the streets with that ass."

I could see the anger flash in her eyes. Juanita had pretended to be so down for my pop. But since his death, the mask had come off and she had shown her true colors.

"I would've been dealt with her fake ass if I didn't think that would be against my pop's wishes," I said.

Just thinking about that bitch got me dumb heated. Most of the money my pop had taken from niggas during robberies and all of his royalties from his CDs were left to Juanita to share with all of his children. So far, none of us had received a dime from her.

"When you graduate from college you'll receive an inheritance," she told me one day, like she didn't realize that college wasn't in my plans. School had been a wrap for me after eight grade when I dropped out and picked up that banger and ski mask.

"That's the one thing I remain mad at your father about," Inez huffed. "He trusted that bougie ass bitch more than he trusted me." She frowned.

"I don't think so." I tried to soothe her, but she waved off my attempt and bit into a chicken finger.

"Yes, he did, but he'll forever be my heart." Just like that, her eyes brightened and a smile replaced the scowl.

I looked at Kamora and wondered if she loved me that deeply as the three of us began to eat.

We chopped it up with Inez for another hour and then it was time for Kamora to go hook up with lil' mama who fucked with Byron.

As for me, I had three things on my agenda: get some Kush so I could get chinky-eyed, collect my street taxes and leave some niggas pants shitty, as a reminder to the streets that I was not to be fucked with.

CHAPTER 5

I put my ear to the door of the apartment and detected several loud voices. That meant Ladell, the weed man, was at home playing some game or another on his X-BOX with a couple of friends. I knocked a few times.

"Who is it?" he answered, probably looking through the peephole.

I stuck my face up close to the door and smiled maniacally like Jack Nicholson in *The Shining*, "Here's Johnny," I said. "Open the door, nigga. You know who it is." I gritted.

The door swung open. "What's good, fam?" He greeted me with a phony smile and extended his fist for a pound. Ignoring his fist, I invited myself inside. I saw two niggas in the living room in front of the big screen television playing NBA live.

"Sup, Trouble?" they said in chorus.

I didn't recognize either of them, but they obviously knew who I was. Good. That meant they more than likely respected my G.

"Ladell, I need some of that good Kush to get my lungs out of pawn," I said.

"I got you, homie."

My hand was in my waist while he walked over to the end table and returned with some Kush in a Ziploc bag. It appeared to be about an ounce. When he tried to hand it to me, I slapped it out of his hand and it spilled out on the floor.

"Don't insult me, nigga!"

"Dog, I'm leaking," Ladell whined like a bitch. "That nigga, Ghost, came through and robbed me the other day."

"A'ight, I'ma deal with Ghost for you because he's stepping on my toes. But don't try to play me like you gave him your whole trap. Nigga, I know you keep two stashed, so go get me what I came for," I demanded.

"A'ight fam, just don't take all my shit. I gotta eat just like you do."

"Man, if I was on that kinda time, I wouldn't allow all this *woo woo woo*. Just give me a pound of that lime green and ya weekly taxes and I'm out."

He walked to the back of the apartment and returned with what looked like a whole pound. I accepted it without complaint.

"See, dawg, I ain't no greedy nigga. Just feed me and we're good." I gave him some dap, then I walked over to the X-BOX and turned it off. His comrades looked bewildered. "What's on y' all minds?" I challenged.

"Nothing, just staying in my own lane," volunteered one.

"Me too," mumbled the other. He was a light-skinned nigga with a face full of freckles.

I looked down at them and thought, *Birds of a feather*. "Well, let me tell y' all what's on my mind." I toyed with them. I could tell that, like Ladell, they weren't killas. "I think as soon as I leave y' all gonna clown Ladell. Saying, *Ain't no way I would let that nigga press me; he ain't bulletproof.* That's the shit y' all gonna talk when I bounce, but y' all frontin'." I put my strap against freckle face's forehead. "Break ya self." He emptied his pockets.

Whap!

I slapped the nigga beside him across the nose with the chrome, drawing blood.

"You too, Bernie Mac lookin' ass nigga. And you bet' not get no blood on that trap."

He produced a band. I snatched it and then I advised Ladell, "Surround ya self with a killa or two."

On the way to the whip, I passed by a group of baby goons who were standing in a circle battle rapping, prolly dreaming of becoming the next Jeezy or the next Swag. I gave them a handful of Kush and bounced.

I collected taxes from a half dozen other spots, making my way over to the Westside where I stopped to politic with a Blood named DeMario.

DeMario and I burned three or four blunts while discussing a lick. I listened as he tried to justify crossing his sister's dude.

"The nigga be chumpin' me off, charging me mafia prices for the work I get from him. Plus, he be doing my sister dirty."

"All that don't matter to me, big dawg. As long as you assure me that he'll have a trap up in his house worth me going after, I'll be there.

Remember, I don't put on my ski mask unless the lick is fiddy bands or more," I stated my ground rules.

"Oh, it'll be much more than fifty gees up in there. But, Trouble, you can't kill him or my sister will lose her mind. The nigga foul, but she loves his ass."

"He bet' not do nothing stupid, then."

"He won't. Their lil' shorty will be there."

"A'ight. Just get me up in there and I'll handle the rest. One question, though. Why you ask me to do this instead of one of your Piru homies?"

DeMario smiled. "Cause he's a Blood, too."

I nodded my understanding.

When I got home, Kamora was still out. I counted the taxes I collected and added forty-five bands to my stash. I now had a little over a quarter-mil.

Sneaker money, I thought.

I wanted to be able to spend that much on a vacation. I also had three sisters to look out for. It was time to step up my game. The plan was to be a multi-millionaire by the time I turned twenty-one. I had eighteen months to reach my goal, which meant that a lot of mothers were about to have to bury their sons.

I threw a pizza into the microwave and sparked another blunt. When I was done eating, I hopped into the shower and let the jet spray massage away the stress I accumulated on the daily, since I lived by the gun.

Twenty minutes later, I was lying in bed in my boxers and I called Kamora.

"Hey, bae," she answered her cell phone in a soft whisper.

"Where you at?"

"In a room with ol' girl, drinking champagne."

"Where is she?"

"In the bathroom."

"So, y' all about to cut something?" I probed.

"It's only business and if you wanna call it off, we can. But don't you want her to lead us to her man?"

"True, but still…"

"Aww, that's cute, you're jealous," teased Kamora, but she was right. I knew the only thing another chick could do was give her some head, but I still felt some kinda way. From the first day we hooked up I believed she had been totally faithful. That was definitely true in regards to myself. "You want me to come home, bae?"

I swallowed my jealousy. It wasn't like some nigga was about to run up in my girl. "Nawl, you good, but I wanna listen. Put your phone on speaker."

"You're freak. Hold on." She laughed.

"Are you gonna do it?"

"Yeah. *Shhh!* Here she comes."

I pressed the mute button on my phone and listened to real life erotica.

"Damn! You got some pretty titties. Can I just taste them?" I heard the bitch remark in a voice thick with lust.

"You don't have to ask, just help yourself," Kamora cooed.

"Mmm. I wanna lick you from head to toe. You are perfect and your tummy is so flat. You must work out."

"I do." She was lying. We had been together twenty-six months and she had yet to do a sit up. Her washboard stomach was due to genetics.

"Spread your legs, baby. Let me play in that honey pot. It's so plump and juicy, and I've been dying to suck your pussy ever since I laid eyes on you."

For a few seconds the phone got quiet. As I was about to hang up, I heard Kamora moan. And I wondered if she was faking it or if she was really turned on. I knew she had been dating women primarily, until she got with me, so the cries of pleasure I heard could be real.

"Take your time and lick it real slow. Yes, just like that," she coached.

I closed my eyes and imagined the chick eating her pussy and my dick sprung to life. Before I knew it, I was stroking myself, turned the fuck on by the fuck noises the were making.

"Eat this wet, young pussy. Make it pour honey down your mouth," murmured Kamora.

"Yes, cum in my mouth while I fuck you with my tongue. Oooh, baby, your pussy taste so good. You're going to fuck around and have a bitch sprung."

"Mmm, that's what I want."

"No you don't. 'Cause I'm telling you, I'll be stalking your ass."

"You won't have to stalk me. The way you're makin' me feel, I'll do the stalking," she panted.

Then the slurping became loud and I could imagine her pussy dripping with wetness. The talking ceased and the moans became louder. My hand slid up and down my dick, unconsciously.

"Ahhh, Sharena, I'm about to cum! Ahh!" Kamora screamed out and I shot a wad of cum clear across the room.

I was stretched out across the bed sweating like a field slave, afterwards.

"What do you think you're about to do with that?" I heard Kamora ask, sounding out of breath.

Sharena responded confidently, "I'm going to strap it on and fuck you like no man ever will."

"Oh no, boo boo! Ain't no dick— real or fake— going up in this unless it's my man's! You can give me head all night, but absolutely no penetration." Kamora shut her down.

"Okay, I can respect that. But you don't know what you're missing."

"Maybe some other time."

"I sure hope so. But I need some dick now! Will you strap on and fuck me real good?"

"I won't say no," replied Kamora.

I sparked another blunt, laid back and listened to Kamora beat that pussy up. She had ol' girl screaming her name. I was laughing my ass off imagining what my shawdy was doing to her.

Once I heard shawdy cry out in ecstasy, I disconnected. About twenty minutes later, Kamora called me on her cell phone on the way home from her little rendezvous.

"Have that dick ready for me when I get home. And you betta make me scream like I had that bitch yellin' and hollerin'! Did you hear her, bae?"

"Yeah, shawdy, I heard her." I laughed.

"I fucked the shit outta her, huh?"

"Girl, you a fool!"

"Yeah, a fool for you. Do I get some of that gangsta shit? Ass in the air, long stroking it from the back, pulling my hair— good fucking tonight?"

"Slappin' that ass, too," I promised.

"Hush, bae. I'm already doing sixty in thirty-five miles per hour zone, tryna hurry home to you."

"Do eighty," I urged.

CHAPTER 6

For the next week or so, all Kamora and I did was chill at the crib and fuck. I guess she was tryna prove to me that what she did with Sharena was strictly business and that I remained her only desire. I already knew that, but I enjoyed letting her convince me. But soon play time was over, and it was time to put my gangsta down on a nigga who refused to respect this shit.

When shawdy saw me gettin' strapped up, I didn't have to say a word. She knew what the mission was because we had been discussing it for days.

Kamora found a tight-fitting T-shirt and pulled it on over her head. Shaking her long hair back into place. She next stuffed a pillow under the T-shirt and then put on a maternity top. "How do I look?" she asked.

"About seven months pregnant."

"Good. That's what we want, right?"

"Exactly."

I watched her grab her banger off of the nightstand near the bed. She checked it carefully to make sure it was locked and loaded and then placed it inside of her Prada bag.

We checked one another's appearance. It was time to roll out.

It took us an half hour to reach our destination. Driving up Panola Road, I was reminded that this was the neighborhood where my pop slayed five muthafuckas inside of a house. Those murders had ultimately led to him being executed by lethal injection. He should've killed seven, I mused, then Lonnie and Delina wouldn't have been able to snitch on him.

"You okay, bae?" whispered Kamora.

"I'm good." I choked up a bit. *Pop, I miss you like crazy, man.*

In the snap of a finger, my mind was back on our mission. I parked down the street from the target's crib and searched for my throw away phone. Once I retrieved it, I found Zeke's number and hit him up. The phone rang twice before he answered.

"You ready to pay your taxes or you're still not convinced that I go hard for mine?" I threatened.

"Fuck you, nigga! I got shoes older than yo lil' young, reckless ass. You betta recognize you outta your league."

"Say no more!" I snarled and hung up. I looked over at Kamora and turned the dome light on in the car. "Shawdy, that nigga still think it's a game. Tell me the truth, baby. Do I look soft or something?"

"Of course not." She leaned over and pressed her lips to mine. "In a minute, he'll recognize that you're a G to the core. Let him keep underestimating you. He'll find out that there's two things for sure—death and taxes."

"No doubt." I flicked off the dome light and drove up the street. Now it was show time.

Kamora put the tiny earbud into her ear and I did the same with mine. We made sure our two-way handless radios were working. Then she got out of the car, and stepped out into the darkening night, looking like a woman well into her pregnancy.

From the car, I heard her knock on the door. When a woman's voice answered, she went into her act. "Is BoBo home?"

"No he's not," the woman replied from behind the door.

"Well, you tell that lying muthafucka that he was supposed to come and take me to my prenatal appointment today and he stood me up again! Tell him that if he doesn't come over to my house by tomorrow, he'll never get to see his baby when it's born." Kamora had the ghetto girl stance going, neck rolling, hands on her hips, as she was getting her shit off.

"Who are you?" the woman inquired.

"His side bitch, but I'm tired of him hiding me from you. That nigga got me fucked up!"

I saw the woman crack open the door. Then Kamora pushed her way inside of the house like she lived there. "Excuse me! Did I invite you into my home?" protested ol' girl.

"No, boo boo, you didn't. But I'm not leaving until you call *our* man and ask him to come home and straighten this shit out."

"Oh, you'sa bold ass bitch, huh? If you wasn't pregnant, I would put this size eight in your ass," threatened the woman.

I listened as Kamora talked the dumb broad into calling her man. She was shouting so loud I could hear every syllable.

"Muthafucka, why is some pregnant ho sitting in my living room claiming that the baby is yours? I don't know the bitch's name, but you betta get here fast and check this bitch, or me and lil' BoBo going back to Savannah— now try me!"

Things were silent for a minute and then I heard her tell Kamora that BoBo was on his way home. Then I heard the woman gasp. I knew that Kamora had the toolie in her face.

"Bae, I have everything under control. I'm about to unlock the back door for you," she spoke into the earpiece.

"I'm on my way," I quickly replied.

I hurried up the street and found the back door unlocked just as Kamora had promised. All lights were off inside of the house except for a lone light that came from a lamp in the living room. That's where I found Kamora and her prey. The woman was seated on the couch shivering with fear. Kamora stood over her glaring down at her with no compassion. I smiled, acknowledging her gangsta.

"Please don't hurt us," the woman pleaded, wrapping her arms protectively around a small child.

"Is that BoBo's son?" I asked.

"Yes. Why?" she answered nervously.

"No real reason, I'm just one of those curious type niggas." My tone was much more ominous than my reply.

She recoiled away from me and held on to her son even tighter, rocking back and forth. I could almost smell her fear. Perspiration ran down her face.

I hummed the tune of one of my pop's songs as we waited for her man to arrive.

Thirty minutes later, Bobo walked into a nightmare. My nine was pressed to his head as soon as he stepped through the door.

Kamora was seated on the sofa next to his woman with her glock to their little boy's head. "Say hello to daddy," she cooed to the infant.

"Yo, what the fuck?" spat BoBo.

I patted his waist. The fool wasn't even strapped, but even if he had been, I had the drop on him. He looked at his woman and I could see in her eyes that she was trying to apologize.

"Don't blame her. Blame your brother, Zeke. All he had to do was share the wealth and I wouldn't be up in your spot like the boogie man," I taunted.

"What does that have to do with me?"

"Blood relations," I answered unmercifully. "Now take me to your stash, and you bet not take me on a wild goose chase." I pointed the banger at his woman. "You! Come tape his hands so I don't have to push his hairline back."

Bobo's wife complied. And once his hands were taped, I made him lead me upstairs to his safe and give up the combination.

With gloves on my hands, I opened the safe and emptied its contents into a pillowcase that I'd snatched off of the bed. I estimated that there was almost a hundred stacks.

"Death and taxes," I said before blasting away half of BoBo's head.

I ran back downstairs where Kamora was having an unusually difficult time silencing BoBo's bitch. I got right up in the broad's grill, placing the banger against her forehead.

"Shut the fuck up or I'ma send you and your son where I just sent his daddy!" I threatened.

Her loud cries quickly lowered to soft sniffling. "Please don't hurt me and my baby," she pleaded while cutting her eyes toward Kamora in hopes of gaining her compassion. But Kamora wouldn't meet her gaze.

"I wish it didn't have to be this way, but we have no other choice. If we let you live, you'll end up pointing us out in court one day," replied Kamora with a softness that I couldn't understand. She was not new to this.

"Oh no. I promise if you don't harm me and my child I'll never identify you to anyone. I don't care about BoBo. I was about to leave him anyway," the woman exclaimed.

Whether or not Kamora bought that, it didn't even matter. The weight from the urn hanging from my chain around my neck reminded me of the consequences of leaving witnesses.

I looked ol' girl in the eyes and said, "I'm gonna allow you a few seconds to get yourself right with your Maker before I send you home to meet him."

Her mouth flew open and she bolted for the door screaming. I reached out and snatched her back by her long, slightly tinted hair.

To Kamora I instructed, "Shawdy, wig call this ho and let's be out." Kamora didn't move, I frowned. "Fall the fuck back, I got this!" I jerked my head back in ol' girl's direction.

"Say a quick prayer, then I'ma let you hug and kiss your baby one last time before you depart. If you go ahead and do this, I'll spare your son's life. But if you don't woman up, I'm crushin' ya baby, too."

She shook her head back and forth as if she could not do it. I placed the tip of the nine against her son's head, hoping that she wasn't gonna call my bluff. "Okay!" she cried out and then mumbled out a prayer.

Kamora rocked the baby in her arms as he began to stir.

"...and protect him from all evil. Amen." Her body trembled as she stepped forward to take her baby out of Kamora's arms. Their eyes locked and Kamora looked away. A few seconds passed and she handed the chick the child without looking up.

The woman accepted her baby and hugged him to her chest. "Pooka, Mama loves you," she cried. Tears dripped from her eyes onto his face as she kissed his tiny lips. "Grow up to be a good, God—fearing boy. And remember that your mama loved you and so did your father." I shook my head. *Didn't she just tell me that she didn't care about his father?*

"A'ight shawdy, ya time is up." I cut her words short.

She turned once again to Kamora and again Kamora could not look her in the eyes. "Please don't let him kill me. Whatever problem he had with BoBo or BoBo's brother does not involve me and my child. That's men's business." Her whole body trembled.

"I'm sorry," said Kamora. The regret was real. I could hear it in her tone. Nevertheless, she wrestled the infant away from the mother.

"Both of you will burn in hell for this!" she cursed.

I snickered. "You'll burn long before we will, bitch!"

The nine popped off. Three loud claps and the whole left side of her face was obliterated. Her body dropped to the floor and I put two more shot in it. I looked up at Kamora and snarled. "What the fuck! You getting soft on a nigga or what?"

"No," she replied, but I was not convinced.

"Hand me the baby," I demanded.

"No, bae."

I raised my arm, the one in which my hand gripped the nine.

"Please, bae!" shrieked Kamora, shielding the baby with her body.

I used the back of my hand to wipe away the sweat from my brow. "Chill, shawdy, I'm not gonna kill lil' dude. I'm a beast, but I'm not heartless."

I could see relief come over her face. This was a side of her that she had not displayed until now, and it made me wonder whether she was truly built for this shit. I decided I'd confront her about it at a later time. In the meantime, she was on some retarded shit.

"I want to keep him and raise him as our own. Look at him, bae. Ain't he cute? And now because of us he doesn't have a mommy or daddy," said Kamora.

"Girl, stop with the dumb shit! I don't know what you've been smoking, but you need to get your mind right before you cause us to get knocked. I don't give a fuck how cute he is, he had to go. Now let's get the hell up out of here." I slung the pillowcase full of money that I had taken from BoBo over my shoulder and walked out of the house looking like a duffel bag boy. And if Kamora wasn't behind me, I was gonna leave her ass. No bullshitting.

By the time I cranked up the whip, she was sliding into the passenger seat still cuddling the baby. "You were supposed to leave him in the house!" I snapped at her. She was really pissing me the fuck off now.

"Bae, I couldn't. Just the thought of him being in that house alone with the bodies of his parents was too much for me. Don't be mad."

Li'l dude began wailing as I drove off. "You better hush him up before I do," I warned.

"Hush, little bitty baby. It's gonna be all right. Give auntie kissy kiss," she cooed.

I shook my head and let out a sigh. Kamora had to be losing her mind. Didn't she realize this was not some fucking game? We had just left two bodies behind.

Two blocks away from the murder scene, I made a right turn onto a quiet residential street and stopped in front of the first house I saw that had lights on.

"Take him up on the porch and leave him." My tone was no fucking nonsense.

Kamora wrapped the baby up in a blanket that she must've grabbed before following me out of the house, then she looked to me for one last appeal. The look I returned convinced her that if she didn't take the baby up on the porch and leave him, I wouldn't hesitate to enforce the alternative. And that option was not pretty at all.

Slowly, she got out of the car and carried the baby up on the porch. I watched her gently lay the baby down, ring the doorbell and then dash back to the car. As soon as her door shut, I pulled off.

At home, I tossed the money on the sofa and whirled around to check Kamora who was behind me. "What the fuck is your problem? The way you acted tonight could've gotten us popped! I taught you to go up top on a muthafucka if they don't follow your command." Spit flew out of my mouth.

"I know. And I'm sorry." Kamora dropped her head.

I put a finger under her chin and roughly lifted her head up so that her eyes met mine. "Don't start acting like no punk ass bitch! I thought you said you were gonna ride for me like Inez and Keisha rode for my pop."

"I am," she said. "But he was just a tiny, little baby."

"Shawdy, I'm not talking about the goddamn baby! I'm talking about the way you was sympathizing for the bitch!"

"I kind of felt sorry for her. When you took BoBo upstairs, she knew you were going to kill him. She begged me to let her slip out of the door with her baby before you came back downstairs. She said that she had been through so much in her life and all she wanted to do was see her child grow up. I can't lie, bae, that touched me," explained Kamora.

I shook my head in amazement. The bitch should not have gotten a chance to tell Kamora her life story, because as soon as she disobeyed the command to shut up, Kamora should have silenced her forever. Ain't no mercy when you run up in somebody's spot.

"You're getting soft, shawdy," I said, walking away to go shower and rinse the blood off ofme.

The hot spray of the water relaxed my muscles, but did little to relax my mind. Kamora's behavior was not something I could overlook. I loved shawdy and I had faith in her gangsta, so I hated to think that what she had shown was a sign of weakness. Because if that was true, I had no choice but to treat her as I would my enemies.

Loyalty to a weak muthafucka had cost my pop his life. I was not going to let the same thing cost me mine.

I closed my eyes and let the water rinse the suds off of my body. When I stepped out of the shower, Kamora was standing there holding a towel out for me. I walked right past her and grabbed a different towel off of the wall rack.

"What happened tonight won't happen again," she promised. Still, I ignored her. She wrapped her arms around my waist and leaned her head against my back. "Bae, the last thing I want to do in this world is disappoint you," she said with such sincerity that it broke through the anger I had put up like a brick wall. I turned and kissed her lightly on the lips.

"If you wanna fall back, I'll understand. Just don't switch up on me until you complete what we're working on with Sharena. I want her nigga so bad I dream about killin' him in my sleep," I confessed.

"I understand, bae, and I'm not going to let you down. I'm sorry about tonight. I don't know why I felt sorry for that lady. Maybe it was because she looked like one of my elementary school teachers who was very nice to me. Or maybe I simply fell for her story. She was so young, and I could tell that she really loved her baby."

Kamora's eyes grew watery.

I sighed. "Everybody has a story, baby girl. Hers was no sadder than the ones that came before her or the ones that will follow. Let her tell her story when she reaches the pearly gates."

"Don't say that, bae."

"Real talk, shawdy."

I dried off and threw on some boxers and then sat down in front of the television and turned on my X-BOX. "Spark up some of that loud," I said to Kamora.

The loud got my head right and slanted my eyes. I fell asleep on the couch thinking about the message tonight's events would send to Zeke. Now he would know that the price for opposing my street tax was the blood of whomever he cared about.

Ca$h

CHAPTER 7

Word on the streets was that Zeke broke down when he learned his brother had been murked. I also heard he had put out a contract on me for a hundred bands. That didn't bother me, because whoever tried to collect it was gonna get sent back to him in a body bag. Muthafuckas was about to find out that I wasn't easy to touch.

I gave Zeke his props, though. Even though I had sent a strong message when I slumped his brother, he didn't fold. I called and asked him, "You ready to pay taxes or do I gotta send you another reminder not to test my gangsta?"

"Little, bitch ass nigga, you can't extort me! I fill cemeteries up with young reckless punks like you," he retorted.

"I hear you talking all this killer shit, but what you saying? You ain't saying nothing, pimp."

"Quit hiding like a bitch and come and see me."

"Oh, I plan to," I assured him and then ended the call.

For the next couple of days, I just kicked back and plotted moves. I wasn't worried about Zeke. Niggas like him had gotten fat off of the game and wouldn't put in any work. That wouldn't stop him from sending someone else to do his work for him, though, so I kept my eyes open and my head on a swivel whenever I was out and about.

The one clear advantage I had over Zeke in war was that I didn't have any soldiers he could knock off. But he sure had plenty niggas whose heads I could splatter to make Zeke hurt. He didn't know my loved ones, so he couldn't get at me that way. All I had to do was protect Kamora and myself from his wrath.

Besides the beef I had in the streets, a few other things were on my mind. More importantly, I wanted to go visit my paternal grandmother who had been committed to a psychiatric hospital in Milledgeville, Georgia. I had gotten so caught up in my hustle, I had not visited her in six months.

I woke up early on a Saturday morning and called the facility to clear the visit with them. Kamora overheard the conversation and asked if she could go with me.

Two and a half hours later, we were being buzzed in to see my grandmother. We were led into a cozy visitation room furnished with a couch, a small table and a pair of cushioned chairs. We sat down and I anxiously waited for the nurse to bring my grandmother out. I was hoping that her mental condition had improved since my last visit.

Kamora and I both stood up to greet my grandmother when she was led into the room. She moved as if she was in her seventies when in fact she was only fifty-two years old. When I hugged her, she felt frail and as brittle as a dry leaf. My heart ached. I was glad that my pop could not see his mother in this condition.

"Hi, baby." She smiled at me.

Her hair was gray and they had her dressed like an old lady, square-toed shoes and all. Even the perfume she wore smelled old and stale.

"Hi, Grandma," I spoke back. I wanted to squeeze her tight to let her know I loved her and that despite her condition and appearance, it was good to see her. But I was afraid I might hurt her. "How you been, doing?"

"I'm wonderful, now that my babies are here to see me. Hello, Toi. Get over here and give your mama a hug and stop acting shy." She was talking to Kamora. This told me right away that she was still delusional. "Terrence, what is wrong with your sister?"

"Nothing, Mama. I'm okay," said Kamora who always played right along with Grandma's delusion. Neither of us had the heart to correct her.

"I told these stupid nurses that my two children weren't dead, but what do these nurses know?" Grandma whispered conspiratorially.

"Not a thing." I agreed

"Terrence, remember that time you hid from me in the dryer and Toi wouldn't tell me where you were? I thought you had run away."

Grandma was confusing me with my father, but I just nodded and smiled.

We all sat down and then Grandma wagged a bony finger at Kamora and said, "Toi, remember when you used to sneak and wear make-up to school? Girl, your tail was so hot I didn't know what I would do with you. I had asked God to give me a husband to help me raise y' all. When I met Raymond, I believed that God had answered my prayer," Her eyes turned sad.

"It's okay, Mama," said Kamora as if she were Toi.

"No, it's not. I almost allowed that man to turn me against my own son. Terrence, Mama is so sorry for that." Grandma looked toward me and began weeping.

Raymond, the man whom she thought was a blessing from God had despised my pop to the point that my pop was not allowed in their house. Grandma had gone along with it and that damaged her relationship with my pop while he was on the streets. It wasn't until Pop was locked up and facing the death penalty that their relationship was repaired. I believe that after my pop was executed, Grandma's guilt helped drive her into a nervous breakdown.

"Grandma, you don't have to cry. I believe that before my pop died he knew that you loved him."

"What did you call me? Boy, I'm not your grandmother. I'm your mama. And don't ever let me hear you say that you're dead. Why does everyone keep saying that? You're not dead! You're not dead! You're not dead!" she screamed.

I reached out to hug her, hoping to calm her down, but that caused her to really go off. "No, don't touch me! You're on their side. You want me to think I'm crazy." She clawed at my face, drawing blood.

The nurse heard the commotion and raced into the room with several male attendants in tow.

"Don't grab her like that!" I snapped at a bulky attendant who was handling my grandmother like a rag doll.

"Sir, we have to subdue her," said the same nurse who had brought Grandma into the visitation room.

"But y' all don't have to treat her like she's a fuckin' inmate. She's barely a hundred pounds. She can't hurt anyone!" railed Kamora.

By the time they removed Grandma from the room, one of the attendants and I were brawling. I caught that big nigga with a quick two-piece that buckled his knees. Kamora jumped on his back and bit a plug out of his shoulder. Together we tore that nigga's ass up.

When we got back to the car, all of my emotions came flooding in unexpectedly. I had vowed never to shed another tear, but seeing

Grandma so mentally deteriorated like that overwhelmed a young nigga. I broke down. "I gotta get her outta there." I cried with my head against the steering wheel. The state hospital was doing her no good at all.

This was my pop's mother. It was as if his spirit inclined me to take care of those he had loved so much.

On the way home, I called Inez and asked her to look into finding a private facility for Grandma.

"Is she still that bad off?" asked Inez, full of concern.

"Yep. And she looks so old and tiny it broke my heart. You ought to see her; you wouldn't even recognize her." I choked up.

"Umph, umph, umph!" She sighed. "Why don't you call Juanita and ask her to help with the expenses. This is the type of thing she should step up to the plate for."

"I'm not asking that bitch for nothing. The only thing she ever gave me was some of my pop's ashes. Anything else, she wants a nigga to live up to her expectations in order to receive it."

"I know, right? The bitch is a hypocrite. Who is she to judge somebody when her ass used to be a nasty ass stripper? That shit makes me so mad. Why your daddy trusted to leave everything to that fake ass ho is something I'll never understand. Deep down, I always knew she was nothing but a bird."

"It's all good."

"Yeah, it is," she agreed. "Because she'll find out that karma is a coldhearted bitch."

"If I don't thrash her ass first, before karma can catch up to her." I snorted.

CHAPTER 8

The anger inside of me was hotter than a furnace. It was time for me to unleash it on those most responsible for what I was feeling.

Ever since my pop was executed, I had been compiling a list of names of people who would feel my vengeance. I'd located and studied their movements for the past two years. Now it was time to strike.

While Kamora was off somewhere with Sharena, I was at the kitchen table reading every page of my pop's trial transcript. I had read it at least twenty times before, so it contained nothing that I wasn't already aware of. Still, my face twitched with fury over those who had testified against him, and those who rejoiced when he was convicted and sentenced to death.

I finished reading the thick file, set it aside and called Inez to discuss the first person I planned to smash.

"Yeah, do that bitch real dirty because she used to be all on your father's dick until he put her on blast to her man, then she hated him. In court when Youngblood was sentenced to death that ho damn near did a cartwheel," she recalled.

"Well, she's about to pay the repercussions. I know where she lives and I'm about to pay her a visit."

Two nights later, it went down. I salivated as I waited outside of my first victim's apartment for the trick she had over this evening to leave. She only fucked ballers, so if the nigga didn't leave soon, it would be worth the effort to clap 'em both. Dude would probably have a few stacks and some nice jewels.

I peered through the glass patio door, about to go on the creep. Luckily for homeboy, he was not spending the night.

He hugged her, rubbed her fat ass through the long T-shirt that served as a nightie and then he bounced. Then she disappeared from my line of vision.

A moment later, I heard music come on from a room in the back. *The punk bitch was probably savoring the dick she had just gotten,* I figured.

Cool! The music would drown out any noise I make.

You won't be giddy for long, ho!

I waited a full twenty minutes before using a glass cutter to cut out a large enough section of the patio door to stick my gloved hand through and unlatch the door from inside.

Once I gained entry, I crept like a panther, not making a sound until my breath was on the back of her neck. Cita stood at the bathroom sink washing her hands. I reached around and covered her mouth as I pressed the sharp tip of a commando knife to the side of her neck. Her body went rigid.

"If you're gonna rape me, just wear a condom and I won't even fight. Just don't hurt me," she replied.

"Bitch, don't insult a G. I don't want any of that sloppy cut!"

"I have money. It's in the bedroom. Is that what you want?"

"Nawl, I want yo life." I removed the ski mask. Cita shrieked as she stared at my reflection in the mirror. I resembled my pop so much that the recognition was instant, even though I had long dreads and a baby face and my pop had worn braids. "Yeah, bitch, it's me." I spun her around and slammed my fist into her face, dislodging a front tooth. She crumpled to the floor and I stomped her head.

I hope you die slow, muthafucka! She had said in court when my pop was sentenced to death.

Cita moaned and cried out in pain. But I felt no mercy for the bitch.

"You're a gutter snipe ho," I said with contempt as I snatched her up off of the bathroom floor and shoved her into the empty bathtub.

She tried to shake the cobwebs from her head and beg for mercy, but I was just as merciless as the jury that imposed death on my daddy. "You wanted him to die slow, huh?"

"I'm sorry," she cried. "Lord knows I'm sorry."

"If you're not, you're damn sho' about to be!"

I plunged the knife in her neck. Blood spouted all over me. I stabbed her repeatedly until she lost consciousness. Then I cut her tongue out of her mouth and threw it in the toilet.

"Next time be careful what you say, bitch!" I cautioned her corpse.

Blood was everywhere, splattered on the walls near the bathtub and all up on the ceiling. I could feel its stickiness on my face, but I paid it no mind.

As I stared into Cita's mutilated mouth, I said, "Pop, I made the bitch pay. She smiled when they sentenced you to death, but she ain't smiling now. I told you I was gonna get all them muthafuckas. This bitch is just the first."

I touched the urn around my neck with my fist and crept out the same way that I came in.

When I got back home, Kamora was there waiting for me.

"Sup, baby girl? How was your night?" I asked, bending down to place a soft kiss on her lips.

"Boring," she replied, then arose from the kitchen table where she had been reading over the transcript that I left out.

"You're not feeling Sharena, huh?"

"No. I'm only doing it so we can get her man, remember? I'm not feeling anyone but you." She reached up to stroke his face and her fingers came in contact with something sticky. She drew her hand back and examined it. "Ewww! Whose blood do you have all over you?"

"A bitch who rejoiced when my pop was sentenced to death."

"Cita?"

"Yep." I nodded.

"I wanted to go along," Kamora whined.

"You're crazy, shawdy," I laughed. "Run me some bath water. Then I want you to wash me up."

When Kamora headed to run me a bath, I called Inez to report tonight's events.

"She deserved it," replied Inez with no remorse. Her thirst for vengeance equaled mine.

"No doubt. I'ma hit you up another time. Let me go wash that grimy ho's blood off of me before it soaks into my pores and turns me sour," I remarked.

"That could never happen. You have the blood of the realest nigga to ever live running through your veins."

"True."

"You didn't leave behind anything that could connect you to it, did you?"

"Nah, I'm good."

"Okay, be safe. I love you."

"Love you, too." I hung up the phone and went into the bathroom. Kamora had bubble bath water waiting for me. As I climbed into the tub, a vision of how I'd left Cita popped up in my mind.

"No mercy," I said as I submerged my body in the scented bubbles.

CHAPTER 9

Later in the week, vengeance was still heavy on my mind when I received a call from DeMario that made me change my focus for a minute. "Dawg are you still gonna do that lick that we discussed?" he asked.

I had to recall that I had agreed to jack DeMario's sister's man. "Yeah, you know I'm always looking to eat, but are you sure you want me to do that? I mean not only is homeboy your family, he's your Blood," I reminded him.

"Fuck that. As long as it don't get out that I set him up, ain't nobody gonna suspect me. Like I told you before, that nigga is on some selfish shit, so it is what it is."

"True. So, when you want me to touch him?"

"ASAP. Because he just got some work in and he's sittin' pretty right now. And guess what?" DeMario said with excitement.

"What's that?"

"I stole my sister's door key off of her key ring today, so you can get up in their spot with ease. Plus, I moved the four-fifth that her nigga keeps on top of the fridge."

"That's all good, but I'm sure he has other bangers around the crib. I want you to bring me that door key, though."

"I can drop it off to you right now. Where do you wanna meet up?" he asked eagerly.

"Slow down, bruh. I'll get with you in a few hours. It ain't no rush. I'm not running up in his spot tonight."

"Dawg, I want you to get at him before he has a chance to sell any of that work."

"Just let me handle this," I said. There was no way I was running up in his brother-in-law's spot without thoroughly checking it out first. DeMario was too thirsty, but I always used caution.

Later in the evening, I met with DeMario and got the door key from him. Then me and Kamora went to case out the spot. We observed it on two consecutive nights before we made our move.

Using the door key that DeMario provided to gain entry to the house was a cinch.

A pretty woman with a jet-black complexion was asleep on the couch. I gestured with my head for Kamora to handle ol' girl while I followed a noise that came from inside of the kitchen.

As soon as I stepped into the well-lit, spacious kitchen, which was equipped with an island, I saw a big ass nigga leaning on the counter with his back to me.

"Blood, turn around real slow and let me see your hands," I commanded. When he didn't move fast enough I growled, "If I have to repeat myself, I'ma empty this clip in your head and then I'ma do your bitch real dirty." That got his attention. He turned slowly to face me. For real, the nigga was about 6'6" and 280 pounds. "You a huge mutha-fucka, bruh, but I'll smash your ass if you try some monkey shit. Ya heard me?"

"Yeah, I heard you." He scowled at me.

Boc! I shot him in the stomach and he crumpled to the floor whining. I walked over to where he lay and pointed the banger down at his head. "You tryna intimidate me, nigga? You want me to body your muthafuckin' ass?" I fired a shot into the floor only inches from his head.

"Please don't kill me," he cried and I noticed he had pissed himself.

"If you don't wanna die you better tell me where all your shit is at."

"Okay, I will," he whimpered.

I made him roll over onto his stomach so I could cuff his hands behind his back. Then I put the banger to the back of his head. "I'm listening. And you know what's gonna happen if I find anything that you didn't tell me about," I warned.

Fifteen minutes later, Kamora and I left the house with a backpack full of money and a knapsack full of blocks. Heading to the car, I saw someone creeping up on us. "Watch out, baby girl!" I yelled and shoved Kamora down just in time to avoid a bust of gunfire.

I dropped the blocks and my banger came alive, spitting rapidly as I shot back at the three niggas coming at us.

Boc! Boc! Boc!

My hammer went the fuck off!

Blocka! Blocka! Blocka! Blocka!

They bussed back.

Wham!

I caught a slug in the chest and it knocked me back, but I stayed on my feet, thankful I was wearing a bulletproof vest.

Shots whizzed around my head as I hurriedly reached down to help Kamora up and dragged her to the car. Both of our bangers were going the fuck off because we was in a desperate gun battle for our lives.

Somehow, we made it inside of the car without getting shot. I jumped behind the wheel and backed all the way down the street so we wouldn't have to drive past our pursuers.

"Bitch ass muthafucka!" I said when we were out of danger.

"It's okay, bae. I held on to the money," she reported.

That didn't mollify me, though. We had gotten jacked for at least twenty-five kilos of cocaine. Though the bpv had stopped the bullets, those clowns clapped at me. I could still feel a sting in my chest.

I rubbed my shit and didn't even respond to my girl. I just continued on to the house in silence. I already had my mind made up on what I would do next.

"I took care of that little business we had together," I said the next morning when I reached DeMario on his cell.

"Yo hold up. Let me walk outside so my people not all up in my business." The line went quiet for a minute. "Trouble, man, what happened over there last night? I'm hearing all type of wild stories," De-Mario asked, talking in a frantic tone.

"I'll tell you about it when I pull up on you. I'm not about to talk myself into the penitentiary on no cell phone. Meet me at Krystal's on Cleveland Ave at 7:30 tonight and I'll bring those ducats to you."

"That'll work."

Since there was still seven hours before my meeting with DeMario, I drove out to Buckhead and checked out some car lots. I was contemplating copping a new whip. Nothing really caught my eye, so I hit the mall and spent three bands on some new gear. A few shawdies were all on my nut sac, but stray pussy was the last thing on my mind.

"Hey, lil' daddy," a sweet voice from behind me said as I was leaving Foot Locker.

I turned and saw a cute, caramel skinned shawdy. She was about 5'5" with ass for days. Next to her stood a darker chick who was just as thick as her friend. They both looked to be about twenty-two years old.

"What's poppin' with y'all?" I asked, looking them up and down.

"Nothing much. We're here from Tampa just trying to find something to get into," the darker one replied.

"Y'all must be getting into some trouble."

"Nooo. Why you say that?" She laughed.

"Because that's what they call me. Anyway, I see how y'all sweating my swag, but believe me this shit ain't what y'all want."

"Why are you so arrogant?" asked the darker chick.

"I'm not, shawdy. I'm just saying that this ain't what y'all want. For real, don't let nobody send y'all on a mission that will end with your funerals. This right here ain't sweet." I lifted my shirt a little to show them the bangers on my waist and then I pushed on.

It could've been just my paranoia, but I wasn't falling for the oldest trick in the book. If Zeke or somebody was plotting, it was gonna take something cleverer than some pussy to catch me slipping.

I left with my hand in my waist and my eyes alert for trouble. Nothing popped off and I didn't spot anyone trying to follow me as I left the mall and merged into traffic.

I put my earpiece in and hit Kamora up. "Hey, bae," she answered.

I told her the business and then checked with DeMario so he knew to be on time. Cleveland Avenue was too hot for me to be waiting around dirty. "I'll be there at 7:30 like we agreed," he assured me.

"A'ight, one." I checked my watch. I had about an hour to kill.

The time was 7:25 p.m. when I spotted DeMario's red '79 Chevy Caprice pull into the parking lot of Krystal's. The spring sun bounced off of the glossed paint of his whip, which was sitting on thirty-inch red rims.

He parked, got out and pretended to be checking the air in his tires. Like the reckless gang-banger he was, DeMario was flagging. His fitted was red, as was his shirt, khakis and sneakers. He rocked so much red he looked like he was on fire.

I scanned the area for trouble before driving across to where he was parked.

"Sup, Blood," he greeted me, slipping into the passenger seat.

"I'm good. Let's do this and be out before po-po roll by and your gear draws heat on us."

"Fuck, APD. Nigga, you ain't know—Suuu-Wooo," he chanted his set's call.

"If that's how you feel. Anyway, I had to pop one in your brother-in-law to get him to cooperate. For real, I didn't realize how huge that muthafucka was until I was right up on him. Bruh's a muthafuckin' giant. But size don't mean shit to a gun. I made that big ass nigga piss on himself like a little bitty baby."

"You're bullshittin'! I knew that nigga was soft." He chuckled. "Blood always talking about he would never bitch up if a nigga jacked him."

"Yeah, a lot of niggas say that shit until that banger is in their face. Then it's the same old thing with everyone. *Please don't kill me*, they all cry."

"Niggas be frontin'. Anyway, what's this I'm hearing about niggas pullin' up on you as you was leaving out the house?" asked DeMario.

I wondered how he had heard about it, but I just downplayed it. "Yeah, bruh, some niggas jumped out on me when I was coming out of your people's spot. They got the work from me, but I got away with the ducats, so the whole lick wasn't lost. Fuck it! You don't miss what you ain't ever had. Feel me?"

"I feel you, dawg."

"I got your half right here." I kept an eye on him as I reached over into the backseat, thinking that don't nothing beat the double cross but the triple cross. I handed him a backpack full of dough.

He opened the bag and peered inside. A big ass grin came across his face. "This is why I fucks with you." He beamed.

"Stay away from the strip clubs or you'll end up sponsoring some bitch a new whip," I joked.

"Shit! Blood, you can't take it with you when you die, so you might as well enjoy it."

"That's one way to look at it," I conceded with a knowing smirk.

"It ain't trickin' if you got it," he rapped.

Then we touched fists and he slid out of the car. He kept his eye on me as he walked back to his flamed-up Chevy, but I wasn't the one who presented danger.

Boc! Boc!

His body dropped and began twitching.

Boc!

One more to the head made it impossible for him to ever get up again.

Kamora hurried to the car and hopped in, tossing the backpack on the backseat as I peeled off. She was a stone cold killa in a skirt, but I hadn't turned her out. By the time we hooked up, she had already slumped three people.

The first body to her credit was that of her stepfather. Dude beat her mother to death in a jealous rage when Kamora was seven years old. She had just turned fifteen when he was released from prison. On the next anniversary of her mother's death, she turned his lights out.

The second person she gave a dirt nap was her biological pops. *"I took his ass out cuz he never acknowledged me as his child,"* she explained.

And the third person was a girlfriend of Kamora's. They had robbed a couple of ballers and then old girl started acting all nervous. So, she figured it was best to end the problem before it blew up in her face.

Kamora was definitely gangsta. We had grown up across the dirt from each other in the projects, both of us were Englewood born and bred.

I looked over at Kamora in the passenger seat and knew without a doubt that she was official.

CHAPTER 10

We had gotten two hundred and fifteen bands from the lick on De-Mario's people. I went over to Inez' house and gave her half of the money to put toward my grandmother's care at a better facility because at Georgia Regional her condition was worsening.

"I found a reputable hospital in South Carolina and they have an available bed. I'll make the necessary arrangements when I get back in town Monday. Swag is flying me down to Texas to catch him in concert with Beyonce," announced Inez.

"Damn, Jay-Z better watch out. Swag might steal BK from him," I said.

"He just might." Inez laughed.

"You wouldn't be mad, would you?"

"Of course not. Why would I care?"

"Well, Swag be doing a lot for you and you might have caught some feelings for him."

I felt the stinging sensation on my face before I realized that Inez had slapped me.

"Don't you dare insinuate that I would disrespect your father's memory by fooling around with someone who was his friend. I'm a woman not a bird," she seethed.

"I'm sorry. I know you're much better than that. I shouldn't have ever let those words come out of my mouth because I know you keep it one hundred," I said.

"I always have and I always will," she replied and then gave me a hug.

Just then, Bianca, Inez' oldest daughter and Tamia, my lil' sister, came through the door. Bianca was carrying a lone shopping bag. Tamia had three. I nodded a greeting to Bianca and she nodded back. Our relationship wasn't very close because I despised Fat Stan, her father.

"What's up, mini diva?" I said to Tamia.

"Hey, Trouble," she replied while setting her bags down.

I checked her out from head to toe. She was rocking skinny jeans and a tight-fitting T-shirt, white and blue Lady Air Max's and she was bejeweled. I shook my head in amusement. At thirteen-years old, she was already high maintenance. In a few years, somebody's son was going to prison trying to take care of Tamia.

"Have you been keeping those nasty little boys out of your face like I told you?" I questioned as I sat down on the couch.

"Yep, sure have." She plopped down next to me on the sofa and rested her head on my shoulder.

"Oh boy, why do I get the feeling my pockets are about to get lighter?"

"Because you love me." She snickered.

"You got that right," I admitted with a smile.

Inez just stood there shaking her head. She knew I could not deny Tamia anything.

"Will you buy me a new cell phone?" asked Tamia.

"No. Lil T, she just got a new cell phone two months ago." Inez jumped in.

"It's all good. My baby sister can get a new cell every week if that's what she wants," I said, kissing Tamia on the forehead.

I pulled out a band and gave it to Tamia.

"Give half to Bianca," I whispered because had I not, Bianca would have refused the money.

"You spoil that child too much," Inez complained.

"I'm just doing what my pops would have done."

"No boyfriends," I reminded Tamia.

"Until I'm sixteen, right?"

"I might change that to until you're twenty-one."

"Nooooo!" she pleaded, causing me to laugh.

"I'm playing. Let me see what all you have in these bags."

While showing me her new outfits, Tamia whined that Inez was going to see Swag and Beyonce in concert and she wasn't taking her along.

"I didn't know you were big on Beyonce like that," I said to Inez.

"I'm not. I really want to see Swag. Besides Lil' Wayne, he's my favorite rapper."

"What about our pops?" I couldn't let her forget him.

"Oh, he was the best."

"Never forget that, Tamia. Our pop was a beast on the mic, and his swag was turned all the way up. Plus, he was a real nigga who did all of the things these other niggas just rap about."

"I wish I could have gotten a chance to know him, but I don't remember him," she said.

"You were too small to remember him when he went away," Inez said.

"Mama, tell me some more stories about him," said Tamia.

For the next two hours, Inez held our attention with reflections of our pop. I knew she was leaving out the stories of Pop putting his murder game down, for the benefit of Tamia. Still, we were enraptured by the tales.

By the time I said goodbye to them, the respect I held for my pop was even greater, and I was even angrier at those who had betrayed him.

I whipped over to Shan's crib, parked, and honked my horn three times. My sister, Laquanda, came out and got into the car with me. I asked how she was doing in school.

"Good. I made straight A's again," she stated proudly.

"Keep it up and you'll be a doctor."

"Yes." She smiled, showing teeth that reminded me of her father, Shotgun Pete. I never liked the nigga, but I didn't hold it against my sister. I held it against my mother.

I asked Laquanda if there was food in the house.

"A pack of hotdogs and Ramen noodles," she informed me.

"That's a fuckin' shame! Your mama need her ass whooped."

"She's your mother, too."

"Not in my eyes."

I gave her money for groceries and made her promise not to give it to Shan for drugs. When I left, I snapped back into G mode. I had another target in sight.

Ca$h

CHAPTER 11

The next nigga on my radar had not betrayed my pop. This nigga caught my attention because he was feasting off of the streets and flossing real hard. Another reason I wanted to snatch him up was because he was from New Orleans. I had a real dislike for out of state niggas coming to the A and tryna run something.

I walked into the club with Kamora on my arm looking like she had just stepped off a video set. Her hair was long and flat ironed and damn near reached her ass. The black DK dress she wore could've passed for body paint. Her jewels cost a couple hundred bands, but they had been bought with our bangers and the blood of our victims.

I was rocking True Religion, a hundred-thousand-dollar platinum Jacob's watch, diamonds in both ears, and of course, the chain and urn that contained my pops ashes.

My dreads had been freshly washed and oiled earlier in the day, and my light trace of a mustache was neatly trimmed. I looked nothing like the young beast that I was.

Kamora and I found a vacant table and parked there. Soon, a waiter appeared and took our order for Patron.

The club filled up quickly because over in VIP, Solo, the nigga I was there to stalk was having a party for some rapper he was backing on his new indie label.

I observed their party through the glass windows that enclosed VIP.

Solo had half the bitches in the room jockeying for his attention. He was a tall, skinny, ugly nigga with a wide spread nose and beady eyes. But because he was the next coming of Big Meech, hoes were all on his dick. Niggas were, too.

"He's going to be real hard to touch, bae. He has so many niggas around him." Kamora observed the scene.

"Yeah, but hard ain't impossible. Besides, we're not gonna rush this. We got other licks to pull off while we plan this one. I'm really just here to get an idea how the nigga roll."

"You want me to go in VIP and slide up under Solo or one of his mans?"

"No, shawdy, we're just watching tonight."

A half hour later, a familiar face popped up in the crowd. It was Criminal, a young nigga from Zone 6 in the city who had gotten five minutes of fame when he spat a verse on one of Swag's tracks.

Criminal's style reminded many of Beanie Sigel. Swag had signed him to a record deal, but Criminal was so deep in the streets Swag had chosen to cut ties with him.

Niggas in the city whispered that Criminal was a fool for throwing away the opportunity to bubble in the rap game, but I understood his choice. He was a true street nigga, like me.

Criminal saw me and pushed through a throng of groupie bitches to make his way to my table. "What it do, bruh-bruh?" he said, taking a seat.

"I'm good, fam'. What about you?"

"I'm making it do what it do. 'Sup, Kamora? You got ya sexy going on real strong tonight, don't you?"

"You know I try to stay looking good for my man," she replied, rubbing my arm.

"I salute that," he said, standing there looking like Juvenile, except his eyes and his gangsta were as cold as mine.

He motioned a waiter over and ordered another bottle of Patron. "So, when was the last time you hollered at ya boy?" Criminal asked and slid into the booth.

"It's been a minute. You know how that nigga is, he stay on the move. But he gets at me through Inez every now and then. He's always tryna get me to put my banger on the shelf and fuck with the rap game, but that ain't my thing."

"I feel you."

"And I feel you, too. I'm not one of those niggas who look down on you because you didn't roll with the opportunity that Swag gave you. Some niggas are born and bred in the streets and that's where they'll die."

Criminal nodded. "Bruh, the streets is all I know. My pop was a street nigga until the day he died. My oldest brother is serving life and fifty years and my baby brother got shot in our front yard and died in my arms. So, the streets owe me and I'ma collect what I'm owed."

"That's real talk, 'cause I feel the same way," I agreed.

"Excuse me. Bae, I'm going to the ladies' room. I'll be right back," Kamora said. She gave me a quick peck on the lips and went off.

The strobe lights flashed around the club as I chopped it up with Criminal. He was probably the only nigga outside of Swag who I respected and somewhat trusted.

As he turned his head to sweat a bitch's ass as she walked by, I noticed a tat on the side of his neck that had not been there six months ago when I saw him last. "You GF now?" I asked.

"Yeah, and I'm about to take us to a whole 'nother level. Before it's all said and done. I'ma put the streets in a vicious headlock."

I didn't doubt Criminal. He definitely had the drive to do it. His reputation alone commanded respect from the streets. Niggas knew he was gangsta with his shit. His set, Good Fellas, was a relatively new gang in the A. They were about money and murder.

"Anyway, what are you doing here? I've never known you to hit the clubs. It must be a nigga up in here you're plotting on," guessed Criminal. He was dead on point, but I kept that to myself.

"I'm just treating my shawdy to a night out," I lied.

Our conversation was interrupted by a commotion going on somewhere near the door. The dee jay announced, "Ladies and gentleman, Jeezy is up in the muthafucka!"

Bitches started losing their minds. The rapper, Young Jeezy, had a crew of real hard head looking niggas as his security team. Like if a nigga wanted some trouble they wouldn't hesitate to serve him. I don't ride no nigga's dick, but since I'm not a hater I gave Jeezy his props. Bruh had his swag turned all the way up. On cue, the dee jay played one of his hits.

"Bruh doing it big. I fuck with him," said Criminal.

"That can be you anytime you want it. All you gotta do is trade the streets in for the studio," I reminded.

He shook his head. "Nawl, I just fuck around on the mic, but it ain't what I do. I'm a dope boy for life. Plus, I pull those hammers."

"I can't knock that, bruh. Let me ask you something. What is your bank like?"

Criminal looked at me like he was wondering why I would get all up in his personal business like that. So, I explained. "I'm asking because I know you're thorough, and if you're with it, I'ma bring you in on a sweet lick."

"As long as we're talking grown man numbers, I'm listening. But I'm not strapping up for no bullshit."

"Bruh, I'm talking duffel bags," I assured him. I took a sip of Patron from the glass in front of me and thought things over for a minute. Up until now, Kamora had been my only partner in crime, and I knew I could trust her completely. If I recruited Criminal into the fold, it would just for this one lick. *But should I trust him?* I wondered.

He was a solid nigga, as far as I knew, but that's the way my pop had felt about Lonnie, who turned out to be a rat.

After careful consideration, I decided I would fuck with Criminal, but I would not leave myself vulnerable to betrayal.

"What you know about a nigga named Solo?" I asked Criminal in a hushed tone that was further blocked out by the music.

"I hear the name in the streets, but I don't know who he is. They say that bruh is moving stupid work," he reported.

"He is," I said. "So, I'm about to go lay him down. He keep a lot of goons around him for protection, so that's why I need your help."

"I'm ready whenever you are. And if we need some help I got a team on deck. Niggas who won't hesitate to pop them bangers."

"Let's just check it out before we involve anyone else," I cautioned, because trusting Criminal alone was a big leap for me. Trusting his mans was unthinkable.

"You're calling the shots, so it's whatever with me," he said.

I nodded imperceptibly toward the booth where Solo and his goons were seated. "You see that big, bald headed nigga over there with two bitches draped all over him? That's Solo. The other niggas supposed to be his crew, I guess. All of them look old and soft to me."

"Yeah, we can crush them with no problem."

"Pump ya brakes. We're not going at him tonight. I'm here just to watch him, because before we strike, we need to find out where his stash is."

"That makes sense," said Criminal.

We observed Solo for the rest of the night without drawing any suspicion to ourselves. Kamora and I were even able to follow him for a distance once he left the bar.

Once I turned off, Criminal kept me on the celly as he followed Solo home. Now that I knew where Solo laid his head, it was just a matter of time before I struck.

The next night, I scooped Criminal up and we drove around the city discussing loyalty.

"You remember my father's story, don't you? The nigga he trusted above all others is the very nigga that sold him out. But he wasn't the only one to flip on my pop. My mother flipped on him, too. So, when it comes to trusting a muthafucka with information that could send me to prison for life, or even to death row, I'm very hesitant to do that," I explained.

"I feel you, bruh," he said.

I pulled into an apartment complex on Riverdale Road and parked three car spaces away from a familiar Range Rover.

"I'm glad that you do, homie. But before we go any further, you're gonna have to prove that loyalty. I believe that you're one hunnid, but the shit we're about to do with Solo is too serious for me to gamble my freedom. See, I'm telling you straight up that whenever we run in on the nigga, I'm not leaving out of there until ain't nobody breathing but the two of us, and whoever we take in there with us. Because I don't have time to be dodging bullets later if Solo finds out who jacked him," I elaborated.

"I feel the same way," he said.

"Another thing," I didn't hasten to add, "if we were to get cased up, you won't ever have to worry about me turning state on you. Number one, I'm not built like that. But more importantly, I'll do most of the killing; therefore, you'll know I won't have anything to bargain with."

"Get to the point, bruh," he said.

I cut straight to the chase. "In order to make me comfortable, I need something on you that you would not be able to bargain away," I stated, turning to look him eye to eye.

Criminal swallowed.

"If I didn't understand your paranoia, because of what happened to your father, I would feel insulted that you're questioning my G." He frowned.

"Trust No Man."

"You can trust me."

"We'll see."

Criminal couldn't help but respect my apprehensiveness. Trust in a nigga had cost my pop his life. I would have been a fool not to learn from my pop's mistake.

"How can I prove my loyalty, bruh?" he asked.

I laid my head back against the headrest and told him how I was putting my press game down on the dope boys and weed man, Ladell. I further went on to explain how Ghost was stepping on my toes by robbing Ladell. "I want you to do Ghost for me."

"Oh, that's all?"

"That's all."

"Bruh, that's easy. In fact, I enjoy slumpin' niggas. Just show me who this Ghost nigga is and where he rests at and it's a done deal."

"He rests in that apartment right there." I pointed.

Criminal pulled out his banger and locked one in the chamber. "How does this nigga look?" he asked, ready to go put in work.

"Nah, we ain't doing it like that. Ghost probably got dumb guns up in his spot, and he ain't slow to use them. Let's just sit out here and hope he comes out before morning." I said.

According to the clock on my dash, it was 10:41 p.m. Hopefully, Ghost was not in for the night. Patience turned out to be a virtue. At about 2:30 a.m., Ghost came out with a thick redbone.

"You get Ghost, I'll do the bitch," I hurriedly instructed.

We were out of the car and up on our prey within seconds. Ghost spun toward the rustling of our feet and looked dead into the business end of Criminal's banger. The .45 erupted with no mercy, snapping his head back and showering his brains up in the air.

The chick screamed, but only once because I ended her cry with two shots to the throat. After watching her crumble to the ground I put another shot in her head.

"Make sure he's dead," I called out to Criminal.

Boc! Boc! He exclamated my point.

When I dropped Criminal off at home I demanded he give me his banger.

"For what?" he hotly protested.

"Because it has your prints on it. That's my insurance that you can be trusted not to flip."

"What's my insurance that you won't flip?" He challenged me.

"My bloodline," I replied proudly.

I could sense some trepidation when Criminal handed over his banger, but he needed not to worry. I came from the blood of a real nigga.

Ca$h

CHAPTER 12

While Criminal stalked Solo, I turned my attention to a lesser mark. A young nigga named Soldier Boy had begun ringing in Southeast Atlanta. Word was he touched up to ten bricks at a time. Soldier Boy fucked with a stripper named Erotica, who ran her mouth a little too much. I had gone to school with this female named Ava who worked at the club with Erotica. Ava knew what my hustle was, so when I ran into her one day at the Golden Corral, out in Forest Park, she put me on the lick.

"Ava, are you sure Soldier Boy keeps his stash at Erotica's spot? Because I don't wanna kick in the door and end up getting nothing but a lap dance," I said, making my intent clear.

"Trust me, his stash is there. Just last night she was complaining about him hiding six kilos in her dryer. She's afraid the Feds are going to kick in her door and arrest her," Ava said.

"Okay the lick sounds easy, but tell me this: Who's at home with Erotica when Soldier Boy ain't there?"

"Nobody. He won't allow her to have company, not even a pet dog."

"Well, when is she usually at home by herself?"

"I can't say for sure, but if you don't see a black Chrysler 300 or Silver Escalade with big rims parked outside, Soldier Boy is probably not there."

"Okay, give me Erotica's cell phone number. Is she working tonight?"

"She's supposed to," answered Ava. Then she scrolled through her cell phone to find Erotica's number. I stored it in my own phone and told Ava I would holler back at her when the lick was complete.

"Don't do me wrong," she said.

"No, lil' mama, I'm not grimy like that."

Ava was surprised when I showed up at the strip club that night. I paid her to spend most of the evening entertaining Kamora and me in our booth, but neither of us was really interested in her performance. We were there so Ava could point out Erotica.

After she had done so, I just kicked back and counted down the hours until the club closed for the night.

Following Erotica was simple. Baby led us right to her front door without realizing she had been followed. I looked around the parking lot for a Chrysler 300 or an Escalade but saw neither. That was good.

I allowed twenty minutes before calling Erotica from a restricted number.

"Hello," she answered, sounding tired.

"Yo I'm tryna reach Soldier Boy. He gave me your number because when I spoke to him earlier his battery was going dead and he didn't have the car charger with him."

"Who is this?"

"His cousin," I lied.

"His cousin who?" she questioned.

"Damn, baby, you ask a lot of questions, don't you?" I laughed.

"I can do that when you're calling my phone at four o'clock in the morning. Anyway, Soldier Boy ain't here, but I'll tell him ya called if he comes by tonight."

"Please do. And tell him I need to see him about some work."

"You tell him that yourself. That's y'all business." She hung up before I could formulate a response.

I looked over in the passenger seat at Kamora and told her that I was going in.

"You stay out here in case he comes home or in case po-po arrives. I'm about to kick in the back door," I said as I felt my adrenaline begin to pump.

"Be careful, bae," said Kamora.

I slid out of the car and found my way around the back of the apartments. Once I found the right apartment number, I pressed my ear to the door, listening for voices. I heard none, so I pulled on my ski mask, eased my banger out of my waist and lifted my foot in the air.

Two kicks busted in the door. I moved swiftly from one room to the other until I found Erotica showering in the bathroom. When she saw me she screamed, but I quickly grabbed her by the throat and choked off the shrilling cry.

Erotica clawed at my hand, so I cracked her over the head with the gun, knocked her out cold. When I slapped her awake she was laid across the bed, bound and gagged. I had covered her nakedness with a comforter.

"Just tell me where the drugs and money is at and I'll be gone. You don't wanna die over Soldier Boy's shit. If he loved you, he wouldn't have the shit in your house no way," I said. Then I removed the duct tape from over her mouth just long enough for her to cooperate.

True to my word, I grabbed the cocaine and a shoe bag full of money and left up out of there without harming her. Back home, Kamora and I tallied up our gain. We had five bricks and seventy-five bands. *Not bad for a night's work.*

The next day, I hit Ava off with Twenty-five stacks and one brick. I warned her not to mention anything to anyone.

"And don't go spending crazy." I added.

"What am I supposed to do with a kilo of cocaine? I don't know anyone to sell it to," She griped.

"Give it back. I'll sell it and bring you fifteen bands," I said.

"Don't keys go for like thirty stacks?"

"Girl, you better take fifteen and be happy," I advised, but she decided to keep the brick and try to sell it for more. I knew she was making a mistake, but I wasn't going to sit there and try to change her mind.

"Do what you do then, lil' mama. Just be careful not to make the same mistake Erotica made. Keep your business off of your lips because you never know whose listening." I lightly lectured her.

Ava thanked me and gave me a hug. All I could do was hope she would follow my advice.

Ca$h

CHAPTER 13

As soon as I got rid of the four bricks I took from Soldier Boy, I returned my full attention to Solo. After watching his movements for almost a month and a half, I decided that tryna run up in his house was not a wise move. Not only was his home a fortress, I wasn't convinced he kept drugs or money stashed there. But our efforts had not been in vain. While following Solo, I drew the conclusion that he met up with his supplier at this little Mexican restaurant in Stockbridge, Georgia, thirty minutes or so outside of Atlanta.

Observing him on two different occasions, I figured out how the move went down. Solo would be driven to the restaurant by the same nigga in his crew every time.

The nigga was light-skinned with light gray eyes that stood out. He drove a white Suburban to the restaurant and parked next to an identical truck, which would already be there when they arrived. They would go inside and have dinner with two Mexicans. One of the Mexicans was small and clean cut and wore business suits. The other one was much younger and rocked a baldhead. I judged him to be the enforcer.

After dinner, both parties would exit the restaurant together. When they drove away they would have already switched vehicles with each other.

"That's when the exchange goes down," I said to Criminal.

"Yep. Solo brings the money and the Mexican brings the work. Then they switch whips. That's clever as hell."

"We're gonna have to smash all four of them and get away from there real fast. And ain't no way of knowing if they have lookouts posted up and down the street. So, we're gonna have to use at least two of your people, maybe more. I'll have Kamora along to watch my back."

"How are we gonna do it?" asked Criminal, who was anxious to set it off. He had grand ideas, and this lick was what he was counting on to kick-start his street dreams.

"We'll wait until they come out of the restaurant. Then we'll wet 'em up, grab their car keys and mash out. That's why we have to have some help because we'll have to get their trucks away from there fast. We won't have time to search them on the spot." I disclosed the plan.

Criminal could get one of his GF comrades to drive the Suburban that I expected the drugs to be in. I would get Kamora to drive the other one away from there since if I was correct, it would contain the money.

"We'll need two more gunners, and we have to find a secluded spot nearby where we can search the vehicles. I'm not chancing letting my girl drive too far in that muthafucka." Criminal agreed with my logic.

When we were alone at home, I bounced the plan off Kamora. "So, what do you think about it?" I asked her opinion.

"It seems sound enough to me. As long as no one panics, we all should be good," she said with less enthusiasm than I'd expected to hear.

"Shawdy, if you ain't feeling this lick we can cancel it."

"No, bae, it's not that. I just worry that one of these times things aren't going to go in our favor."

"Hush, before you fuck around and speak that shit into existence."

Kamora hushed, but I was still uptight about the lick right up until it went down a few weeks later.

The evening came when it was show time. We were all prepared—wasn't no turning back. I parked outside of the Mexican restaurant with Criminal in the passenger seat. The two gunners Criminal brought along were inside of an electronics store next to the restaurant. Kamora and another GF dude were inside of the restaurant, waiting patiently for the evening to unfold.

As soon as Solo and them walked out of the restaurant and reached their trucks, we were on them like a trained hit squad. My yoppa spoke first. I chopped Solo down in an instant. Beside me, Criminal's four-fifth joined in and I saw the baldheaded Mexican double over and fall to his knees. Criminal ran up close to him and smashed him. The smaller Mexican pulled out a banger and fired off a lone shot at the two GF gunners before they blasted him over the hood of a Camry parked next to the Suburban.

Solo's mans with the gray eyes ducked low and took off running in the opposite direction. I blasted after him, but the nigga got away.

By now, Kamora and the other designated driver were out of the restaurant rambling through both Mexican's pockets in search of the truck keys.

"I got them!" announced Kamora.

I looked on the ground and saw a second ring of keys. Solo's man had dropped them. I pointed them out to the GF dude and he snatched them up.

"Let's get up out of here!" shouted Criminal.

"Hold up," I said. I aimed the yoppa at the large glass window of the restaurant and let loose. Nosy muthafuckas caught a face full of lead.

I tossed the AK-47 into the backseat and then dragged Solo's body inside.

"Yo what you doing, bruh?" asked Criminal. I could not see his face because like me, he wore a ski mask, but his tone told me that he was not feeling that move.

"I got this," I said.

We drove off and met up with the others at the designated spot. After we found what we were searching for inside of the two Suburbans, we set them both ablaze and quickly mashed out.

At a house in Rockdale, owned by the sister of one of the GF gunners, we split up the drugs and money. Kamora and I got half and Criminal got the other half. I left it to him to break bread with his Good Fellas homies.

On the way home, Kamora asked, "Bae, why are we riding around with a dead body in the trunk?"

"I'ma take care of that," I promised with no further explanation.

At home, we showered together and then exalted over our score. Real talk, neither of us was in love with the money as much as we in love with the rush that we got from deading a nigga.

We then laid in bed, sharing a blunt and watching television. I felt Kamora's hand encircle my dick and stroke it up and down.

"Can I get some of my dick tonight?" she asked.

"If you gotta ask, it ain't yours."

"Oh, it's mine. That's for sure." She slid down under the covers and put her lips around the head of my manhood.

"You like the way I suck your dick?"

"Mmm hmm."

"What about when I spit on it and slurp it up?" *Puwt!* She did exactly what she was talking about.

"Suck this dick, baby girl. Show me you got a fool head game."

That's all the encouragement Kamora needed. She put her head game down something serious. I held her by the head and tried to hold out, but she kept saying, "Give me that hot cum, nigga" in between slurps.

The next thing I knew, I was exploding in her mouth.

"Mmm, you taste good, bae. Now I'ma need you to dick me down."

I was definitely game for that. I fucked Kamora into a deep sleep.

When I awoke in the morning, she was still sleeping peacefully. So, I left a text on her phone telling her I would be back later.

CHAPTER 14

I drove down to the hood to holla at Tommy Gun, a hustla whom I had known since Pre-K. TG was getting to the dough real good because he was fucking with a made nigga who had stupid work on deck.

I pulled up on TG in front of his baby mama's house on Constitution Street. He was waxing his silver F-150. Rick Ross' *Push It* was booming from the truck. TG eyed me, a bit leery, as I hopped out of my ride and walked up on him. He knew I was pressing many of the d-boy.

"Fam, I come in peace," I announced. We touched fists.

"Nigga, we go back like noodles off the same fork. I would never press you," I spoke sincerely.

I could see him staring at the diamond encrusted urn that hung from my chain.

"Put it on, Youngblood," he said, testing me.

"I put it on my pop," I vowed.

The tenseness in his face automatically dissolved. He knew I would not break a vow sealed with my father's name.

"Homie, you got the city shook. Po-po ain't even gotta close a nigga's trap down. Muthafuckas scared to open up 'cause they fear Trouble. But, fam, you should put the toolie down and get money with me," he proposed.

"Nawl, I ain't no d-boy."

"I hear you. So, what you wanted to holla at me about?"

"I got a proposition for you."

"Let me hear it."

"Supposed I said I had forty-six bricks and you can get 'em for fifteen a piece?" I tossed at him.

I saw him doing the math in his head.

"Well, problem number one is I don't have that kind of stacks on deck. Problem number two is that the agreement I have with my connect is that I won't get work from anybody but him."

"Who's your connect? Solo?" He didn't have to answer. I knew what I knew.

"Do you have any work at the moment?" I asked.

"Nawl. My people must be out of town picking up a new shipment because I haven't heard from him in a few days."

"Well, it won't hurt you to take a look at what I got. Just take a peek. You don't have to commit to anything."

TG followed me to my car. I walked around to the trunk and opened it. He stood next to me and peered inside at the bundle under the blanket.

"Check it out," I said and uncovered the bundle. Solo's lifeless eyes stared up at us. I saw the color drain from my homie's face.

"You gonna fuck with me?" I smirked and shut the trunk.

"I guess I don't have a choice, do I?"

"Oh, you do. I'm not coming to you on no gorilla shit. Just give me a hunnid and fiddy stacks up front and you can pay the rest after you slang the work."

He nodded his agreement and we sealed it with a fist pound.

"TG, let what you saw in my trunk be a warning to you of what will happen if you tell anyone about it," I threatened.

"Homie, I'm like Stevie Wonder. I ain't seen shit."

I didn't trust Tommy Gun not to ever open his mouth about what he'd seen. I believed if he ever got bopped up on a serious drug charge he might try to bargain his freedom with what I had shown him. Therefore, I buried Solo's body somewhere it was unlikely to ever be found. Then I torched my ride to get rid of all forensic evidence.

I still had ten more bricks on deck. We had struck gold when we hit Solo. I sold three of the ten blocks I had left to one of Inez' relatives and told him to give the money to her.

"That's for being a true rider for my pop when he was alive, and for doing what you do for all of his seeds," I told her.

Another three bricks were sold to someone Kamora knew. I fronted the remaining four to Scarface and Manky, two partners from around the way.

Then I took Kamora on a weekend cruise to Jamaica. Unwinding in Jamaica from our deadly escapades was exactly what Kamora needed because shawdy had been very tense lately. We spent a full week lying on the beach smoking ganja and listening to reggae.

We hit various nightclubs and, of course, we dined at different restaurants, enjoying the spicy Jamaican dishes. Hell, we even attended a soccer match. We both were two shades darker by the time our vacation ended.

When I returned, I collected taxes along with some of the money TG owed me. He was pushing work well and only had twenty bricks left.

Manky and Scarface were another story. All of a sudden, they wouldn't even answer their cell phones. This went on for a week.

"I can't believe these niggas tryna test me," I told my shawdy.

"Is it time to clack up?" she asked with a slight smile and raised brows.

"Not yet, I'ma see how it plays out." I was trying to give them the benefit of the doubt.

An hour later, I whipped over to Big Ma's house. I was glad to see that Shan wasn't over there. I hugged and kissed Big Ma and then we sat and talked for hours. She even told me about her past drug addiction, being honest about the foul things she had done to get more crack.

"Poochie," I addressed her, teasingly. "I bet you was something else back in the day." I knew about her indiscretions with my pop, but I never judged her.

"Hmph! But the good Lord brought me through. He'll do the same for your mother, you'll see."

"The good Lord can't bring my pop back."

"No, he can't. You just have to trust that He makes no mistakes. I've always believed that the Lord took your father so you could learn how not to live," she lightly preached.

A lot of good that did, I thought.

Big Ma must have read my mind. "God does everything on His own time and He's always on time, no matter what it seems. You'll fall on your knees and turn your life over to him one day," she prophesied.

"Well, he better hurry 'cause I'ma die young," I said.

"Boy, hush your mouth. Only God can say how long you'll live," she scoffed.

"Seriously, Big Ma. My pop was just twenty-nine years old when they killed him. I'll never see that age. But while I'm here, I'm gonna take care of and protect those I love."

I pulled out thirty stacks and placed them on the cocktail table in front of us.

"That's for a down payment on a new house. I want you to move to the suburbs because you stay too close to where I do dirt. I'm afraid that someone might hurt you to get back at me."

"God is my shield and my sword."

"Please, Big Ma, do it for me," I begged.

"Oh no!" She stood firm. "I can't accept that. If I did, it would be condoning whatever you did to get it. The Bible teaches that it is easier for a camel to go through the eye of a needle than for a rich man to enter the Kingdom of God."

I wanted to argue, *Crackers wrote the Bible*, but I held my tongue.

"Lil T, the love of money is the root of all evil. Don't you see what the pursuit of it makes you do? But only God can judge. All I can do is love you and try to share His word with you."

I stood up. I had heard enough.

"I feel you, Big Ma," I said.

"Take the devil's money with you on your way out."

I just smiled and shook my head.

CHAPTER 15

The next day, I was at the crib telling Kamora how Big Ma responded when I tried to give her the down payment on a new house.

"At least she's not a hypocrite," said shawdy.

My cell phone lit up on the dresser in the middle of the conversation. "Excuse me, shawdy, let me catch this call," I told her.

"It's okay, bae."

"Sup, nigga?" I grumbled at the caller.

"I got that check for you," replied Manky.

"Meet me at that liquor store on Boulevard, the one that has a mural of my pop painted on the side of the building."

"A'ight give me an hour. And yo don't kill me, man."

"I ain't gonna do you dirty, nigga. Just have my ducats. Where's Scarface?"

"I'ma tell you 'bout that," he said.

I rolled dolo because Kamora had gone to dinner with Sharena. She believed she was close to getting ol' girl to lead us to Byron.

I pulled up to the liquor store and honked my horn. The owner came out and chopped it up with me for a second or two and then went back inside.

Manky arrived ten minutes later. I waved the nigga over to where I stood, leaned on the hood of my car, watching everything that moved.

"Where's my dough, nigga?" My tone was cyanide, and my hand was inside my Polo jacket, gripping my banger.

"Be easy, man. Give me a chance to pay you and explain." He held his arms up in front of his face as though his arms could stop a bullet. "I got that in a shoe bag under my seat."

I followed him over to his car, watching him carefully when he reached under the seat. Had he pulled out anything other than a bag I was gonna spill his thoughts on the ground. I accepted the bag of money and we walked back over to where I was parked.

Then Manky broke it down to me.

"Trouble, I was gonna pay you your money off the rip because we got off of all four bricks in a day and a half. But Scarface was on some sideways shit. He said *fuck you, we keepin' the money.* I tried to tell his stupid ass that you weren't the one to try. But after he got those bands in his pocket he started thinkin' he was gonna be the next Big Meech."

I nodded.

"I couldn't really say shit because you hit him with the work. Shid, he chumped me off with one brick and kept the three for himself. Still, I hustled my half of what was owed for the four. I didn't want you to come gunning for my ass."

"Why wouldn't you answer my calls?"

"Man, I didn't want to have no excuses. So, I turned my phone off until I had what I owed you."

I pulled my jacket closed while I considered his explanation. Winter was coming in fast and the wind was biting. My dreads blew about my head like twigs from a tree.

"Get in the car," I said.

Manky hesitated. He must have feared I would take him on one of those rides that niggas never returned from.

"I'm not gonna slump you, man. I'm just tryna get out of the cold." I assured him.

We both got in the car and talked for a while. After I made myself clear, I let him bounce.

On the way home, I received a call from Tamia. Inez was in the hospital.

"What happened?" I asked.

"Bianca's daddy jumped on her," answered my sister.

On the way to the hospital, I couldn't help but count the many ways my life mirrored my pops'. A nigga had beat Toi down and my pops went snap over his sister.

Inez wasn't my sibling, but she was a surrogate mother to me. And it was about to be hell to tell the preacher, as we say in the Dirty.

I sat in the emergency room for hours until Inez was released. My blood boiled as soon as I saw her. The whole left side of her face was swollen and her left eye was black.

"That nigga gonna pay for this. If I don't put something on that ass, my pop was a bitch, and you know that's not true," I remarked while pushing her to the car in a wheelchair.

While driving Inez home, I asked why Fat Stan had jumped on her. "Because he's a hater," Inez replied. "He said I was a fool for still being in love with a dead man. He called Youngblood a coward— said he had given up on his appeals because he couldn't do the bid. So, I spat in that fat muthafucka's face! I'm not going to let no nigga talk about my boo, because if he was here, that bitch ass nigga wouldn't have said it to his face."

"He sure wouldna' called my pop a coward to his face, or he would've got the whole top of his head pushed back. My father coulda did the bid, but he showed those crackers he wasn't afraid of the needle, either. Like he said, *Either let me fly or give me death!* And that's some real nigga shit. Something Fat Stan's lame ass can't understand." I defended my pop, though I was preaching to the choir. Inez knew better than anyone that my pop feared nothing. "Anyway," I said with my lip curled, "where does that bitch ass nigga rest at? It's easy for his fat ass to knock a woman around, but I'ma see if he's so muthafuckin' hard when the odds aren't in his favor."

"He stays in one of those new lofts on Memorial Drive. You'll see his black Tahoe parked out there or his black Impala," she said.

"A'ight. Let me stop at CVS and get your prescription. Then I'ma drop you off at home so you can get some rest. Don't worry about that nigga. I'ma teach his ass about putting his hand on you. Nigga must don't know— you're more of a mother to me than the one that birthed me."

It was more than a thirty-minute wait for Inez' prescription to be filled. I paid for the pain pills and then drove her home and helped her in the house.

"Take care of your mama," I told Tamia.

I said nothing to Bianca. I didn't even look at her because in just a short while her father was gonna look way worse than Inez did.

"Have Tamia call me if you need anything," I said to Inez. I gave her a hug and then bounced.

Back in the car, I hit up my nigga, Criminal. "Sup, bruh-bruh," he answered.

"What you up to, pimp?"

"Just blowing some Kush with some of my fam. I been on a 24/7 grind ever since we did that, so now I'm just unwinding. Sup? You sound like you got some problems."

"In a way, I do, but it's not business. It's personal." I told him the deal.

"Shid, nigga, I fuck with you the long way, so let's go see this fat ass nigga. I'ma bring four of my homies with me, a'ight?" offered Criminal with no hesitation. I appreciated the love and it earned him more points with me.

"That's what's up, bruh. Y' all meet me at that carwash on Moreland where Tay got killed."

They needed no further direction. He knew the spot well.

Tay was a young nigga who was ranked the number two high school point guard in the nation. Some fool had robbed and killed him over some sneakers last year. The whole city had been torn up over Tay's murder because he wasn't a street dude.

"We're on our way," said Criminal.

It was dark outside the loft, except for the lights that illuminated the parking lot. Fat Stan's Impala was parked, but the Tahoe was not there. We waited patiently for almost three hours before we saw the Tahoe pull up. Criminal was ready to pounce.

I put my hands on my elbows. "Slow down, killa. Let him park and get out. We don't want him to get spooked and pull off." My adrenaline was racing, too, but the nature of my profession had taught me not to spring too quickly. I had done that once, early in my jack boy initiation and the vic' had gotten away. Now I had the patience of Job.

As soon as Fat Stan hopped down out of the Tahoe and lumbered toward the entrance of the building, Criminal was all over his ass.

With the black hoodie pulled low and tight over his face, he whipped out the four-fifth and cracked Fat Stan in the mouth. Fat Stan tried to run, but two of Criminal's GF homies blindsided him.

"*Whap!* They knocked him on the ground.

"Hold up! What I do to y' all?" he cried while trying to block blows and feet that came crashing down from all sides.

"Shut the fuck up, lame ass nigga, and take this ass whoopin' like a man," barked one of the GF dudes. They were stomping a mud hole in his ass.

Criminal busted his head open with the butt of the four-fifth, drawing more blood with each lick. Then I stepped through the crowd undisguised.

"You like beating on women, huh?" My tone was menacing. Fat Stan looked up and recognized my face. "Stupid nigga," I said. "Didn't you know when you put your hands on Inez, I was gonna come and straighten it? It don't matter how long my pops has been dead, Inez is still his woman. Plus, you called my father a coward." My nine came out ready to cough.

"Lil T, I'm sorry, youngin'. I swear I'll never hit her again. Just don't shoot me," cried Fat Stan.

Now that he was up against a man, all the bitch in him came out. He might as well have worn a pink thong up under the Evisu jeans he had on.

"Don't beg me, nigga. I ain't got no muthafuckin' talk!"

Boc!

The nine clapped and he made a sound like a whale crying. He held his hip and writhed in pain.

"Please, Youngblood!"

"Nigga, keep my daddy's name out of your mouth!"

Boc!

"Owww!" he yelped again and grabbed his other leg.

"Sing my name to the police and you'll never live to testify," I warned.

Criminal added, "Mob shit!"

Bow! His four-fifth sounded like a small canon. More blood gushed from Fat Stan's leg.

"Don't test my G," I warned him one final time.

Ca$h

CHAPTER 16

I might be a psychopath, I thought. Because one night after wilding out on Fat Stan, I took my sisters out for pizza and a movie as if last night never occurred. Then, less than twenty-four hours after a fun night out with my sisters, I was back on the G shit. Fat Stan's blood had barely dried on my hands when it was time to put my gangsta down again.

This time it was for keeps. My shawdy was parked outside of Manky's mother's house. If she didn't hear from me in forty-five minutes, my instructions to her were to puff mom's wig out.

I was outside of Manky's front door with my ear pressed to it. Inside, I could hear Manky's and another voice. I recognized Scarface, having a debate.

"Man, you ain't cut Michelle Pierce. Quit frontin'!" I heard him laugh.

"Dawg, you ever known me to lie on my dick?" asked Scarface.

"Hell yeah! All the time," Manky said.

"Well, I ain't lying now. For real, fam', I been hittin' it for two weeks. I love that bitch."

"It's still M.O.E. right? Let's cut that ho together, cuz."

"Hell to the nawl. I would rather see yo dick in my mama's mouth than to let you cut lil' buddy."

Manky laughed again. "Dayum, it's hittin' like that?"

"It's wet like the sea," boasted Scarface.

I listened as Manky switched the subject. He convinced Scarface that he was about to call up some Decatur hoes for them to fuck. I strained to hear his whole conversation, but I was getting impatient. Although I couldn't see them, I could imagine he had his cell phone to his ear, capping it off.

"Yo, what's up, shawdy? Y' all got some big asses? 'Cause ain't nothing but big dicks ova here," Scarface shouted.

"A'ight, baby girl y'all know how to get here. We'll see y' all in fifteen minutes," Manky said loud enough for his voice to carry out to me.

I checked the time on my wrist. Then I called Manky's cell phone. When he answered, I advised, "Don't get dumb. Remember: If I get it, your people get *got*, too."

"I know. Just holla at me tomorrow." He seemed to be playing his role to perfection.

Exactly fifteen minutes later, I rapped on the door. The irony of the situation was when he cracked the door opened. Jay-Z's joint *It Was All Good Just a Week Ago* was playing on the CD deck.

We grew up in the hood, my dawg and me/ we used to hustle on the block for all to see/ problems I called on him he called on me/ shit wasn't quite equal I broke him off a piece.

I was wearing a bulletproof vest up under my coat in case that message was for me. I wouldn't die alone if the cross was on. I raised the yoppa, and Manky stepped aside to let me in.

"He's in the bathroom. I have his strap, he left it on top of the flat screen," he whispered.

My eyes darted from right to left. I was wary of a setup, but not in fear. I ducked off into the kitchen out of sight, but I could peep around the refrigerator and see Scarface when he reentered the living room.

"Where those hoes at?" asked Scarface, anxious for some pussy that was not on the way. "I thought I heard a knock at the door."

"That was my neighbor," Manky lied.

"Oh. What's taking those bitches so long to get here?"

"Just chill, dawg."

"Yeah, you're right. Check this out. Shit been shady between us lately. I know it's because you disagree with how I handled that work we got from Trouble. But peep game, bruh. That nigga don't put fear in me. What? I'ma let another man have me shook? Never dat! Fuck, Trouble. He got guns. We got guns. Ya feel me?"

I saw Manky nod his head.

"Damn, shawdy, you look like you 'bout to cry," Scarface said. "Trouble ain't got you shook, do he? Not killa Mank. Fam, let me find out you done went soft," he cracked.

"Oh shit!" he shrilled when I stepped out of the kitchen with the yoppa aimed at his chest.

"Sup, Scar? You're slippin', homie. I got guns. You got guns. Ain't that the slick shit you was just poppin'? Go for your gun, nigga, so I can chop your punk ass down."

He stared at the AK-47 in my hands.

"I was only kickin' the bo-bo wit' my nigga, Mank. We was gon' pay you. Wasn't we, Mank?"

"Your man already squared up his debt. You're the bitch that thought you could hold out on me. Fool, Manky put ya ass in the re-mix."

He looked at Manky, his closest friend and uttered, "Nawl, bruh. Say it ain't so, you snake muthafucka!"

"Homie, I'm not a snake. I begged you to pay Trouble, but your greedy ass wouldn't do it. So, you made your own bed."

Blocka! Blocka!

Manky shot his man in the forehead and the chest. Scarface's body dropped to the floor in a grotesque twist. Now Manky's debt to me was paid in full.

I hit Kamora on her touch screen. "It's over, shawdy. You can go home. I'll see you in a few."

"Okay, are you blowing my back out tonight, Daddy?" she rasped in a voice thick with seduction.

I jokingly replied, "I'm not your daddy, I'm ya Grandpa."

"Bae, you so crazy." She laughed.

For three straight days and nights all Kamora and I did was make love, blow Kush, eat and sleep. My touch still inflamed her like they very first time, I still thirsted for her body and loved to hold her in my arms after we pleased each other.

Of course all that marathon fucking came with a price.

Five weeks later, Kamora announced with a proud smile on her face that she was pregnant.

"Don't tell me that shit, shawdy," I responded angrily.

"Bae, why you gotta holler?" whined Kamora.

"I'm not hollerin'! How the fuck did this happen?"

"Uh duh!"

"Don't get slick out the mouth! You know what the fuck I mean. You were supposed to be on the pill."

"Listen, nigga! I was on the fuckin' pill. So maybe I forgot to take a pill sometimes, because a bitch isn't perfect. We run around killing people twenty-four seven, and we stay blunted— what do you expect?" Her fuse was short, too.

"I expected you to handle your business," I said. "You already know." We agreed that we weren't bringing a child into this world as long as we were doing what we do."

"Terrence, I don't feel like solving a riddle, so will you please just give it to me uncut. Do you want me to get rid of our baby?"

Now I knew shorty was steaming. She never called me by my government name. Her eyes teared up as she awaited my response.

"Shawdy, you know what we agreed on," I shot back.

"Yes—or—no! Do you want me to get rid of the baby?"

My tone softened, but my decision did not change. "Yes."

Kamora burst into tears and ran off into the bedroom like a white girl. I sat in the den of our spacious condo and threw back shots of Hen dog straight to the head. I got so drunk I tripped over my own feet when I stood up.

Steadying myself, I made my way back to our bedroom using the walls to hold me up. The bedroom door was locked. I knocked, but Kamora wouldn't open the door.

"Sha—shawdy—let—me talk to—you," I slurred. Still, she wouldn't respond. I put my ear to the door and heard crying.

I was cold-hearted, but to my girl I was never that way. What hurt Kamora hurt me. I couldn't change my decision, though. At the rate we were going, we both could be dead at a single tick of the clock. It would be unfair to bring a child into the midst of that uncertainty.

I slid down the floor, placing my back against the bedroom door and tried to think. I looked down at the urn that hung from the chain around my neck and silently spoke with my daddy.

"Yo, pop, this is the same shit you went through with Inez, ain't it? I guess it don't matter how gangsta a woman is, she's still a female and she still has emotions. Did you ever regret not pressing any of your baby mamas to have an abortion? Probably not. Nigga, you was slinging dick like crack." I chuckled. "Man, this shit is crazy. My wifey is in

there crying her eyes out, and it's breaking a nigga's heart. What is a young nigga to do?"

I sat there trying to think of the right way to deal with the situation. The sound of Kamora crying had my head fucked up, at first. Then I got upset because Kamora should've never put me in this situation. Our agreement was supposed to have been tacit.

I stood up and banged on the door. "Open this bitch up or I'ma kick it down! Think I'm muthafuckin' playing!" I barked. The Hennessey was controlling my tongue.

When Kamora didn't respond, I followed up my threat by thrusting my shoulder into the door with such force that I broke the doorframe. Then I kicked the door in with my foot. The funny thing was Kamora didn't even budge. She remained stretched across the bed with a pillow covering her face.

"Are you gonna have an abortion or not?" I asked.

Still, she refused to respond.

"You, know what? Fuck—this—this shit. I'm—out!" I slurred.

Somehow, I made it to the strip club without getting pulled over. Inside, I found an unoccupied booth and waved Ava over.

"What's poppin', baby boy? What brings you to my place of employment?" she asked.

"I'm just passing a little time. Tryna clear my head really," I confessed.

"You want to talk about it?" she offered, but I didn't wanna talk.

"Nah, I wanna see a fat, pretty pussy. I wanna see titties bouncing and ass cheeks clapping. C'mon, show me what you're working with." I pulled a coupla bands.

Ava smiled and began swaying her hips. She moved closer and used a knee to spread my knees wider so that she could get even closer.

Moving in tune with the music, she removed her string bikini top. Her titties were two perfect orbs, not too big but more than a mouthful. Her dark brown nipples looked taunt and edible. She cupped her titties and lifted them close to my mouth.

"You like?" she purred.

"Fuck yeah."

She opened her legs and pulled her thong aside just enough to give me a peek at her treasure. Then she spun halfway, grabbed her ankles and made that ass jiggle one cheek at a time. I smacked that big booty and leaned back for the rest of the show.

While Ava gave it up, I took her in real good. She was short and thick with a very pretty face and seductive eyes. The hood version of Rhianna, but much thicker. Her pussy was like a camel's toe. Plus, it was clean and shaven.

"Pop that pussy for ya boy," I prodded.

She did not hesitate. She started poppin' that pussy. I stuffed money in her garter and whispered my mack game in her ear.

"You just wanna fuck tonight." She laughed.

"I don't wanna fuck. You got it wrong, lil' mama. I am gonna fuck you tonight. And I'ma have you walking bowlegged when I'm done," I boasted.

"This ain't what you want."

"Why ain't it?"

"Because I'll have you talking in your sleep. I'm telling you right now, my pussy is so wet and tight you'll go crazy when you get up in it."

"Girl, please." I chuckled, waving the waiter over. "Bring me a bottle of Patron." I handed the waiter $200 and she headed to the bar to get my bottle.

A half hour later, I was feeling good and ready to see if Ava's shit was as fiyah as she advertised. "Can you leave?" I asked.

"I told you this ain't what you want," she repeated with so much sassiness I couldn't back out. "Give me fifteen minutes," she said.

Twenty-five minutes later, we were headed to a hotel. As I drove I checked my cell to see if Kamora had called or text. She hadn't, so I turned my phone off and shoved it back inside my pocket.

I drove to the Fairfield Inn and rented a room for the night. Once we were inside, I pulled out some Kush and Ava and I blazed two blunts. I was already feeling guilty because I knew what was about to go down and I had never creeped on Kamora. So, I forced myself not to think about it, which wasn't hard to do now that Ava was standing up and removing her clothes. As soon as she bared those succulent breasts, I stood up and said, "Hit the brakes, lil' mama. I'ma drive this car. All you gotta do is enjoy the ride."

She wrapped her arms around my neck and whispered in my ear, "I love a nigga to take control."

"That's how I rock." I kissed her neck while sliding her pants off.

"Hurry up, nigga. I've been wanting you since we were in middle school."

"*Shhh.* Be quiet. I'ma do all of the talking. Let me feel this fat pussy." I eased my hand inside of her thong and palmed her mound. I softly squeezed it before running my finger up her hot, wet slit.

"*Ssssss!*" she sizzled when I drew tiny circles around her clit with my finger.

I concentrated on her love button until I felt her body quiver, then I slid two fingers deep inside of her sugar walls and slowly moved them in and out. She was so wet her juices squished down my arm. I drew my fingers out and held them up to her mouth.

"*Mmmm.* You like to watch me taste my own pussy, don't you?" she moaned.

"Didn't I tell you to hush?" I drew back and slapped her across her face. That shit must have turned Ava on because she looked at me like she wanted to eat a nigga up. I pushed her down to her knees. She knew what I wanted.

She took my dick out and stroked it up and down while kissing the head. Ava looked up at me as she licked the underside of my hardness then took me deep into her warm mouth.

"Suck that muthafucka like you want it to be yours," I said.

Ava's slow neck game was wicked. I was up on my toes like a muthafuckin' ballerina. I then thrust my dick further down her throat, causing her to gag.

"Yeah, this that grown man shit!" I boasted.

A few minutes later, lil' mama was swallowing my cum. I had to grab a hold of her head to keep from falling. A nigga's legs were weak and the alcohol had my head spinning.

"Dayum, shawdy, you ain't slip nothing in my drink, did you?" I asked, now stretched out across the bed.

"Hell no, I would never do you like that. You must don't know that I really want to fuck with you. On all levels," professed Ava.

I was kinda drunk, but liquor couldn't make me lie. I kept it gutter at all times, that way I wouldn't have to deal with the bullshit later.

"Shawdy, you know I got an old lady. And on the real, I ain't never fucked around on her, so I can't tell you that I'll fuck with you like this beyond tonight. You feel me?"

"I feel you. I guess I'll just have to make this memorable, then."

"Do what you do." I pulled off my gear and welcomed Ava to the dick.

Shawdy damn sure did her thing. She rode my dick up and down, slow and fast, frontwards and backwards. When guilt about creeping on Kamora tried to surface in my thoughts and fuck up the mood, I pushed those thoughts right out of my mind and went deeper inside of Ava. We fucked like we were running a marathon and then we fell asleep sweaty and satiated.

In the morning, I dropped Ava off at home and headed to my spot wondering if Kamora would be able to read the guilt on my face when I walked through the door.

CHAPTER 17

Standing in doorway of our bedroom, I could see Kamora's figure under the covers. I kicked off my Jordans, pulled off my socks and stepped out of my jeans. I slid under the cover and Kamora scooted to the edge of the bed away from me.

"I see you still on some emotional shit. And I thought you was gangster," I said to the back of her neck. She hugged the pillow tighter and continued to ignore me.

"I see you ain't built like I thought you was," I added, hoping to stir up some kind of response out of her. It worked, but the response was not the one I had hoped for. She started sobbing into the pillow.

"I want to keep my baby," she cried.

Shawdy was fucking with my emotions. I said, "C'mon, Kamora, don't switch up on me in the middle of the race. We already talked about this, and I thought we both agreed that we wasn't having no kids because with the way we're living, ain't nothing in our future but death."

"We don't have to live that way."

"You may not, but I don't have a choice. I'm gonna avenge my pop."

"And then what, bae?" she asked, rolling over on her side and looking into my eyes.

"After you avenge your father, what will you do? What type of life will we have with all these murders on our conscience?"

I stared at her in straight disbelief. I couldn't figure out where she was coming from with that type of response. Shit, she had already bodied three muthafuckas before we hooked up, and together we had been dropping niggas with no regret. Now she was on some next shit.

"I ain't got no conscience, shawdy. Muthafuckas didn't feel no type of way about killing my pop, so I don't give a fuck about them. Now either you bustin' ya gun right next to me or you're falling back. Which one? I need to know how you're rockin'."

When she took too long to answer, I said, "I thought you were theBonnie to my Clyde, but in a snap of a finger you're some new bitch that I don't even recognize. I can't fuck with you no more 'cause you sound like you're capable of testifying against me like my mama did to my pop."

"Nigga, I'm not your dirty ass mama! If I'm nothing in this world, I'm loyal to your black ass. Don't you dare compare me to a snitch bitch!" Kamora was seething.

"I don't know what or who you are, shawdy."

"Wow. Is that really how you feel about me? I thought I had already proven to you that I'm a real ass bitch. And I thought I would never see the day when you would discount all that I've shown you. So maybe I don't know you like I thought I did," she countered.

I glared at her. "Maybe you don't."

I slid out of bed and put my clothes back on. My banger was on the floor next to my Jordans. I picked it up and snapped one in the chamber.

"Something tells me I ought to do you right here, right now, or it's gonna come back to hurt me," I said in a threatening tone.

"Would you really take my life?" asked Kamora.

I saw the hurt in her eyes and heard it in her voice, but I could not allow it to cloud my judgment.

"You damn right I would. Before I let you sell me out I would murk you with no remorse.

"Wow!" was all she said, but the look in her eyes said everything else.

When I considered all that we had been through together, I lowered the banger and shoved it inside of my waistband. Not another word was spoken between us the entire time I was packing my gear.

Once I was through packing, I said, "Shawdy, I can't force you to have an abortion, but I can't stay with you if you don't. I believe—"

"Why, bae?" Kamora interrupted.

"Because the baby will be what they'll use to make you flip on me."

"Never, bae."

"I can't take that chance. So, you have to decide right now what it is you love the most. If it's not me, I'll walk out the door."

She broke down again. "How can you ask me to choose between you and your own seed?"

"What you gonna do, shawdy?"

114

She wiped at her tears and looked at me with an expression that was intense and unbreakable. "I'm not killing my child," she replied.

I tried one last time. "If I walk out of that door, I'm not coming back. I put that on my pop."

"Goodbye, T. I'll always love you."

I gathered up my bags and headed for the door hoping that Kamora would run up behind me and beg me to stay. Hoping that shawdy would come to her senses and realize that having a child was the wrong move, but my hopes were fruitless.

At the door, I turned and said, "I only took half of the money out of the stash spot. The rest is yours."

"I don't want it."

Now I knew Kamora had lost her mind, or else she was allowing her emotions to control her words. I just shook my head and walked out to my whip. Before pulling off, I looked up and saw Kamora toss a duffel bag outside.

Oh, hell to the no! I said to myself.

I jumped out and went to retrieve the duffel bag of money. Too much blood had been spilled to stack that check. I wasn't about to let the dough just sit there.

I felt a pain in my heart as I drove away from there. Kamora and I had been ride or die with each other from the moment we first kissed, and now it was over in the blink of an eye.

From that night forward, it was like a part of me was gone. Now, I really had that *fuck the world* attitude.

Ca$h

CHAPTER 18

"Yeah, fuck the world!" I shared my feelings with Inez. I was sitting on her living room couch blazing a blunt. My head was still spinning about Kamora.

"Boy, you're trippin'. What do you expect? Of course, she don't want to kill her baby."

"I expected shawdy to keep it gangsta. How is she gonna be Bonnie to my Clyde in a maternity dress?"

"Maybe she doesn't want to be Bonnie. Can't she just be Kamora? You have to understand that pregnancy is something very special and sacred. What if your mother had aborted you?"

"What? I should've aborted her ass," I argued and Inez couldn't help but laugh. We both knew that Shan was only the vessel through which I came into this world. A mother she was not.

"But you can't compare Kamora to Shan," objected Inez. "Kamora will probably make a good mother. And for you to break up with her because she doesn't want to abort her baby is dead wrong. I expect much better of you. See, that's what I loved about your father. It didn't matter how he felt about those other women who had children by him, he always loved and provided for all his kids. That's what a man does, Lil T. I know you're a gangsta in the mold of Youngblood, but there was a soft side to him when it came to his children. If it wasn't, Shan wouldn't be alive today, and he would've probably never gotten caught for those murders. But when he broke in the house to kill Shan, he ran into you in the hallway. He just could not kill her in front of you."

"He should have," I stated.

"That's neither here or there. It must not have been in God's plan for it to happen." Inez waved off my comment.

"I didn't know you believed in God." I coughed, choking on Kush smoke.

"Of course, I believe in God, boy."

"You don't go to church," butted in Tamia who had just come downstairs into the living room.

"Church is in the heart," replied Inez. "Now go back upstairs so I can finish talking to your brother.

117

"Okay," said Tamia. But before she left she turned to me and held out her hand.

I placed a couple hundred dollars in it and she skipped off. I caught a glimpse of Bianca glaring at me from the staircase. *Whatever, shawdy*, I thought.

When the two of them vanished back upstairs, I picked back up on my conversation with Inez.

"I thought Kamora was a pitbull in a skirt, but she ain't no killa. She just did what she did to impress me."

"She did it out of love for you. Don't you ever think she just enjoys all of that. She was doing it because you needed her by your side," reasoned Inez as she uncrossed her legs then crossed them again.

"Is that why you set up King for my pop? Or did you do it because you're a true rider?"

"I did it because I would've done anything for him. That's how deep my love was for him. But don't get it twisted. I never pulled the trigger. I'm not no killer. And even now, all these years later, I still have nightmares about what I did. Women aren't like men. We have fragile emotions and a guilty conscience when we hurt someone."

"You think my pop had a conscience?" I asked.

"Definitely. But not for the enemy."

I nodded my understanding, leaned back on the couch and gathered my thoughts. When they were clear, I blurted out, "If Kamora has the baby, I'ma do what a man is supposed to do, but I can't fuck with her like that no more. She broke her word to me."

"Lil T, you're being unfair to her."

"Well, life is unfair, then you die." I grunted as I lifted myself up and headed for the door.

As soon as I stepped off of the porch I was swarmed by APD! "Get on the ground! Get on the fuckin' ground! Now!" they shouted.

In the backseat of a police cruiser, headed to jail, I was suddenly thankful that I had absentmindedly left my nine on Inez' coffee table along with the bag of Kush I had been smoking.

This was one time being high saved my ass, because the nine indeed had been used in a murder. Still, I wasn't out of the clear. I was being arrested for some reason or other, and it damn sure wasn't no misdemeanor shit. Not with the way APD and plain clothes detectives bum rushed me.

I figured Bianca had dropped a dime on me. Fat Stan had probably told her that I had shot him. Yep. And that's why shawdy was standing on the staircase grilling me.

"Well, I guess shit could be worse," I said to myself in resignation. I didn't like it one bit, but at least I wasn't being snatched up on a body charge. I could make bond on this.

Downtown at the Pretrial Center, I was taken into a cold room and made to wait over two hours before someone came in to talk to me. I knew that it was one of the tactics they used to unravel a muthafucka because it had been tried on me once before. *Me unravel, though? Imagine that!*

I had my feet propped up on the table and my hands behind my head when two detectives walked into the interrogation room. One was a short, fat black dude in his forties, I guessed. The other was about 5'11", medium build, brown skin and kind of put me in mind of P. Diddy. He wore a thick, platinum chain around his neck and he was dressed like a street nigga who was in his mid-thirties and still had swag. I recognized him immediately. On the streets, he was known as Smooth. His sullied reputation preceded him.

It was rumored that Smooth robbed and extorted some drug dealers and provided protection for a few others. And it was said that he wasn't above fabricating evidence to ensure a conviction. It was well-known that Smooth got just as much hood pussy as the hood superstars. In other words, Smooth had his hand in a whole lotta shit, and his badge gave the nigga immunity.

Looking at Smooth and his little fat partner, who had just introduced himself as Thomas, I felt my throat dry up, but I disguised my nervousness like a true street veteran.

If they were waiting for me to break the ice, I hoped they packed a lunch and a change of clothes.

Thomas grilled me with the most intimidating face, but my expression remained unchanged. That seemed to bother him. He swiped my feet off of the table with his arm and pushed me over in my chair.

"I know all about you, you little thug!"

I got up off of the floor, up-righted the chair and sat back down without responding in any way.

"I know who your father was. We executed his murdering ass, didn't we, Smooth?" Thomas said to his partner, trying to blow me. But I remained calm and quiet.

"Oh, he's hard. We'll see how long you last when I send you to prison for life. You'll be somebody's bitch in no time at all."

I found a spot on the wall and stared at it. There wasn't a nigga on God's green earth that could make Trouble his bitch. Three life times behind bars couldn't bring a bitch out of a nigga, unless there was a bitch hidden inside of him all along. Thomas was just talking because he had a tongue and didn't know what the fuck else to do with it.

Smooth threw several enlarged black and white photos on the table in front of me. They were crime scene photos of BoBo, Zeke's brother, and his girl.

"The way we're hearing it, that's your work, lil homie."

I remained silent.

"Terrence Whitsmith Jr, aka Little T, aka Trouble, aka Coward. Do I need to go on?" asked Thomas.

I didn't remark. I listened to them read my street file for twenty minutes. Some of what they said was accurate, but other things were bullshit that snitch nigga blamed on me, although I had not committed that crime.

"We all know about you, Trouble. You have all of the drug dealers afraid. Now really, I don't give a rat's ass about some worthless piece of slim drug dealer. You all can kill each other and I wouldn't lose one night of sleep. But when you kill innocent women and make their children orphans that's when I gotta nail your ass." Thomas went on and on.

When Thomas grew tired of talking, Smooth took over, employing a much kinder interrogation technique.

"Maybe you were put in a situation where you felt you had no choice but to kill them. I can understand that," he said.

As before, my expression remained blank. These two fools didn't know who they were tryna run that routine on. Although I was young, I knew the rule – keep your mouth closed.

120

Two hours later, they had work themselves out. That's when I finally spoke.

"I'd like to call my lawyer," I said.

It turned out that Bianca hadn't dropped a dime on me about shooting Fat Stan, which was good because it would've complicated my relationship with Inez and Tamia. But someone had dropped a dime about BoBo, and only two others besides myself had known that I smashed the nigga and his bitch.

Kamora knew, but I didn't even waste time considering her. Shawdy had nothing to gain and everything to lose had she done that. The only other person that could've dropped a dime on me was Zeke.

On the outside, Zeke talked all that killa shit like he would rather take it war than pay street taxes. But he must have feared me inside so much that he was trying to use po-po to get me off the streets.

Old heads knew that we 90's babies were quick to murder some shit. For the most part, we owned the streets because most of us had nothing to lose. Our mamas were crackheads and our pops were either in prison or dead. So, we were off the muthafucking rack, dumb-wild with that banger in our hands. We feared nothing and no one because we had nothing and no one.

On the other hand, old heads like Zeke had wives and families that they always had to consider. Seldom did they want to go all out and risk losing everything that they had hustled so many years to get. So, they were no match for the new generation of killas, like myself. Besides, I had the true G blood of my pop in my veins.

From the interrogation room, I was taken up on the sixth floor and detained for suspicion of murder. Up on the floor it, was like a hood reunion. All of the homies were up there waiting to be sent over to Rice Street to await trial for whatever they were in jail for. Most had body or armed robbery charges. I chopped it up with them, but I mentioned nothing about my own charges. *Trust No Man* was still the code I lived by.

A day later, Swag's lawyer came to see me at the jail. "I'll have you out of here in forty-eight hours. They have nothing on you. So just relax and keep your mouth closed," he cautioned.

"Will do," I assured him.

Two days later, I was back on the streets. Swag picked me up in his black Aston Martin. Every female deputy at the jail was all on his dick as we left the Pretrial Center and hopped in his whip.

"I see you're still thuggin' it," Swag said to me as we drove out to his estate in Buckhead.

"Unc, you know how I rock, so it ain't nothin' to discuss. I appreciate you sending that lawyer down to see me, though."

"That wasn't shit. But for real, Lil T, one of these times I'm not gonna be able to get you out. That's what I'm tryna prevent, because before your pop departed I promised him I would look out for you."

"Unc, my pop didn't depart. Those crackers executed him. Let's keep it gangsta," I corrected him.

"I know that, Lil T. I was right there when those muthafuckas stuck the needle in his arm. And like I've always told you, your pop died like a soldier. That's why niggas still talk about him to this day. But I know that before he died, he was worried about you. I'm not tryna take the gangsta out of you. That's something that was passed down to you through your bloodline. I'm just tryna get you out of the streets because the true gangstas are behind a desk in a plush office high up in the skyline," said Swag. But he could tell that I wasn't tryna hear no lecture, so he let it rest. "Anyway, I'm doing a concert up in New York this weekend with Trey Songz. You wanna roll with me? We'll go fuck some of these up North bitches since I heard you and Kamora broke up."

"I might roll with you. I'll let you know," I said.

"Man, it won't hurt you to get away from the A for a weekend. In fact, that's what you need to do because you know po-po is watching you."

"Yeah, I feel you. Let me see where Kamora's head is, first, and I'll let you know." I gave him my word then called Kamora.

Her head was in the same place it was the last time we talked. No matter what I said she would not change her mind.

"I'm not killing my baby. Lord knows I've done a lot of dirt, but that is something I will not have on my conscience." She stood firm.

"Well, I'm through dealing with you, shawdy." I said.

"If that's how you feel. But I'll always love you and be waiting for you to come back to us," she said.

I hung up the phone.

"Let's go bone us some New York bitches," I announced to Swag. He smiled and gave me some dap.

"Can I call Criminal and invite him, too?"

"Yeah, I fuck with Criminal," agreed Swag who was always one hundred.

Ca$h

CHAPTER 19

The weekend in New York turned out to be just what I needed to get Kamora off of my mind. Those up North bitches couldn't get enough of our Dirty South swag. I dicked about eight bitches in three days and went through a whole box of Magnums.

When we got back to the A, I flipped on the switch and got right back into beast mode. I loaded up the yoppa and set out to send a message to Zeke that siccing po-po on me would not get me off of his ass.

It was pitch dark outside, but I didn't give a fuck. I drove down to Zeke's main spot in East Point and turned it into tattered wood.

A mile away was another one of his spots. I saw a nigga walking up on the porch, whom I recognized as one of Zeke's workers. I aimed the yoppa out of the window and did the boy real dirty. A smoker across the street ducked behind a parked truck. I knew he could describe my whip and may have peeped my tag number, so I hopped out of the car and ran over to where he was ducked down. His eyes bulged when I got up on him.

"I ain't seen nothing, my man," he cried.

"Me either," I said and sent him off into the afterlife.

I heard sirens but somehow avoided po-po. I guess if there was a God, he was watching over me. That's what Big Ma always said.

I wasn't a religious dude, but I believed there was a power higher than me. My pop had been a Five-Percenter at the time of his death and had not believed in any God other than the Black man. I knew that Juanita's fake ass had introduced him to that culture. Since it had bred a counterfeit ho like her, I could not embrace it. My only belief was that there was a heaven for a G, where no slimy muthafuckas were allowed.

I quickly got out of the area where I had just lit up the night. Not really having a destination, I decided to go by Ava's. When I got there, she had company of the female persuasion, some butch broad that looked like Ray J.

"I'll pull up on you another time," I suggested, but Ava nipped that in the bud.

"No, you won't. Now that you're here, I'm not letting you go no-where. Hold up a minute, let me tell this she-male that she has to bounce," whispered Ava.

"Don't let me interrupt y'all," I said, plopping down on the couch and inhaling the scent of vanilla incense that wafted throughout the living room.

"Whatever." Ava sauntered off into the room where her little fake dude friend had just gone.

I sparked a blunt and waited for the show. A minute later the butch ho stormed past me, right out of the door.

"I don't get it. Don't she know that her strap on can't compare to this python," I cracked, grabbing my crotch.

"I know, right?" Ava didn't hesitate to agree.

For a whole week, I chilled with shawdy and realized she was good people. Her sex was dumb good and she knew how to cater to a nigga's every need. At night, she went to work at the club and I hit the streets with my hoodie, scarf, gloves, and banger.

In the day, we hit the malls or different restaurants because micro-wave pizza pockets were the limit of Ava's culinary skills.

One day while we were at the Golden Corral in College Park, we ran into Kamora and Inez. The hurt was written all over Kamora's face, but she didn't show out.

I nodded at Inez then took Ava somewhere else to eat. Back at her crib Ava asked, "Do you still love her?"

"I don't love nobody, shawdy. So, I'm telling you right now, don't fall in love with me because I can't love you back. I'm on a whole different mission and love ain't nowhere in the equation."

"But you have to love someone. What about your mother? Don't you love her?" Ava asked.

"Fuck no! I mean, I love my sisters and I love Inez and both of my grandmother's but that's it."

Ava took in my answer and seemed to be dissecting it in her mind. "You love Kamora, too. You're just mad at her," she concluded.

"I don't love her. She betrayed her word to me. That's a sign that she'll betray me in other ways, too, but I'm not giving her a chance to do that. Fuck a bitch!" I exploded.

After that, Ava retreated from that subject. I pulled her down on my lap and said," "Just enjoy this gangsta shit I put on you while it lasts. When it's over, it's over. No regrets."

"Okay." She brightened up. "I still want you to have these." She held up a set of door keys.

Shawdy, you're sprung already." I smiled and accepted the keys.

A couple days later, I was rolling down Glenwood, having just collected taxes from a nigga out toward Decatur.

A detective's car got behind me and turned on its flashing lights. I drove on for another block or two, allowing myself time to slide my banger in the hidden compartment in the driver's door. Once I had done that, I pulled over at a well-lit and heavily populated service station. I didn't trust po-po.

I recognized Smooth. I wondered what the outcome of this would be. I didn't know why he had pulled me over, but I knew I wasn't letting him cuff me.

I let my window down with my driver's license, car registration and insurance already in hand. A group of people stood around anticipating any type of excitement. If Smooth planned to arrest me, I was about to give them the show they seeked.

"What's up, Trouble?" said Smooth in an unofficial tone, like we were friends.

"Talk to my attorney."

"Why would I need to do that? You committed any crimes lately? Oh, my bad, that's an everyday thing for Little Youngblood."

"Keep my pop's name out ya mouth. And I don't got time to kick it. Check my papers and let me bounce. Time is money."

He laughed but it was fake. "Money," he repeated. "Now the love of that is what we have in common. Let's make a date to talk. We could be very beneficial to each other."

I looked at him like the fool he was and then I told him that I don't fuck wit' po-po, at all. "Besides, I'm straight legit these days," I lied.

"And a cow's pussy ain't beef," he quipped. I pretended not to get his point so he moved on. "I have a real lucrative offer for you, but it's not wise for me to be seen talking to you. Meet me on the corner of MLK and Ashby in two hours. I'll be in a black Silverado. You can follow me somewhere where we can talk privately. This is on the up and up. I'm offering you a license to commit crimes without having to worry about ever being arrested. Think about it." He walked back to his car and I drove off.

Two hours later, I was nowhere near MLK and Ashby— fuck the dumb shit. Instinct told me that Smooth was trying to do me dirty. Besides, the only thing po-po could do for me was draw a chalk line around my victims.

I pulled up on a boy outside a house of Flat Shoals that I'd heard was doing stupid numbers. Before he peeped the move, I was breathing in his ear.

"They call me Trouble. Does that name ring a bell in your mind?"

"Yeah, I heard of you."

"Good. Then you already know my get down, so don't make me act a fool. You got a baby mama?"

"Yep."

"Do you take care of your child?"

"Yeah."

"You wanna live to see him or her grow up?"

"Yep."

"Well, go inside and tell your homies that Trouble is outside their door. Tell 'em to send five bands out, and I'ma expect that same amount every week. If anyone besides you step out that door I'ma yop 'em down and hold you accountable," I warned, before allowing him to go deliver my message.

I ducked off, peeping out from behind a dumpster when he came back out of the house. I had the yoppa clacked, ready to leave carnage behind.

"Bring it here," I called out.

He was probably squeezing his ass cheeks as he followed my voice, but he did as I commanded. I pocketed the street tax and he walked back inside, shoulders slumped. I'm sure he felt punked, but the alternative would have been death.

Back at Ava's crib, I broke shawdy off a few bands. She was playing her role without pressing a young nigga, so I didn't hesitate to bless her.

"What did you ever do with that brick you had?" I asked, thinking about it for the first time.

"I gave it to a friend to sell for me and he ended up shitting on me," she admitted.

"Was you fuckin' him?"

"No," she replied a little too quickly.

"Shawdy, if you gonna be down, you can't lie to me. I don't feel no kinda way if you was fuckin' him or not. I just asked because I'ma make the nigga pay you. But if you care about the nigga, I'm stay out of it."

"Okay, I slept with him a few times, but I don't have any feelings for that bitch. He played me out of my money, and now he comes to the club and acts like he don't owe shit."

"A'ight. Don't lie to me no more. Now what's the nigga's name?" I smacked her on that phat ass.

"They call him Trap. He be on Gresham Road."

"I'll find him and get your money. Now come show me how you like to curl a nigga's toes."

"I'm down with that." She lowered her eyes erotically and sunk to her knees.

In no time at all, she had my dick out and it was standing firm. She slowly licked the head and then began popping it in and out of her mouth.

"Do it real sloppy, baby girl."

"Okay, daddy." Ava slurped my dick noisily until I was standing on my toes and shooting cum down her throat.

Afterwards, we fucked like there was no tomorrow. But of course there was a tomorrow, and good pussy and head couldn't resolve all of the things I had on my agenda.

As if I didn't already have enough on my plate, my sister, Laquanda, called me crying. I asked, "What's wrong?"

"Mama tried to make me suck this man's thing so he would give her some rocks," Laquanda cried.

"I'ma kill that bitch!" I shouted. "Stop crying, baby, I'm on my way to get you."

I kissed Ava before leaving out of the house, but I paid no attention to her pleas for me not to murder Shan.

Fuck that! Shan had crossed the line.

But when I got there, the only thing that saved her from death that night was that she wasn't at home when I got there.

I helped Laquanda pack her things and we set out for Big Ma's house. On the way there, I thought I detected a car following me.

"Get down and don't raise up until I tell you to," I ordered Laquanda. Anticipating drama, I grabbed the banger out of the hidden compartment.

The car continued behind me for another mile and then it turned off. I bent a few more corners to make sure I had shook whoever might've been following me. Then I continued out to Big Ma's.

Once I got Laquanda settled, I bounced. Finding Shan was the only thing on my mind. But when I got back at my car, the muthafucka wouldn't start. "Fuck!" I sighed and kept trying the engine with the same result.

Finally, I gave up and entered Big Ma's house, complaining about the car not starting and the foul shit Shan tried to do to Laquanda.

"Take that as a sign that God doesn't want you to leave out of here tonight," Big Ma said. I wasn't tryna hear that, though, God should've told Shan something before she did that fuck shit.

I had to beg Big Ma for her keys to her car because I think she had a premonition that something bad was going to happen if I left.

"What will you do if you find your mother tonight?" she questioned me.

"I don't know," I admitted.

"Look in my eyes and promise me that if you find her, you won't lay a hand on her. Just bring her over here."

"I promise," I grumbled. It was the first time I ever lied to Big Ma.

It didn't matter. I searched every crack house in the hood for Shan but could not find her. It was 3 a.m. when I gave up and went to crash at Inez' house. I planned to take Big Ma's car back to her tomorrow and have my own car towed to a mechanic's shop.

When I got to Inez', she was up watching television.

She flicked the remote control to the news channel. They reported the latest on the murder and mayhem in the A. That wasn't a concern of mines, my sister's situation was more important.

I sat down on the edge of the sofa and put my head in my hands. *How can a mother bring herself to prostitute her own child for drugs?* I wondered.

"Is Laquanda okay?" inquired Inez.

"I guess so," I responded dryly and then looked up at the television.

A news reporter stood outside of a house that was engulfed in flames.

"Neighbors say that they saw a car pull up to the house. Two men got out of the vehicle and tossed what is believed to have been gas cocktails through the windows. So far, firefighters have pulled two un-identified bodies from the fire. That's all we really have now, Don."

The next camera shot showed my car in the driveway of Big Ma's house.

"Oh, my God!" cried Inez.

I flew outside and hopped in the car. Inez was right on my heels in her pajamas. I floored the gas pedal and sped over to Big Ma's house. *There had to be some kind of mistake,* I told myself.

When I got there the fire trucks were just pulling away, but a throng of neighbors remained standing across the street from Big Ma's house, which was now little more than a charred wooden frame. It seemed unbelievable that this could have happened so fast.

I let out a loud scream and pounded my fists on the steering wheel.

Ca$h

CHAPTER 20

The organist was strumming a melody with a plaintive cry when I entered the church doors with Ava's hand in mine. All heads seemed to turn in our direction and stare. I wondered if they all knew that one of those closed caskets on the altar was meant for me, instead of my beloved Big Ma and sister.

Approaching the front of the pew, I stopped to look up at the picture of Big Ma that sat atop her dove white casket. Even in the photo, she stared back at me with love in her eyes.

The ache in my heart was immeasurable. I glanced over to Laquanda's picture that sat on a three-legged stand next to her soft pink casket. I could hardly breathe, my grief was that intense.

We found our seats in the front row, next to relatives whom I barely knew. All three of my sisters sat directly behind me. They had been of no relation to Big Ma or Laquanda, but I knew they were there for me.

I looked over my shoulder and saw Inez sitting next to Tamia. Kamora came up to me and gave me a hug. I did not see Shan anywhere in the gallery. That bitch was probably somewhere in a crack house on the very day of her mother and daughter's funeral.

The minister stood at the door and greeted the many mourners that filled the church. Then he took to the podium and the service began.

"Fret not thyself because of evil doers. Neither be envious against the workers of iniquity. For they shall soon be cut down like grass, and wither as the green herbs. Trust in the Lord and do good. Commit thy way unto the Lord. Trust also in him and he shall bring it to pass. Cease from anger and forsake wrath. Fret not thyself in any wise to do evil: For evil doers shall be cut off, but those that wait upon the Lord, they shall inherit the earth."

I was not tryna hear that shit.

"I have seen the wicked in great power," the pastor said, "and spreading himself like a green bay tree. Yet he passed away."

I blocked out the sermon when he said "Vengeance is mine, so saith the Lord," because I knew what I was gonna do. "How long will good Christian folk and little teenage girls suffer at the hands of sinners?"

"Not long," the church chorused.

"Not long, I tell you, brothers and sisters. Soon will be the day of the coming of the Lord. You better get ready."

I stood and walked up on stage. Then I placed my hand on top of Big Ma's casket and bowed my head, speaking lowly.

"Big Ma, I'm sorry. This wasn't supposed to have been you." Tears threatened to break through closed gates. *"I know I haven't turned out to be what you hoped I would be. But still, you loved me. Your arms and your doors were always open for me no matter what I did. I hope you know that I loved you and I took everything you ever told me to heart. You did everything you could to steer me away from the life I live, but my pain and anger is too great. I guess the only good about it all is that now it can't cause you anymore sleepless nights. Rest in peace."*

I knew I said gangsta don't cry, but I was wrong. A stream of tears slid down my face as I thought of my grandmother dying in that fire. My whole body shook with silent sobs.

I took a few weary steps over to my sister's casket and for the first time in my life, my knees buckled. Placing both hands atop of her casket, I pulled myself up. I laid my head on the closed lid and began to weep.

"Laquanda, bruh-bruh—is so—sorry." I bawled shamelessly.

I had slipped badly. I should've never discounted the car that tailed me that night. Guilt overtook me, causing me to sink to my knees under the weight of it. My chest heaved as I sobbed.

I felt a pair of delicate hands on each arm, helping me to my feet. "It's going to be okay, bae." Kamora comforted me. Tears poured from her eyes and she wrapped her arms around me.

"I know your pain," added Inez. She laid my head on her shoulder like a loving mother would.

The mournful melody playing on the organ brought an outburst of cries from behind me.

A familiar voice shouted from the rear of the church. "It's your fuckin' fault they're dead! Momma and my baby ain't never done nothing to nobody. Whoever did that to them was after you! I can't stand your ugly ass!" Shan stood in the doorway of the church, looking jacked up.

As she stormed down to the stage where I stood, I could see her dress was old and soiled. The heels of her shoes leaned to the side and her hair was slicked down with so much grease it looked like a shiny skully.

"Let me at that muthafucka!" she yelled, obviously forgetting she was disrespecting the church. Inez held her back. "Bitch, get your hands off of me!" she spat. Sharp gasps from the pews spread like wildfire.

"If this was any other place and time I would do to you what I should've done a long time ago." I stepped right up in Shan's face.

Since she couldn't get to me, she turned her crack induced fury on Inez and cursed her like only a project chick could.

Inez said nothing back. But Shan got too bold when she slapped Inez in the face.

The two of them tore up the stage, and there was nothing I could do to stop them.

"It's a shame how black folks disrespect the dead," one woman said.

"Sister Poochie would be so embarrassed if she was here to see this," the neighbor added.

Hearing that, I stepped between Shan and Inez and forcefully separated them.

"Get the fuck off of me!" Shan spat.

I knew there was no calming her so I turned and appealed to Inez. "Y'all can't do that here. Please!"

"You're right," she agreed. She shot Shan a cold stare and then she turned and quietly walked out of the church.

All I could do was express my apology to Big Ma and Laquanda in a silent but tearful prayer.

The service continued without further incident. When out concluded, we all filed out to proceed to the cemetery.

At the gravesite when they lowered the caskets into the earth and the preacher announced, "Ashes to ashes, dust to dust." He didn't just bury Big Ma and Laquanda. Along with them he buried whatever bit of soul I had left.

The streets of the A were about to see the repercussions of turning a young nigga heartless.

For two weeks after we buried Big Ma and Laquanda, all I did was get high and drunk. Ava finally got fed up with the drinking and called Inez over. The two of them poured out every bottle of liquor I had in the house and flushed a half pound of Kush down the toilet.

"Are you giving up?" Inez challenged me.

"Nawl, just let me grieve in my own way and I'll be a'ight. You don't know how I'm feelin'."

"Oh, I don't? Do you know how many times I wanted to give up when they killed your father? Every day I thought about taking my own life to end the pain. But I knew Youngblood wouldn't have respected that." She picked my chain up of off the coffee table and held it up close to my face. "You gotta rep this no matter what. Sad as it is to say, sometimes that battle doesn't go in your favor. You've made a lot of families shed tears over their loved ones. It was your time to shed some. I'm sorry that I happened like it did, but let this be a lesson to you not to ever leave an enemy breathing or they'll come back to haunt you."

I covered my head with a pillow to block out the raw truth of her words because they made me face the guilt I felt over exposing Big Ma and Laquanda to danger that ultimately cost both of them their lives.

"Ava, baby, will you please allow me some privacy with Lil T? I need to tell his muthafuckin' ass some things he might not want you to hear," Inez said.

"Okay, I'm going to run to the store. I'll be back in thirty minutes. Is that long enough?" replied Ava.

"That's plenty," said Inez.

"I'll be back, Lil T. Can I bring you something?" asked Ava.

"Nawl, I'm good, shawdy," I mumbled from up under the pillow.

As soon as Ava left, Inez turned straight gangsta on me. She was something like I had never seen her before. She snatched the pillow from me and screamed, "Get your ass up and go straighten out your business! While you're over here wallowing in grief, the nigga that killed Big Ma and Laquanda is out there pounding his muthafuckin' chest in victory. I know the shit hurts, but you got to make him hurt worse. Your father didn't crumble when niggas killed his sister to get at him. He was beyond crushed because Toi was his heart. But he still did what he had to do. And he didn't stop until a lot of families were crying. If you're not built the same way, then take the chain from around your neck and give me my man's ashes."

I saw fire in her eyes.

She searched the room until she found two of my bangers. She shoved them toward me and demanded to know, "What the fuck are you going to do? Are you Youngblood's son or are you your mama's boy?"

I took the nine and the four-fifth from her and exclaimed, "Like father, like son."

"Well, prove it! Every time I turned on the news somebody better be getting zipped up in a body bag or you stay the hell out of my face." She stormed out without awaiting a reply. I had nothing to say anyway. My bangers were gonna talk for me.

By the time Ava returned, I was in beast mode. Lying out on the bed was the entire cache of weapons I had accumulated over the past two years.

I had two Tec 11's, two yoppas, a Calic, a street sweeper, an AR-15 with an infrared scope attached and a dumb assortment of semi-automatic hand guns.

Ava looked at the deadly artillery and then looked up at me. I studied the windows to her soul to see if there was fear. What I saw was the soul of a rider. I pulled her into my arms.

"Are you my bitch?" I asked her flat out.

"Yes, Trouble, I'm your bitch," she answered.

"For how long?"

"Infinity."

"A'ight, from now on don't let no other nigga or bitch touch what's mine. You understand me?" I pulled her into my arms and nuzzled my nose in her hair.

"Yes, and I haven't since we've been kicking it like this."

"That's what's up. Now, not only must you keep the pussy on lock, you gotta padlock your mouth. What you see me do must go to the grave with you. If po-po ever snatch you up, don't say or answer shit. Just ask to call your attorney. And if a nigga ever snatch you up and try to force you to call me, don't do it because he's gonna kill you anyway. If that scares you, now is the time to fall back." I tilted her head up and stared deeply into her eyes.

"I'm not afraid, daddy."

"A'ight, gimme some tongue and then sit over there out of the way. Niggas are about to be shown why they call me Trouble." I kissed Ava.

She sat down in the overstuffed chair adjacent to the bed and watched me check each of my weapons to make sure they were ready for the war I was gonna bring to my enemies.

"I'm going all out, shawdy," I said as I aimed the AR-15 at the wall and looked through the scope. Everything on it seemed to be in fine order, so I set it down and picked up the four-fifth.

"You're supposed to go all out because what they did to your grandmother and your little sister was not called for," replied Ava.

"I begged Big Ma to move. Something kept telling me that somebody would try to get at me through her. But if Shan hadn't done that foul shit, none of this would've happened because I never would've taken Laquanda over to Big Ma's house that night."

Ava just listened. I guess she was uncomfortable speaking against my mother. But the truth is the truth.

"Don't get it wrong," I said, "I know that it was my beef that came to Big Ma's front door, and that's a burden I'll carry on my shoulders until they toss dirt on my casket. But I wouldn't have been slippin' if Shan would'na tried to prostitute Laquanda that night. I swear, I should go kill that crack head bitch."

"Baby, I don't like to hear you talk about your mother like that. Why don't you try to get her some help?"

My head snapped up from what I was doing and my nostrils flared. "Is you stupid? If that bitch was on fire, I wouldn't piss on her! She's the reason my pop got executed. She helped those crackers convict him and put him to sleep like they do stray dogs! What did my pop ever do to that bitch but stop fuckin' with her grimy ass after she fucked his mans? And what type of mother would sell her daughter to a muthafucka for some crack? Hell no, that bird ass, gutter trash ho ain't nothin' to me!"

Ava had no comeback.

My chest heaved rapidly and my blood was boiling. "Where's my cell phone?"

Ava found it up under the bed.

I unlocked it and checked my text messages. Then I checked my voicemail. You have four new messages.

First message: *Yo, bruh, I'm just lettin' you know when it's time to ride, I got your back. Get at me.*

I recognized Criminal's voice.

Next message: *Bae, I'll always love you. Please don't forget that. I know you're hurting right now and so am I. I loved Big Ma and Laquanda, too. If you need me for anything you know where I'm at. And if you still want me to handle that business I started on with Sharena, I'm ready. She's been calling every—*

I clicked to the next message. *Fuck that!* Kamora had shown a flaw. Her word wasn't platinum.

The third voicemail was from Swag asking if I could call him. He claimed that it was very important. But I would have to get at him later. Right now, I was on that other shit.

Next message: *Sometimes the hunter becomes the hunted. I warned your reckless, young ass to fall back. Never forget that you got family, too. Now go visit their graves and fall back off me before I send some more pain at your ass.*

That voice belonged to Zeke! I tried to climb through the phone to get to his ass. "Bitch ass nigga, quit hiding and come out on the front line! Talkin' that killa shit when the whole A knows that money is your only power. When was the last time your tool went bang? You ain't no killa. You pay niggas to protect your thong!" I growled into the phone." Spit was flying everywhere.

Of course, Zeke wasn't on the other end. I would have to hit the streets and find his bitch ass, and it wasn't going to be easy. But in my rage, somebody was dying tonight! I strapped up.

"Don't go to the club tonight. I want you here when I get back," I said to Ava.

As I left out of the door, I already knew whose life I was gonna take.

Ca$h

CHAPTER 21

I sent a powerful kick to the center of the apartment door, and it went flying in and slammed against the wall. I stepped through the door with both my gloved hands around the four-fifth. Criminal was on my heels with his semi-automatic banger out and ready to cough at the squeeze of the trigger. Outside in the car was one of his GF homies.

The black scarves around Criminal's and my face told the surprised nigga on the couch what the business was.

"I got dope and money. Y'all can have it all, just don't kill me," he immediately offered.

"Where's the shit at?" I barked while keeping a close eye on him. There was always the chance he had a banger under the pillow on the couch.

"Everything is outside in the trunk of my car."

Boc!

I shot him in the shoulder.

"Don't play with me! Where's the shit at? If you lie to me again I'ma spray your thoughts all over that wall."

"Okay! The money is in the linen closet in the bathroom, inside a purple and black pillowcase. Ooh! Aw shit, my shoulder is burning like fuck!"

"Tough luck! Where's the work?"

"Under the kitchen sink. There are two blocks and a couple four ways. Man, don't wipe me out, please. I just got out of prison a few months ago, and I'm tryna get on my feet."

"Yo, bruh, who is this nigga talking to?" I asked Criminal.

Criminal hunched his shoulders.

"Go, check it out. Be careful, somebody might be in the back," I warned my nigga.

Five minutes later he returned with the work and the ducats.

"C'mon y'all, I'm a street nigga, too. Respect the hustle and leave me with something to bounce back with," cried Trap. His voice was irritating the shit out of me.

"Did you leave my bitch anything to bounce back with?" I snarled.

"Who's your bitch, fam?"

"Figure it out in your next life, nigga." I spat and then popped three in his head.

I kept the money and gave Criminal and his man the work. When I got back to Ava's, she was in bed watching The Real Housewives of Atlanta. I opened up the pillowcase and poured the stacks out on her legs.

"I keep my promises."

"What's this for?" she asked, looking puzzled.

"I collected from that nigga who shitted on you about that block. Count the bands and tell me how much it is."

She unwrapped the rubber band from around a stack and began counting one bill at a time. "Hold up, hold up!" I stopped her. "You ain't gotta do that. Trust, each one of those is $1,000. Just count the stacks, shawdy. Damn, you're green as lettuce," I joked.

"Leave me alone." She feigned a pout and looked cute as hell doing so.

"You're a pretty muthafucka."

"Thank you."

"Yeah, you're my bitch," I said.

"I sure am. I'm nobody's but yours. And if you can find a better bitch than me, you better marry that ho."

"Talk that shit, shawdy." I chuckled.

"I'm just keeping it gangsta."

"We'll see," I said.

Ava exclaimed, "You have forty-three stacks or bands. Whatever you want to call them. Forty-three thousand dollars."

"Yep. Yep," I remarked, satisfied. "You can have it all."

"Are you serious?"

"Yeah, shawdy. I don't want any of it. You got what I want inside those booty shorts. Stand up and take them off. I wanna see my bitch in her birthday suit."

"Whatever you want, baby," she purred demurely as she seductively stripped down to nothing but pussy, ass and titties.

That dark, pretty muthafucka had a fine body. Her pussy poked out from between her thighs like a sweet honeydew melon.

"Shawdy, you a bad ass bitch."

Ava blushed.

"You wanna bend me over and fuck me?" she rasped.

"Yeah, shawdy, I wanna put my stamp on that pussy. Turn around and let me show you how boss my dick game is. I ain't never fucked you like I'ma fuck you tonight." I used the remote to click on the music.

Kem came on, completing the mood. Ava put her elbows on the dresser and tooted her ass up. I squatted down and spread her chocolate ass cheeks. Then I slowly ran my tongue from the rooter to the tooter.

I circled the opening to her brown eye with the tip of my tongue. Then I tenderly probed the inside. She began moaning and grinding her ass on my tongue. I was on some real, freaky shit tonight. I pushed my tongue as deep as it would go, then I jabbed it in and out.

"Ooh, baby, baby, baby. You're fucking my head up," she cried.

I ate that ass like a sweet potato pie.

"Put your dick in there," she cooed.

"A'ight, you know I got a python. I'ma have your ass wearing a pamper like a 22-year-old baby."

"You'll have to go slow." She coached.

I did as she wanted. I was slow and gentle, still she was hollering and screaming like the dick was splitting her in half and I had only gotten the head in so far. When I pushed deeper, Ava screamed and snatched the dick out of her ass. "What's wrong, shawdy?" I laughed.

"Fuck that! Your dick too goddamn big. Fuck around and have my ass in the ER."

"I told you, you couldn't handle this shit. I'm not one of those lil' dick niggas who be coming to the club. Lie down and give me some of that fat, wet pussy."

"Anytime." She smiled as she swept the money off the bed and onto the floor.

I woke up the next morning with Ava draped all over me. I climbed on top of her and gave her some of that fiyah, early morning dick. Then we took a shower together and fucked some more.

"My stuff is sore," she groaned, while lotioning her body back in the bedroom.

"That's what happens when you fuck with a G. Next time you better get one orgasm and call it a night. Because if you get greedy I'ma have you walking with a permanent limp around this bitch," I boasted because I knew I had fucked her well.

I threw on my $800 True Religion jacket over the T-shirt I wore with my pop's picture sewn across it. I was also rocking True Religion jeans and a new pair of Adidas. The four-fifth was on my waist and a nine was in the small of my back. It was time to hit the streets. I picked up my cell phone and saw ten missed calls from Swag. *Damn, what's so urgent?* I wondered as I hit him up. He answered right away.

"Damn, lil' nigga, what took you so long to hit me back? I've been tryna reach you all week," he complained.

"I been going through some things since the funerals, but I'm good now. What's the business?"

"I hate talking over phone, but I'm way out in LA, and this shit is too important to wait. Can you fly out here?"

"Nawl, unc, I got too many things poppin' off here in the A to come out there now. Maybe I'll be able to get away in a couple weeks."

"No, that won't work. You could be dead by then."

"Anybody can get it any day, but what you saying?"

"A nigga named Zeke got a hundred bands out on your head. There's a DT named Smooth who is supposed to have the contract now. One of my security dudes used to work for APD and he heard that from a very credible source. The department is already investigating Smooth for armed robbery, taking bribes, planting drugs and guns on niggas. Everything you can name. They say the nigga is real slimy, so you better lay low."

"I'ma lay low, a'ight." I replied sarcastically.

Smooth is out to bury me, huh? That's why that nigga tried to get me to meet him on MLK that night. He was gonna slump my ass.

"Lil T, you still on the line?" asked Swag.

"Yeah, I'm still here. I was just thinking. I'ma pull up on you later. Let me strategize."

When I hung up from Swag, I knew what I had to do. And I knew that it could not wait.

CHAPTER 22

"Fuck it, bruh. You gotta get that nigga before he gets you. Just because he wears a badge it don't make him immune to being murdered. He's crooked as hell anyway. Last year he planted a gun and a half block on my dude, Black Rain. Got him fifteen years for nothing. I'm with you. We'll just have to do it real smart, because you know how hot shit gets when a po-po gets killed," said Criminal.

We were on I-20 East in the new Chrysler 300 he had just copped.

"Bruh, I'm not asking you to help me murk homeboy. That would be asking way too much of you. I know you got love for a nigga, but you don't owe me that type of loyalty. You and your mans are doing y'all thing, building up your numbers and making noise in these streets. Just like you said it would happen. I'm not gonna ask you to risk all that for me. All I need is for you to have your people keep their eyes and ears open and help me catch Smooth somewhere with his pants down. I'ma handle it from there."

"I got you, bruh."

Days later, I told Swag the same thing. For the time being, I gave Smooth my full concentration because he was the biggest threat of all.

Weeks passed by without any news from anyone. I was getting restless sitting in the apartment all day. I used Ava's laptop to go online to the Georgia Department of Corrections and pull up Lonnie's picture and info.

I stared at the screen with hate so intense my vision blurred. Lonnie had the untrustworthy face of a snitch. He was now in his early forties and was serving life without parole. I saw he was at Macon State Prison in Oglethorpe, Georgia.

"Who is that, baby?" asked Ava, standing over my shoulder.

"The bitch nigga that snitched on my pop."

She read Lonnie's jacket and then she concluded, "He's not ever getting out of prison. I don't see what he told for."

"He told because he had bitch in him."

"Hmmph! Well, I bet his ass is suffering, knowing he won't ever get out."

But he's still breathing and that's way more than he deserves, I thought.

I clicked off of the screen. I could not take looking at that bitch nigga's face another second.

That same night, I dreamed I had got locked up and sent to Macon State Prison where Lonnie was. I stepped off in that coward's cell with a shank in both hands. He didn't even recognize me. That infuriated me more.

"Nigga, you sent my pop to death row." I jogged his memory as I began stabbing him over and over again.

"Ahhh! Trouble, what are you doing?" Ava screamed as she lay in bed beside me.

When I woke up, I was poking her violently like my fingers were shanks.

"My bad, shawdy. I was dreaming about stabbing that rat nigga who told on my pop."

Oh, okay. You had scared me for a second."

She then wiped sweat from my forehead and laid her head on my chest and we fell back to sleep, holding each other.

That same day, Swag called to tell me Smooth had been arrested. It was all over the news. They called him an alleged rogue cop. I kept abreast of the situation. That's how I found out several days later that Smooth had been released on a $250,000 bond.

My trigger finger started twitching. He was fair game now. A civilian just like me! And I needed to get at his ass more than before. Because now he was dismissed from the police force and facing serious legal problems. The $100,000 on my head probably looked better than ever. I felt in my bones that he would come after me.

One of the hood chicks that Smooth messed with was a lady named Pudding. It was crazy because Pudding had babysat me often when I was in grade school and I had developed a mad crush on her.

"Yeah, me and your pop used to laugh about that," Inez recalled with a smile.

"Small world."

"Yes, it is."

For a few days, I contemplated approaching Pudding and offering to pay her fifty bands to set up Smooth. But that would've left me vulnerable, so I nixed that idea and reverted to a time worn truth: When stalking prey, just wait for them to show up at their bitch's house. Pussy sets the best trap even when it is unintentional.

I watched Pudding's apartment for a week before I broke luck.

The night I pulled into the complex and saw Smooth and Pudding sitting in his Silverado truck immersed in deep conversation, I knew it was now or never.

I circled around and parked a short distance away. By now they were out of the car and headed toward Pudding's apartment.

Luckily for me, Smooth didn't go inside. He hugged Pudding at the door and then walked casually back to his truck, bracing himself against an unusually brisk November wind.

I slid out of my whip with a singlemindedness. My AR-15 was down by my waist, locked and loaded.

I raised the assault rifle, looked through the scope and located Smooth. I moved my arm over to the right a bit until the infrared beam was in the center of the back of his head. Then I squeezed off four successive rounds.

The shots rang out like tin trays clapping together. Smooth's head snapped forward violently, and his body slid down the side of the car.

I hopped back in my car and backed up the street.

The assassination of Smooth did not bring the type of heat on the city that it would've brought had he still been on the force and in good standing. He had dirtied his badge and brought shame to the APD so they did not comb the A looking for his killer. They gave lip service to finding the culprit, but that was the extent of it.

"I see you crushed that nigga," said Criminal.

We were cruising down Gresham Road in my SUV. A week had passed since I had bapped Smooth.

"Nawl, bruh. That wasn't my work. I wanted to smash that ass, but obviously somebody wanted him worse than I did. What I'm hearing is that the police got him," I said.

"They probably did."

I don't know why I lied to Criminal, I just did. He must've bought my lie, because he changed subjects. "Trouble, I'm not tryna get in your personal business, but I ran into Kamora the other day and she's fucked up over how you just cut her off," he said.

"Leave it alone, bruh," I replied.

"Fam, you ain't being—"

"Bruh, leave it alone," I repeated.

There was no one Kamora could get to speak on her behalf and change my mind. I had closed that chapter. Criminal correctly interpreted that debating the issue was pointless, so he let it go and we drove on in silence for a few minutes.

We left the hood and hopped on I-20 East until I reached the Rockdale exit. We barely avoided getting side swiped by a dairy truck as I made a last second turn into a BP station to get gas.

After refueling, I got back behind the wheel and quickly explained things to Criminal as I pulled back into traffic. I drove past a ranch styled crib out in a quiet subdivision and pointed it out to Criminal.

"That's where Byron lives," I said. It was one of the last pieces of info Kamora provided me with before our fallout. "Now all we have to do is figure out a way to get up in that bitch. The nigga is getting to the money, so I know he got a stash up in that bitch. Probably some of them thangs, too."

"Let's eat, bruh," said Criminal, meaning that he was ready to pounce on the lick.

"We'll do that, but let's check it out for a few weeks. He ain't going nowhere. Meanwhile, what's the business with those Mexicans out in Buford you're beefing with? You wanna go body some of those muthafuckas? I don't like their asses no way. They all over the A like they own this bitch."

"Those niggas do think they're running shit. Yeah, let's go chop some of them down."

Late that night, Criminal, two of his GF dudes and I rode out to Buford Highway and smashed five Mexicans. I didn't give a fuck if the ones I shot weren't involved in the beef with Criminal or not. They were thug looking esses and that was good enough for me.

Niggas run the A! They better bow down to it.

CHAPTER 23

I put my bangers up on the shelf long enough to spend Thanksgiving with my sisters. I picked Eryka and Chante up and took them over to Inez' to spend the day with Tamia. Ava came along because her family was torn apart and scattered everywhere.

Inez threw down. She baked a turkey so fat and juicy the meat melted in our mouths. She also cooked baked chicken, dressing, collard greens, cornbread, candied yams, macaroni and cheese, green beans and banana pudding.

We all ate until we couldn't eat another bite. Then we sat around and talked about our pop. My sisters wanted a chain and urn like mine and I promised to get them one each.

"I'll call Juanita and ask her if she'll give them some of his ashes. She probably has them out in the garage. I can't stand that bitch!" said Inez.

Tamia rolled her eyes up at the ceiling. Chante and Eryka laughed.

"She'll give us the run around. Watch and see," I predicted.

Just then we heard the front door open. In came Bianca and her daddy. He was on crutches. He looked at me and I slid my hand in my waist.

"Daddy let's go back to your house," said Bianca, interrupting the tension between Fat Stan and me.

They left back out and Tamia took Chante and Eryka upstairs to her room where they could talk about boys, probably. I could tell her lil' ass was on fiyah.

"She gonna make me hurt some little boy," I said.

"Oh, Miss Thang is hot! Hot! Hot! But I'm going to cool her off or kill her ass, one. I'm way too young and fly to be a grandmother," added Inez.

"Miss Inez, you are young and pretty. Can I ask ya why you don't have a boyfriend?" Ava chimed in.

Inez stood up from the table and went and took my pop's picture off of the mantel. She came back clutching it to her heart. She held it up for Ava to see. It was a photo of my pop holding Tamia when she was a baby. *Damn, I was his spitting image.*

"You see that man in that picture, Ava? I loved him more than life itself. He was everything I wanted in a man. But he's dead now, and I just can't imagine giving my body to another man. I would feel so— icky," explained Inez. A tear slid down her cheek. "I miss your father so much." She wept.

I hugged her and wept inside with her. Ava was crying, too.

The doorbell rang, stopping the tear that threatened to fall from my eye. Inez dried her eyes and then went to answer the door. She returned with company.

"What's up, Kamora? You already know Ava, so introductions ain't necessary," I said.

Kamora looked at Ava like she wanted to choke her, but Ava didn't blink. Pregnancy agreed with Kamora. She looked radiant and her skin was beautiful. Her hair was in long braids and she wore loose pants and a maternity top. I could see her stomach poking out a bit.

"Inez, we enjoyed Thanksgiving dinner. We're gonna bounce now. Chante and Eryka are spending the night. Are you gonna take them home tomorrow or do I need to come scoop 'em?" I stood up to leave. Ava followed suit.

"Y' all don't have to leave because of me,' Kamora said.

"We were about to leave anyway. Take care of yourself and let me know when you go in the hospital to have the baby," I said.

"Why?"

"Just let me know," I repeated.

As I was leaving out with Ava's hand in mine, I looked back at Kamora and thought I saw tears in her eyes. I felt some kind of way because we had a lot of history and if my anger were put aside, I knew I still loved her. However, I could not allow emotions to override principle. That was one of the many ways I was just like my pop. We both loved hard, but the slightest betrayal got you cut the fuck off. Disloyalty was unforgivable.

After Thanksgiving weekend was over, I dusted off my bangers and refocused on my many missions. I hit the streets and put my press game down hard. Nobody backed out on paying their taxes. I guess they could see zero tolerance in my eyes.

Now it was time to make Zeke feel the pain he had caused me. I had found out he had two nephews that played football for Washington High. I found out exactly who they were and I followed them from practice. A few blocks away from the school I pulled up to them and called them over to the car. Since I called their names, they felt less worry about approaching a strange car.

"Who is that?" one of them asked as they stepped closer.

"I'm a friend of your Uncle Zeke. I just wanted to congratulate y'all on the win last week."

"Man, we didn't win. We lost 12-0."

"Oh, Zeke told me y'all won. It don't matter, though, stay at it and don't fuck with the streets. Here's some sneaker money." I held a fist full of bills out of the window.

When they reached for the money, I let it slip from my hand and blow to the ground. "Damn, my bad." I feigned an apology.

They bent to pick the money up and I reached in my waist. The banger came up spitting fire.

Boc! Boc! Boc! Boc! Boc! Boc! Boc! Boc! Boc!

I squeezed off nine shots in just a few seconds. Both teenagers were sprawled out in the street. I had no mercy. Laquanda had been even younger. I hopped out and stood over them. One of them was lying still with the whites of his eyes showing. Still, I aimed the Glock .50 down and put a hole in his forehead.

His brother was trying to crawl up on the curb. I kicked him in the side and he collapsed on his face.

Boc! Boc!

You touch mine, I'll touch yours.

I didn't even allow my gun to cool off. Two nights later after receiving an unexpected call from Kamora, I was at it again. But this time it was to avenge my father. The hands on my watch moved at a snail's pace. After twenty-eight minutes and eleven seconds I could wait no longer. I moved like a cat burglar as I crept up to the front door of the one-level house.

The knob turned easily and I slid inside, quietly pulling the door up behind me. I already had a Sig Sauer in my right hand, ready to pop.

With my left hand, I removed the Glock .50 from my waist as I adjusted my eyes to the soft lighting inside.

Damn, I had forgotten to ask where they would be! I followed the sound of Donnell Jones playing on a stereo, which led me to a bedroom down the hall on the left.

I cracked the bedroom door open and tipped inside. The smell of sex was in the air. Sharena had her mouth glued to Kamora's pussy. With his back to the door, Byron was hitting Sharena doggie style. I crept up close behind him and placed the felony ends of both bangers to the back of his head.

"What the fuck!" He flinched, and then looked over his shoulder.

"Please make me murk you," I whispered.

"I won't. I'll do whatever you say." His voice quaked with so much fear he sounded like a woman.

"Good, just don't ask me not to kill you. Every nigga that has ever said that to me has gotten a negative answer. Pull out and lay face down on the floor, dick in the muthafuckin' carpet."

Byron backed out of his bitch. Sharena was so into licking Kamora's sweet kitty that she didn't even realize an intruder had invaded their fantasy until her pussy was left unattended.

"Why you take it out, daddy?" she complained without looking back.

Byron couldn't respond. He was butt naked on the floor with my Air Force 1 on the back of his neck. I quickly tucked one of the bangers back in my waist, grabbed a fist full of Sharena's hair and snatched her face up out of Kamora's wet-wet.

"Owww!" she yelped.

"The party is over, bitch!" I snarled.

"Dang, bae, she was just about to make me cum," grumbled Kamora.

I looked at her reproachfully.

"Whateva, boy. You know I was just joking."

The banter did not distract us. We were pros by now. I held the Glock on Byron as Kamora removed the roll of duct tape from her overnight bag and then taped his hands behind his back and his ankles together.

"What about his mouth?" she asked.

I nodded affirmatively.

Kamora placed a strip of tape over his mouth and then bound and gagged his ho the same way. "Boo Boo, did you think this sweet candy came without a cavity?" she taunted as she stepped into her clothes.

I could see the terror in the couple's eyes as we sat them up on the bed. I sat on the edge of the bed between the two. Kamora propped herself up on the edge of the dresser.

"Byron, I wanna tell you a true story about the realest nigga that ever lived," I said. A short while later, I concluded with, "Your mother helped get him executed. Now you have to pay for her deeds."

I wasted no more time. A bullet in the forehead from point blank range did to Delina's son what her testimony did to my pop. The tape covering Sharena's mouth muffled her scream.

"This ain't about you, Miss Lady, so get yourself together and do as I tell you. If you cooperate, I promise not to kill you. Byron is gone, as you can see. There's nothing that can bring him back, so now you have to think about saving yourself. Do you understand?" She nodded vigorously.

I removed the tape from over her mouth and demanded she tell me where Byron kept his stash.

"There's a small safe with about eighty thousand dollars in it in the room across from the laundry. The combination is 38-35-01. It works like a typical lock," she stammered.

"What about cocaine?"

"Four kilos. They are in the dryer under a load of clothes."

I put the Glock to her temple. "You want me to believe that's all Byron had? Bitch, don't insult my intelligence."

"No!" she shrieked, thinking I was about to turn her lights out. "I wasn't trying to insult you. It's the truth. That's all that Byron has here. His real stash is at his mother's house in Virginia."

My ears perked up. "Where in Virginia does his mother live?"

"In Portsmouth, but I don't know her exact address," she claimed.

I looked on the dresser and saw what I was looking for. I pointed to the cell phone on the charger and asked Sharena if it was hers or Byron's.

"That was—his." She sniffled.

I retrieved the phone from the charger and asked Sharena for the code to unlock it.

"I don't know the code," she said.

I gave her the benefit of the doubt because Byron was probably the type of nigga who had a bunch of sideline hoes. He would not have given his woman the code to unlock his phone.

"For your sake, you better know his mother's phone number," I warned.

She told me that Delina's number was programmed in her phone under Byron's Mom.

"My phone is in my purse in the bathroom," Sharena said.

Kamora dashed off to get it. When she came back with the cell phone and handed it to me, I went to Sharena's contacts and found what I was looking for.

I text: *this is Sharena. Text me your address. Byron wants me 2 mail u a gift.*

A few minutes later, a return text came through with: *1803 High St, Portsmouth, Va 23704.*

It was all I needed from her, so I text back: *Thanx.*

And soon after Delina replied: *Welcome. Smooches.* I cut the phone off and put it in my pocket and then I went to Byron's stash.

Two gunshots echoed through the house as I bent down to unlock the safe. I didn't have to go investigate. No witnesses was the policy.

Yeah, I had promised not to kill Sharena, but Kamora hadn't.

I emptied the safe, went into the laundry room and got the kilos out of the dryer. Then together, we wiped all of our prints from every spot we touched.

"Strip the bed, we're taking the sheets and pillow cases with us," I said, mindful of leaving behind forensic evidence.

I hadn't had any intentions on using Kamora to help me get Byron. The plan had been for Criminal and me to handle it. But when Kamora hit me up and told me she had it all set up, I could not let the opportunity pass. Avenging my pop meant everything to me.

Driving back to Kamora's place, I gave it to her raw. "I appreciate what you did, but it changes nothing between us. You broke your word to me and I cannot forgive that."

"Bae, I don't understand. It's not like I'm having the next nigga's baby. This is your seed inside of me," she protested.

"It don't matter, shawdy," I said.

"You think Ava is a better bitch than me? How many niggas has she bodied for you? None probably. And you're parading her around like she's earned something. That's the thing that hurts, but I'm going to handle this like a lady. Time will tell who the real bitch is."

"It always does."

I dropped Kamora off at home. Before she got out of the car, I offered her the eighty bands we had taken from Byron. I would keep the blocks.

"No, I'm good. I didn't do it for that, I did it for your father."

She had to know that would touch a nigga's heart.

"I feel you, shawdy. But accept the money for the baby."

Kamora reconsidered and accepted the money.

"Take care, bae," she said and ran into the house.

Ca$h

CHAPTER 24

"I handled that," I said to Inez, passing her a copy of Atlanta Journal Constitution. The newspaper was folded open to the relevant article.

Three days had passed since Kamora and I slumped Byron and Sharena, but their bodies had just been discovered in the house the night before. Inez read the story thoroughly.

"Now Delina will know how it feels," she remarked unsympathetically.

I believed that my pop's execution had turned Inez' heart just as cold as mine. I tossed twenty bands on the table. "That's just a little something for you and Tamia."

"Thank you. Where is Ava?"

"She's at the nail shop getting pampered. Can you believe she tried to get me to go along and get my shit done, too?"

"What!"

"Close your eyes and try to imagine that! I'm too G'd up."

"That's too funny." Inez laughed.

Just then, Tamia and Bianca came busting into the house. When Tamia noticed me, she came and sat on my lap.

"What's good with my little sister? You getting your cute on today, I see," I said.

She was rocking pretty pink Coogi leggings with some fresh white lady Air Max's that matched her pink and white long Coogi sweater.

"Yep, and the haters can't stand my pretty girl swag," she bragged.

"Oh, my God! I think I'm going to throw up." Bianca gagged in jest. Then she looked at me, rolled her eyes and walked off.

Inez mouthed, "Never mind her." I hunched my shoulders. Oh well, I couldn't be mad at Bianca for catching a 'tude with me over what I did to her father.

"She'll get over it," Inez said aloud.

"What are y'all talking about?" asked Tamia.

"Grown folks shit," I responded in a playful tone.

Inez sent Tamia to her room to do her homework and to allow us some privacy. Once Tamia was out of earshot, Inez asked if I had wiped Byron's place down real good before leaving.

"I told you my hair fibers are what tied me to that thing I did with your father in Kentucky," she said.

"Relax, I took care of all of that."

"Are you sure?" Worry was etched on her face.

"Chill. You know I stay on point," I reminded her, but I knew she was just double-checking because she didn't wanna see me cased up.

Leaving Inez' crib, I turned on the radio in my car and listened to the latest on the growing murder rate in the city. There was a mention of Byron and Sharena's murders, but no mention of any suspect. I soaked up everything being reported, making sure I was not a suspect in the case. Satisfied that I was not, I pushed in a Jeezy CD and headed out to Swag's studio in Roswell.

I was buzzed in after ringing the bell twice. The strong scent of exotic weed filled my nose as soon as I stepped inside.

A dozen niggas along with just as many dimed up chicks was up in there partying. Swag was seated on a couch getting dome from a bitch in front of everybody. Lil Mama had no shame! I smirked and accepted a blunt from a shawdy with a platinum colored weave that hung down to her ass.

"What's your name, Lil Daddy?" she asked, eating me up with her eyes.

I peeped shawdy's physique. She was built like Ciara, the singer, but I still didn't give her the satisfaction that I'd trick off with her.

"They call me Trouble."

"Do you rap?" she inquired, eyeing the icy chain and urn piece around my neck.

"Nawl, I wrap niggas up, though."

"Okay, nice meeting you," she said and jetted off in search of a rap dude.

When I saw that Swag was done getting his dick sucked, I went over to him with a smirk on my face. "Sup, unc? Nigga, you act like you're still in your twenties." I laughed.

"Shit don't change," he said, rolling up a blunt.

"I see. Y'all doing it up in this muthafucka. Naked bitches everywhere. You living the life, fam. For real, you need a reality show because this shit right here is made for TV."

"Oh, I'm working on that. That's why I was out in L.A," he said.
"Yo, you still fuck with Criminal?"

"Yeah, me and bruh eat noodles off the same fork."

"You're not GF, are you?"

"Nawl, but I contribute to their campaign. Why?"

"Nothin'. I just can't see you being down with that because like your father, you're your own man."

"Fa' sho but those are my niggas. I mean, it don't matter to me what set a nigga represents. It he's real, he's real. I fuck with GF like that because of Criminal."

"I feel you. Call bruh up and tell him to come out here. I wanna get that nigga on this track with T.I. He'll fall through in a minute."

I hit Criminal up and told him the business. He was in the middle of a transaction but promised to come to the studio when he was done.

Two hours later, he came through with a couple homies. They all knew Swag, so it was like a reunion.

Not long after Criminal arrived, T.I. and his mans showed up. To paraphrase something Jay-Z said about another rapper, T.I. came through like hurricanes do. And the bitches damn near fainted. Swag introduced him to me. I dapped him, but I ain't no groupie nigga.

"This Youngblood's son?" T.I. asked Swag.

"Yeah, that's him," Swag said.

T.I. didn't say another word, he just raised his arm and saluted me. I returned the salute. The rest was understood. T.I. was straight business. He ignored the groupie bitches and stepped into the recording booth. When he spat his verse, it was clear to all of us why he was known as the King of the South. I wondered if Criminal would be able to hold his own following the sixteen bars T.I. had just dropped.

Criminal was no slouch. Plus, he had real street stories to draw from, and his delivery was unique and flawless. My nigga spat pure venom. "Mob shit!" chanted his fam.

He made us all proud. This was bruh holding his own with T.I. Swag did the last verse and he kept it turned up. The song was sure to be a hit. I didn't leave the studio until three in the morning. Then I had to get up at seven to catch a 9:30 a.m. flight. Inez and I were taking my sister to New York to Christmas shop.

Ducats weren't an issue. My bank was in order. I had been doing licks for years and stacking my money. Tommy Gun had paid me off for the forty-six blocks I had hit him off with months ago. Plus, I was still collecting taxes from Ladell, and a dozen other niggas.

In New York, my sisters purchased so much shit we had to get it shipped to Georgia. The last thing I bought them was the platinum chains and urn they wanted.

Juanita had promised to send some of our pop's ashes, but the bitch was procrastinating.

"If they're not here soon, we're flying out to Las Vegas and taking them from her ass," I promised Inez.

She was with it. She was chomping at the bit to get her hands on Juanita. And I was biting at the bit to get back to the A because shopping with four women will exhaust a nigga.

When we got back home, we all drove to South Carolina to visit Grandma Ann in the new facility Inez had gotten her moved to.

Grandma looked better, but her mind was still gone. That spoiled my holidays and visiting Big Ma and Laquanda's graves further darkened my mood.

My only relief was to go out and look for a few of Zeke's people.

On successive nights, I murked a couple niggas Zeke fronted work to.

A day later, gunners caught me riding down Ralph McGill and tried to ambush me. They murdered my whip but failed to assassinate me. Although this time I did not walk away unscathed. I had caught a slug in the shoulder and another in my left hip. I was on the shelf for a minute but not long. And even wounded, my gangster remained official.

CHAPTER 25

Things quieted down a lot in the city over the next few months as I recuperated. But with winter fading away, I knew things were about to get turned up again. Things remained the same with me. I was still pressing niggas and plotting on my enemies. So far Zeke had managed to outrun his fate, but hunting him down and spilling his every thought on the pavement remained a priority. It was no longer about the street taxes he refused to pay— now it was personal.

I rode in the passenger seat checking out the hood as Ava drove. It suddenly struck me that some sort of tragedy had occurred on damn near every block we passed. More than a few of those tragedies had my hand prints all over them. I could picture the bodies sprawled out on the pavement leaking blood in the gutter. *I had no remorse for those who had been in the game.*

No apologies because my murder game had been wittier than theirs. My regret was for taking the lives of a few people who posed no threat to me. I looked to the sky and hoped that if there truly were a power greater than me, He would understand. I guess Big Ma's years of uttering gospel had seeped through, if only just a little bit.

Then the skies opened up and the angels began to cry. I wondered which of the raindrops that pelted down on the windshield were Big Ma's tears.

Then something on my old block caught my attention. Two teenagers were beating a woman.

"Stop the car, shawdy!" I shouted. Ava hit the brakes and I was out the car in an instant with my banger already out and down by my side.

"Back the fuck up off of her!" I barked. I didn't recognize either boy.

"Nigga, mind ya own goddamn business and stay the fuck up out of mines before you get a beat down, too," threatened the biggest of the pair.

I raised my arm so that the Glock was pointed at his dome. All of the bass drained from his voice. "Man, this junkie ho stole—"

Bap!

I slapped him in the mouth with the banger. "That's my mama, bitch ass nigga! I don't care what she did. Don't you ever put your hands on her again. Understand me?"

Bap!

I split his eye. He fell down on the ground next to Shan. His mans tried to jet, but I shot his legs out from under him. He fell on his face screaming like a punk ass nigga.

I turned my attention back to the one I had cracked across his head. "You think it's gangsta to beat up a fiend? Nigga, show me where your heart at?" I spat dead in his face.

"Put that gun down and I'll whoop yo ass, too!" He snorted.

My knuckle game was nice, but niggas in the Dirty didn't fist fight. "You got some balls, huh?" I sneered.

Boc!

I shot him between the legs.

"Now you got a pussy!"

"Owwwww!" He clutched himself and yowled in pain. I snatched Shan up off of the ground and pushed her into the backseat when we made it to my car.

By the time I hopped in the front, Ava was back behind the wheel, ready to zoom off. Inside of the car was silence. I was mad at myself for coming to Shan's rescue, but I told myself I had done it for Big Ma.

"You need to get ya life right," I grumbled.

"Who the fuck are you talking to?" Shan said.

"I should've let them niggas beat you to death!"

"Next time, do that! Nigga, if you see me in a fight with a bear, help the bear!"

"Oh, now you wanna talk shit? Ava, pull over. I'm putting this bitch out in the rain."

"No, Trouble." Ava drove on.

"Stop the fucking car!" I yelled.

"Wait. Let us at least get out of the neighborhood in case someone called the po-po." She was thinking for me.

When we reached a safe area, she pulled over to the curb. "Get out!" I gritted without turning around in the seat to look at Shan. She was straight pitiful. I could not believe I had come out of her womb. What my pop had ever seen in her was a mystery to me.

I heard the back door open and then I felt my chain being snatched off of my neck. It dangled in Shan's hand as she ran through the rain.

Though I now had a permanent limp, I ran her down in less than ten strides, but when I tried to take my chain back, she held on to it for dear life. It was as if the chain represented her only way to get some crack. Still, it did not mean as much to her as it meant to me.

"Let it go!" I tussled with her.

Her grip was strong and desperate. I yanked it away and the urn slipped off of the chain and clunked onto the ground. The small lid popped open and my pop's ashes spilled out and washed away in the rain. I fell to my knees and tried to save whatever hadn't spilled out. When I reached for the urn, Shan kicked it away.

My mind snapped.

I pummeled her with both fists. She was curled up on the ground whimpering under the assault. I felt nothing but rage. I snatched my banger out and pointed it down at her.

You ugly little bastard. You're gonna end up on death row just like your daddy. I should've flushed your ugly ass down the toilet. I'm glad they executed his ass.

All of the insults she had hurled at me drummed in my head. What she said about me didn't matter. It was the way she spoke and felt about my pop that festered my hate. Now she had committed the ultimate disrespect to his memory. I looked down at her with no pity.

"You ain't shit!" I said. "You hated my pop because he was a nigga wit' principles too strong for a rat like you to live up to. He didn't do shit to you and you violated him! He should've murked your ass when he had the chance and saved me a bullet!" I spazzed.

I was about to pull the trigger when Ava's cry made me hesitate. "Nooo, Trouble! Don't do it." She held on to my arm.

"Let me go, shawdy. This bitch don't deserve to live."

"She's your mother."

I wasn't tryna hear that fuck shit. Ava clung to my arm so that I wouldn't do it, but my mind was set. I slung her back and forth, trying to shake her loose. She would not let go, though. Finally, I threw her to the ground. My moment had come. I was about to put Shan out of her misery, once and for all.

Suddenly, Ava did the only thing that could've stopped me from slumping Shan. She crawled on top of her and covered her body with her own. I took my finger off of the trigger and tucked the banger back in my waist. Rain poured down on us all. I picked the urn up off the ground and saw that it was empty of my pop's remains.

"Just tell me why you hated him so much?" I snarled as I looked down at Shan. She didn't respond. "You're pitiful. I don't have to murk you, you'll smoke your own damn self to death," I said with disdain.

"Get up, shawdy. I'm not gonna shoot her," I told Ava.

"Promise me," she demanded.

"On all that I love," I avowed.

I understood why Ava had protected Shan's life with her own. She had lost her mother to cancer at a young age. Mothers were sacred to her.

"You should've let me put that bitch out of her misery." I drove off, leaving Shan in a downpour of rain.

"You don't really feel that way. Because if you did, you wouldn't have done what you did when you saw those boys beating on her."

"Whateva, shawdy. All I know is that I hate that slimy ass bitch," I said.

"Don't talk like that. She's still your mother, regardless. I would give anything to have my mother here with me. It wouldn't matter if she was a crackhead, a drunk or a two-dollar whore—as long as I could go to her sometimes and just lay my head on her lap. I'd cherish those moments," lamented Ava.

I felt the same way about Big Ma. If I could just lay my head on her lap everything would be all right. But no matter how I tried. I could not feel that same love for Shan. I hated her more than Ava was capable of understanding.

"You should've stayed out of the fuckin' way and let me kill that rat ass bitch," I said as I recalled that Shan had tried to prostitute Laquanda.

CHAPTER 26

"Umph ump umph!" Inez shook her head in disgust when I told her how my pop's ashes had been spilled and washed away. "That woman is a hot ass mess!"

"I'm telling you, if Ava wouldn't have done what she did, I was gonna push Shan's little ass ponytail all the way back."

Inez laughed and then said seriously, "I'm glad that you didn't. If for no reason than it would've caused Poochie to roll over in her grave."

"Fuck that, I was gonna put Shan in a grave of her own," I said, firing up a blunt.

A week later, we were inside a hotel suite in Las Vegas, not far from where Juanita resided. Inez had accompanied me there on the airplane. We stayed up most of the night talking.

In the morning, we rented a car and drove to the address we had for Juanita. On the way to her house, I called to speak with her, but I did not let her know we were in town. I just wanted to make sure she was at home.

I was still on the phone with her when we pulled up to her crib. "I gotta call you back," I said in a hurry and hung up.

Juanita stayed in Summerlin in a large stucco home with a cobble stone driveway. The luxuries my pop's CD royalties provided her were obvious. The lawn was as tight as a fresh hair-cut with a sharp razor line. A Benz was parked in the driveway and one of those new Cadillac trucks. I knew that Juanita had become a psychologist and made a sweet check of her own, but intuition told me that what I was looking at came from my pop's dough.

When I made the comment to Inez, she replied, "You damn right. This trick out here ballin' and don't want to do anything for you or his other children. That's what burns me up!"

I had to tell Inez to pipe down as we approached the door. She regained her composure and rang the doorbell with a fake smile plastered across her face. I chuckled at her Dr. Jekyll/ Mrs. Hyde antics because she was looking like a mad-woman moments ago.

Finally, Justice answered the door looking as nerdy as he sounded over the phone. All he was missing was a pair of suspenders. *This little soft looking dude couldn't be my pop's son. We needed to take this shit to the Maury show,* I stood there thinking.

"May I help you?" he asked. He didn't recognize me. We had only met once, right after my pop was executed.

"Sup, lil' nigga? I'm Lil T, your brother."

He looked at me with nothing in his eyes. There was no bond between us.

"Mom, Little T and some woman is at the door," he called to Juanita. She came to the door right away.

Instantly, I knew how she caught my pop's eye. Her appearance screamed Basketball Wives.

"Terrence Junior, what on earth are you doing way out here? Inez, is he running from the police" she asked, looking alarmed.

"No, he's not. May we come inside?" Inez scoffed.

"Yes, but I'm afraid you can't stay long. I was about to go to the gym with a friend." She stepped aside and let us in.

Justice was watching me like he thought I might steal something.

The interior of the house was as impressive as the outside. The furniture looked rich and shiny and the floors were polished like glass. On the walls, I saw framed pictures of Juanita and Justice, but not a single picture of my pop. My nose flared.

"Have a seat," offered Juanita.

Inez accepted the offer, but I remained standing. I didn't want to sit on that bitch's perfect sofa.

"Mom, would you like me to get tea or maybe bottled water for the guests?" my half-brother asked.

I couldn't help it. I busted out laughing. *What type of dude had Juanita raised?*

"Bruh, loosen up. Pull your pants down and let 'em sag off your ass a little. Your swag is all wrong. Don't you know who our pop was?" I said.

"Pull my pants down like a hoodlum, you mean?"

"I'm sayin', bruh, they're up to your chest." I snickered. "C'mere, let ya big bruh hook you up." I loosened the lil' nigga's belt and adjusted his pants.

"Justice! Pull your pants up on your behind. You're not a thug." Juanita scolded him.

Our pop epitomized a thug. How is she hating on that? I asked myself. And she was from the projects not so long ago. How the fuck did she get all brand new? I could see her wanting the best for Justice, but she was raising a lame. I shook my head.

Justice sat down on the sofa beside Juanita.

"So, what warrants this visit?" she asked looking at the watch on her wrist like she was pressed for time.

I explained our presence.

"Well, if you've managed to lose the ashes of your father that I gave you, why would I give you more? It seems you're not responsible," said Juanita.

"He didn't lose them," Inez said.

"Six in one hand, half a dozen in the other."

"Come off that high horse and speak English!" Inez snapped. "Don't make me pull your card."

"I got this," I said, jumping back in the conversation. "Juanita, I'ma make this short and simple. 'Cause for real, my patience is zero. My pop left you a stupid check and instructed you to take care of his children with it—"

"I will when you demonstrate that you will do the right thing. I've told you this before."

"I'm not demonstrating a damn thing. I don't need you to take care of me. But what about my sisters?"

"I've set up trust funds for each of you."

"Did you set up a trust fund for me when I was in prison and you wouldn't even send me commissary money?" Inez said. "Didn't Youngblood trust you to do that?"

Juanita said nothing.

I cut straight to the chase. "All I want is my pop's ashes. Now, we can do this the simple way or it can get ugly. Don't make me leave here today with your blood all over me."

Juanita seemed to weigh my seriousness and her conclusion saved her life. She went into another room and returned with a black porcelain urn.

"Take it and go! And please stay out of our lives!" she said as she shoved the urn into my hands.

I grilled her, but my mission was complete. Fuck everything else. I locked eyes with Justice, who was about ten or eleven years old.

"It ain't even about you, lil' dude," I said.

At the door, Inez half spun and gave it to Juanita. "Queen Africa, huh? Ain't that the shit you was kicking when Youngblood was alive? You were supposed to keep his tribe together. Didn't you vow to do that? Bitch, you're a fraudulent ass ho, and I never liked you in the first place."

Whop!

She punched Juanita dead in the mouth, knocking her on her high-class ass. "That's for stealing my man. And this is for mistreating his children!" she kicked that bitch in her side.

Juanita grabbed a hold of Inez' leg and pulled her down. They rolled on the floor of the vestibule tearing into each other like two felines, but Juanita was a Persian while Inez was an alley cat.

"Bitch, all I did was fight when I was locked up," Inez said as she got on top of Juanita and pinned her down.

"Get up off of my mother!" cried Justice, trying to intervene.

I snatched his lil' ass up, "Fall back before I make change."

I held him in a firm but non-violent choke hold while Inez punched his bougie mama in the nose several times. When she stood up, Juanita's blood was all over her blouse.

"Don't make me fly back out here to get another piece of your high yellow ass!" Inez huffed.

I let go of Justice and smirked down at Juanita, who had finally gotten the beat down she deserved.

Justice dashed upstairs in a huff. I guessed that his soft ass was going to cry on his pillow or something.

A minute or so later, he returned with a banger in his hand. He pointed it at Inez first and then trained the banger on me.

The little nigga didn't utter a single threat, he just stood there trembling with fury. His eyes were slits and his jaw was set so that his mouth was a tight line. He seemed ready to pop that toolie. I smiled because baby bruh was finally letting his nuts hang. Our pop's blood had risen to the top.

"Justice, you put that gun down, right now!" barked Juanita.

Justice grilled me for a full minute before letting his arm drop to his side. The tension in the room quickly evaporated. Inez looked at Juanita and Juanita lowered her eyes. A fresh ass whooping seemed to soften Juanita's whole attitude.

"I'm sorry that I couldn't remain as strong as you," she blurted out to Inez. "I tried, but holding on to those memories and the love I had for Youngblood was affecting my health. Remember, I was right there when they put him to death." Tears streamed down Juanita's face.

I felt a little sorry for her. She looked at us both with pleading eyes. "If I hadn't let go, the grief would have killed me," she said.

Inez had heard enough, she turned and walked off to the car.

"Lil T, will you please forgive me?" Juanita asked tearfully.

"I'll try." That was the best I could do.

Ca$h

CHAPTER 27

Back in the A, I dropped ninety bands on a new platinum chain and urn. Now my swag felt complete again.

I made my rounds, checking on Eryka, Chante and Tamia. I poured some of our father's ashes into each of their small urns and watched them proudly rock their chains. Now it was back to the streets.

I collected taxes without trouble. By now, all but the most foolish niggas knew it was cheaper to pay me than to bury their whole squads.

I was on Moreland, about to put my press game down on this new spot, when two cars whipped up on me. My banger was out in a flash.

"Nah, homie, it ain't like that. We come in peace. We're Criminal's family."

They stepped out of vehicles empty handed. I kept my eyes on them and saw the GF tats on their faces and I relaxed a bit. Long story short, they wanted to recruit me into the GF to help out in a serious beef they had with a clique of esses-Mexican thugs.

"Real talk, I'll slump an ese on GP. But I can't fuck with your offer right now; I got my own thing going on." I declined.

"I respect that," said the one doing the talking.

I spoke to the one who looked familiar. "What's good, lil' homie? I'm Trouble."

"I know who you are, fam. I went on a lick with you and Criminal. Real recognize real."

"True. Listen, I can't get down with y'all on no clique shit, but if shit gets too hot, hit me up and I'll drop a few of those bitch ass Mexicans. They ain't running the A. They better take that shit back to Cali, Texas or wherever else niggas let 'em regulate. This the Dirty we'll eat their lil' short asses alive."

I gave him my number to lock into his phone. "Real recognize real," I said.

We touched fists and I left there imagining the fierce team GF would be if I joined their ranks. Those thoughts didn't linger long, though.

The next night, I donned a ski mask and kicked in the door of one of Zeke's stash houses I had learned about.

"Oh, Jesus! Please don't hurt me," pleaded the gray haired elderly woman whose face my banger was pointed in. Then she started hyperventilating.

"Calm down, I'm not gonna hurt you unless you force me to. Would you like a glass of water?" I asked.

"Yes, please."

"Where's the kitchen?"

"Back that a way." She pointed.

I had been watching the house for days, so I knew she lived alone. I turned my head in the direction she pointed for a split second; next thing I knew, granny had a .45 shoved into my spine.

"Drop that damn gun or I'll cripple you for life," she threatened. I stalled for a minute. "Drop it!" she hissed.

"No, you drop yours!" Criminal's voice came from behind Grandma.

That distracted her for a pause. I turned, grabbed her wrist and easily wrestled the gun away from her.

"You slick ass, old bitch!" I barked and knocked her on her ass.

Criminal pointed the banger down on granny's head.

"No, bruh!" my voice boomed. "You gotta respect grandma's gangsta." I tossed him the duct tape. "Tape her up so she don't pull nothing else out from under that house coat."

Once granny saw she had no win, she gave us no more problems. We left there with twelve bricks and twelve pounds of Kush, but found no dough.

"Now you see why I watch your back." Criminal pointed out to me. "Grandma almost caught you slippin'."

"Yeah, she did," I said as we split up the lick.

***

I hit Manky with three of the bricks on consignment and sold my other three to Tommy Gun. All of the Kush, besides what I kept for my personal use, went to Inez, free of charge. She had clientele she had been serving for years, dating back to when my pop was alive.

While I was at the house, Fat Stan drove up to pick up Bianca. He didn't come inside. He waited outside in his car. Bianca was in her room getting dressed. Tamia was on the phone with Eryka.

I hopped up and headed for the door.

"Lil T, what are you about to do?" asked Inez, looking alarmed.

"Going to go find out what's on this nigga's mind," I replied. I was out before she could try and stop me.

I saw fear in his eyes when I got to his car. A scared nigga will murk you fast, though. So, I wasn't slippin'. My shit was in my hand, already click-clacked. I wasn't trying to chump the nigga, but neither was I gonna tip toe around him. If he wanted some payback, we could set it off right now.

"You got something you wanna settle with me?" I confronted him, straight up, no chaser.

"Nawl, I just came to take my daughter to get her driver's license. I'm through with all that."

"You sure? 'Cause we can do it here and now and get it over with."

"Like I said, I'm through with it."

I eyeballed the nigga, trying to read him. Something in the way he looked at me told me that the nigga still held animosity, and the shit wasn't over with. But before I could challenge him on it, Bianca came bounding up to his car.

"Hey, Daddy. Sorry to keep you waiting."

She climbed in the car with Fat Stan and they backed out of the driveway and drove off.

Pushing his punk ass out of mind, I went back inside to kick it with Inez and Tamia. We played different games on the Wii until the sun went down. Then Inez made some shrimp fried rice. We ate while watching American Gangster on DVD. In the middle of the movie, we heard a car pull up to the house.

"That's probably Bianca. Tamia, go open the door for your sister," said Inez and Tamia sauntered off.

A burst of gunshots tattered the front door and shattered the picture window. Tamia screamed. I jumped up and tackled her to the floor and then pulled her away from the gunfire.

"Y' all stay down!" I barked as I ran toward the back door.

I hopped down the stairs off of the back porch in one leap. I bent the corner of the house, bustin' off with my toolie at the dark vehicle that had just pulled off. "Nawl, bitch muthafuckas, don't run now!"

Boc! Boc! Boc! Boc! Boc!

I blasted at its taillights.

Once the car was out of sight, I hurried back inside to check on Tamia and Inez. They both were unharmed, but Tamia was crying and she had peed on herself.

"Look, I gotta bounce before the po-po arrive. Don't stay here tonight. Go get a room somewhere and call me and let me know where y'all are," I told Inez.

On my way to my car, I said to myself, "So that's how he wanna play it, huh? Nigga just buried his goddamn self."

If I wasn't living it, I would've sworn it was a movie. Everywhere I went guns went off! Didn't niggas know if they aimed at me and missed, I was coming back at 'em with a vengeance? Didn't they know I go hard in the muthafuckin' paint!

"Yo, what's going on, lil' soldier?" asked Swag, calling from Brooklyn where he had gone to record something for Jigga. I assured him it was nothing that I couldn't handle.

"Just the hand I've been dealt," I added.

"True that. But you can play it how you choose. Can't you see that your luck is beginning to run out? How many more times do you think the bullet will miss you?"

"Fam, I'm synonymous with death." I brushed off the lecture.

"I hear all that slick shit, pimp. And I believe you really don't care nothing about dying young, but others around you might wanna live. What if Inez and Tamia would've caught a bullet? Haven't you learned anything from what happened to Poochie and your sister?" His words hit me like a punch in the face.

"Nigga, you must want me to come through this phone," I shot back.

"Dawg, ain't no bitch in me. I'm just giving it to you raw. What? The truth hurts?"

"I guess it does," I reluctantly admitted before hitting the END button.

I hit Inez up and told her to go house shopping. We argued back and forth because she felt that moving would be allowing someone to make her tuck her tail and run.

"Ain't nobody did that shit but Stan's fat ass," she surmised. "I'm not letting him make me catch out."

So, I knew what had to be done, immediately. Whether Inez was wrong about Fat Stan being involved or not.

The night was quiet and still, but I was out on the prowl. No ski mask. I creeped his fat ass getting out of his Surburban in front of his mama's crib in Oakland City.

"Guess who's behind this tree?" I taunted as I jumped out shoving the sawed off under his chin.

"Lord, have mercy!" He damn near fainted.

"The Lord might have mercy for ya fat ass but I don't," I said. "Watch how high I blow the top of your head."

He would not get a second chance to gun at me.

***

Inez didn't attend Fat Stan's funeral. That caused instant problems between her and Bianca. Compounding the trouble, Fat Stan's mother, was screaming to everyone who would listen, "I know who killed my son."

Detectives snatched Inez up and took her downtown to interrogate her. Tamia called me crying, afraid her mother wasn't going to be released. Ava and I went over there to calm her down. When we arrived, Bianca wouldn't let us in.

"Go away! I know you killed my father!" she screamed at me through the door.

A few seconds later, I heard her and Tamia thumping like cats and dogs. I broke a window, climbed inside and broke them apart. Tamia looked to be the most tore up of the two, but she wanted another piece of her sister's ass. That was our pop's blood in her veins.

Bianca screamed, "I hate all of you!" and ran out the front door. I sent Ava to bring her back, but she could not find her.

Inez returned an hour later and we told her what had happened. "She's probably over his mother's house or with her boyfriend," she guessed. Bianca had started dating a year ago, when she turned sixteen.

Inez called several numbers in search of Bianca, but no one had seen her. Inez wasn't really worried. She said Bianca would come back home when she calmed down. Inez walked us to the car and told me how the detectives tried to press her.

"Do you wanna go back to prison? That's what they kept asking me. I told them that they better check a bitch's file."

"They don't know," I agreed.

"Anyway, I feel like they'll be watching me now. So, you can hook me up with that house."

"I got you. Just let me know when you find one you like." With that, I hugged Inez and told her to get busy with the house search.

"I'm jealous," Ava whined once we were in the car.

I told her I was going to buy her a mansion one day.

"All I need is you," she purred.

"You just want me to hit it," I teased.

"You know me too dang well." She smiled and then sucked her teeth.

A couple hours later, the wail of my cell phone woke me up from the *good pussy* coma I was in. Ava's thigh was draped across my leg, and her head was buried in my chest. Her hand was still wrapped around my dick like it was too precious to let go. I had put it on her ass good last night.

"Hello?" I answered the phone without looking at the number.

"Fam, what's poppin'?"

"Who dis?"

"Criminal, bruh."

"Oh, what it do?"

"Come fuck with me. I got something to tell you. Real talk."

"I'll meet you at Greenbriar," I said.

"That's wassup. One," he agreed.

"One."

I woke Ava up with a kiss, stanking breath and all. She whined about me getting out of bed, but understood once I told her the business.

I hopped in and out the shower in fifteen minutes flat. It was warm outside, beast season, so I just threw on a pair of cargo shorts, T-shirt and some throwback Jordan's and then accentuated my look with my chain, of course.

I had cut off my dreads and rocked a short-faded Mohawk with designs on the sides. That was the style, and although I was skeptical of rocking it at first, a nigga's swag was on a milli when I tried it for myself. I kissed shawdy goodbye, then I bounced.

When I got to Greenbriar, Criminal was already parked where he knew I would come. I wondered what bruh wanted to holla at me about. He got out his ride and slid into the passenger seat of my whip.

"What's it shaking like?" I greeted him.

"'Money, murder and mayhem,'" he proclaimed.

"I'ma bend a few corners while we talk. Is your truck gonna be good right there?" I asked.

"Niggas know better," he stated simply.

I drove off and Criminal started talking. He told me he had heard from a reliable source that two Decatur niggas were running their mouths about throwing Molotov cocktails inside of a house they thought I was in because my whip was parked in the driveway.

"Oh yeah? Who is the niggas?" I insisted on some names.

"Nigga named Crucial from Candler Road. The other nigga is named Juwan, but you don't have to worry about him, I already got at him for you."

"I owe you two for that one. Those niggas burned my grandmother and sister to death in that fire."

"I remember," he murmured in a sympathetic tone. "That's why I wet that nigga's whole chest. Check out today's AJC if you don't believe me."

I didn't respond. My thoughts were on Laquanda and Big Ma suffering in that fire.

"I owe you," I said as I dropped Criminal back off at his truck.

I drove straight to the store up the street and bought that morning's edition of the Atlanta Journal Constitution. I went to the metro section, where I found proof that Juwan Davis had gotten his cap pushed back sometime last night.

I hit Criminal up.

"Sup, fam'?" he answered.

"I forgot to ask you where that nigga Crucial hang out at?"

"On McAfee. He's a tall, red nigga with dreads, drives a black old school Camaro or a two-door Caddy with the brains blew out," he concluded, meaning the Cadillac was a drop top.

"Thanks, bruh," I said before I hung up.

I shoved my phone down in my pocket and thought about murking Crucial in a manner just as heartless as he had murdered my Big Ma and Laquanda. Tears welled up in my eyes as I imagined how they had suffered in that fire.

Crucial was gonna suffer, too.

CHAPTER 28

The murder of Crucial's mans must've alerted him that he was next. For more than a month, I stalked the nigga's hood and every spot he was known to frequent, but he could not be found. Mad niggas knew who he was, and that he pumped work for Zeke, but they did not know where he had gotten ghost to. The spot where he usually pumped was being overseen by someone in his place. It mattered none to me, I was closing that bitch down. I caught one of Zeke's workers making a drop to the house and did him real dirty.

A night later, I hit a spot of Zeke's on Hollywood Road. That same weekend, I followed two other workers to the Chinese restaurant on Jonesboro Road and left them nodded in their truck. I was on a roll.

I found out that one of the top niggas in Zeke's clique was Nafi, a young head banger about my age, whom I had went to school with. I knew Nafi's people real well. I got the word to Nafi, through his cousin, that I needed to holla at him ASAP.

Two days later, we sat across from each other at a table at the Waffle House on Moreland Avenue. I was facing the window, though Criminal had the parking lot covered. Wearing a burgundy and black kufi, Nafi nodded his head in greeting, "Asalaam Alaikum."

"Alaikum As-Salaam." I paid my respect to his faith.

"My dude, Trouble. How have you been? Besides being a hot boy?"

"I'm gucci. What about you, ock?"

"Just been tryna get mine and get out," he said.

"I feel you. So, let me give it to you straight: Me and your connect got a big problem with each other."

"Yeah, I heard. But what that got to do with me?"

"The same thing it had to do with Big Ma and my sister, Laquanda!"

He looked at me strangely, confused by my statement.

"I'm missing the connection, T. Maybe I'm slow. Spell it out to me so I'll understand. 'Cause right now I'm lost."

"Zeke sent the niggas who burned down my grandmother's house and killed Big Ma and my lil' sis."

Nafi's eyes got wide. "'You sure about that?" he asked.

I told him about the voice mail Zeke left on my phone after the fire. He let out a long whistle.

"I wouldn't wanna be Zeke," he said, correctly reading that *kill or be killed* look in my eyes.

"Nawl, you sho' wouldn't. And you don't wanna be on his team, either. 'Cause my gun don't discriminate. If I gotta murk a hundred pawns to get to the king, that's how it's going down. That nigga touched people that I loved. I'll never rest until they play that organ for his bitch ass."

"Homie, I don't have beef with you. True, Zeke put me on my feet when I came home from a bid, but we're not tight like that. I'ma just fall back and get back on my square. Allah will see me through."

We chopped it up for thirty minutes more and then said our good-byes.

"Stay out of this, Nafi," I warned him.

"I will," he swore.

"You heard all of that?" I spoke into the cordless mic that was taped to my chest under my T-shirt.

"I heard it all, bruh," Criminal said from the parking lot.

"So, what you think?"

"Trust no man!"

A few seconds later, I heard the familiar clatter of Criminal's four-fifth. A throng of people rushed out of the Waffle House and gawked down at Nafi's body, allowing me to slip away unnoticed.

The next day, I received an unexpected call from the very mutha-fucka who had sworn he would not fold. I laughed at him when he of-fered peace.

"Youngin', I wanna have a sit down with you and see if we can't end the bloodshed," offered Zeke.

"Nawl, bitch nigga, I don't want no muthafuckin' peace. I want blood! If you want this to end, shoot yourself in the muthafuckin' head and let me read about it in the newspaper."

I hung up and immediately had Ava to have my number changed. Big Ma and Laquanda hadn't lost their lives at the hands of Zeke just for me to settle the beef with a handshake. That had me fucked up.

Rusty ass nigga should've bowed down to my pedigree from the start. Now it was too late.

I went on about my business as usual until Criminal hit me up.

Later that same night, we squashed four Mexicans at an apartment complex on Tara Boulevard. Criminal offered me five bands for rolling with him, but I turned the dough down.

"One hand washes the other," I reminded him.

Problems that I could solve with a bullet was like water off of a duck's ass. It was other shit that twisted my face.

Inez called me sounding down and out about Bianca. Weeks had passed and Bianca still hadn't returned home.

A friend of Bianca's had told Inez that Bianca had hooked up with an older dude who had her stripping in the club, tricking off and popping X. She wasn't my blood sister, but the love I had for Inez extended to her. Plus, I had killed her father, so I felt some pity for the girl. I found out where Bianca danced and went to handle that lil' bit.

When I showed up at Pin Ups, the strip club where Bianca was working under a false ID, she had no holla for me. I looked in her eyes and saw she was zoning.

"Shawdy, on the real, if it was up to me you could shake your ass on stage forever. If you like it, I love it. But this ain't the right way to go about it, and it's tearing Inez apart. Now you can walk up out of here with me on your own, or I'll drag your ass up out of here. You got two minutes to decide." I checked my wrist.

Bianca called my bluff. Clad only in a thong, she stood planted in the same spot. So, I showed her that I didn't issue idle threats. She kicked and screamed as I threw her over my shoulder and headed for the door. Of course, security intervened, telling me to leave her alone. I sat her down and pulled one of the toy cops to the side.

"Bruh, that's my people and she ain't even seventeen years old, too young to be up in this bitch shaking and selling her ass. I'm not no snitch, so you ain't gotta worry about me sending the po-po up in this spot. But peep game, fam. I'm about to tell you some real shit. If you let her back up in here, I'ma murk y'all niggas one at a time until I erase all of y'all. They call me, Trouble. Ask around," I said.

When dude stepped aside, I walked out of the club and looked around for Bianca. She had disappeared.

CHAPTER 29

I guess I should've expected niggas to come at me on some bitch shit. They were scared to get at me themselves, so they did what a coward does. I looked in my rearview mirror and saw detective vehicles close on my bumper. Behind the DTs car was APD. I sensed I was about to get pulled over, and I knew if there was a warrant for my arrest, it would be for more than jaywalking. I hit Ava on the jack and spoke calmly.

"Po-po behind me. I don't know for what but it can't be good news. If this is it, shawdy, stay up."

"Where are you at?" she asked. "I'll meet you."

"Fall back. I got this." I clicked her off before she could protest.

The squad car's flashing lights came on behind me. I ignored them and continued on at a moderate speed, trying to reach a good spot to bounce on 'em or throw down at 'em.

My thoughts then jumped to Ava. I could see my cell phone on the seat between my legs lightning up with missed calls. I knew shawdy was going crazy with worry. I believed if this was the end of the road for me, she would do the right thing with my things that were in her possession.

I slammed on brakes at the intersection of Georgia Avenue and Pryor Road, threw the car in park and was out in a flash, banger backing me up.

With a limp, I dashed through screeching traffic and hit a side street doing a hunnid on foot. My Forces were smoking. A nigga kind of felt punked running with a banger, but common sense overruled my ego and foolish pride in this instance.

I cut through backyards, jumped fences and stepped in dog shit, but I got away with the help of an old black woman who hid me in the trunk of her car and drove me to a motel out on Fulton Industrial.

"I would rather fall dead than see another black person get locked up. My son has been in prison twenty years for some shit he didn't even do," she'd explained before wishing me good luck.

"I'm sorry to hear that. But I appreciate you helping me." I blessed her with five bands and thanked her with a kiss on the cheek.

"I sort of feel like Harriet Tubman," she quipped with a snaggled tooth smile. I laughed, although I didn't know who Harriet Tubman was. "Take care of yourself, son. Don't let these crackers and the Sambo's catch you. Because once they lock you up, they don't like to let you go. My baby, Dexter, has been locked up for twenty-seven years. Now you know that's a shame. I don't care what a man did wrong, twenty-seven years is long enough." I went into my pocket and gave her another two hundred dollars.

"Send that to your son for me." Tears trickled down her wrinkled, brown face.

For an extra fifty dollars, I was allowed to register a room without presenting my ID. I hit Ava up and told her my whereabouts. Shawdy said she'd be there in twenty minutes. Next, I called Inez and told her the business.

"Let's hope it's not too serious," she said.

"They had a DT with 'em, so that's about a body or armed robbery. Some bitch nigga probably took out a warrant on me, tryna get me off of the streets," I guessed.

I was still on the phone with Inez when I heard a soft knock on the motel room's door. I hung up and let Ava in. She closed the door and rushed into my arms.

"I'm happy to see you, too, shawdy," I teased.

"It's not funny, Trouble. I was scared I might not see you again because I knew you wouldn't go down without a fight. I kept calling and calling and calling you, so I could come wherever they pulled you over and give those bastards the surprise of their lives. But you would not answer the phone." *Whap!* She hauled off and smacked me across the face. "Boy, you had me going crazy!" She broke down crying. I kissed her sweet lips and wiped away her tears with my thumbs. "Make love to me," she whispered.

"A'ight. Let me take a quick shower, I'm sweaty."

"So! I want you inside of me now."

"Sweaty balls and all?"

"Yep. Funky ass nuts and everything." Ava said as she pulled off her shorts. I tried to make love to shawdy, but that's not what she wanted at the time— she wanted to fuck.

She was naked in a flash, and on all fours before I could protest, giving me a hellava pussy shot. She flipped over onto her back once she'd seen me unbuckling my jeans. I went in, ready to give shawdy what she was craving. She pulled me onto her and began kissing my earlobes and whispering to me seductively.

"Pin my legs back and make it hurt so good," she pleaded. "I want to feel it in my stomach."

I pinned her legs back and stepped to my business. "I'ma kill you with this dick," I said, stroking deep and hard.

"Umm! Kill it, baby." I went deeper. "Do you love your pussy? Does it grip your dick tight enough?" she rasped with pleasure.

"Mmm hmm," I grunted.

"Don't ever leave me, Trouble. Promise me you won't leave me," she cried as I banged her back out.

"What if I die, shawdy?"

"I want to die by your side."

"That's this good dick got you talking like that."

"No, it's not. I wouldn't want to live without you. Promise me you'll never go away."

"Stop talking crazy, shawdy. Didn't I tell you from the getty up not to get sprung? Just wrap your legs around my back and enjoy what we have now. Tomorrow ain't promised."

When it was time for me to bust, I pulled out and shot babies all over her stomach. *No more accidents.*

The following Tuesday, Inez found out Bianca, with the help of Fat Stan's mother, had sworn out a warrant accusing me of aggravated assault. *Okay. But why the DTs?* I hired a prominent attorney, Barbara Moon to find out.

"They want to question you about the murder of Stan Montgomery and other murders, including that of an ex-police officer that was killed some months back. These are very serious accusations and I advise you turn yourself in so that we can begin to address them," she said after looking into things on my behalf.

"Am I charged with murder in any of the cases?" I probed.

"No. No murder charges have been filed against you, as we speak."

"Which means that things could change once I'm in custody?" I read between the lines.

"Yes, they could. But I don't expect that they will. I expect that you'll be officially charged and booked on the assault charge. They'll want to question you about the other stuff, but of course, as your attorney I will not allow them to."

"A'ight. Last question. If I turn myself in, will I get a bond?" I asked, because if the answer was *no*, I was hanging up the phone.

"I'm sure the judge will set a bond, but it will be excessive due to the fact that you fled from the police. However, I'll argue that your subsequent surrender mitigates that," she replied in legal jargon.

"What's excessive?"

"Maybe $150,000."

That was peanuts because I would only have to put up ten percent.

"I'll come to your office tomorrow, and we can go from there. But if I don't get a bond, I'm gonna be real pissed off," I said.

"You'll get a bond," she assured me.

"I stayed up all night smoking loud and directing Ava on what to do with my cache of guns, just in case the po-po raided the crib.

When morning came, I surrendered to the muthafucking law.

CHAPTER 30

I was out on bond in three days, I could not believe the lies Bianca had told in the warrant. It was easy to conclude she was also behind the po-po's wanting to question me about Fat Stan's murder. But she could not be guilty of pointing them in my direction for the other murders I was questioned about. That could have only been done by Criminal or Zeke.

I discounted Criminal because he participated in the murders. Also, every single murder they questioned me about was related to Zeke's people.

The nigga popped all that gorilla shit about him regulating the game before I was in diapers and then when my gun got too hot for that ass, he dropped a dime on me.

"I want that ass almost as bad as I want Lonnie's." I said to Criminal.

Feeling the eyes of the law might be on me real strong, Ava and I changed addresses under the cover of nightfall. We now resided in North Druid Hills.

As fate would have it, we were out at the mall shopping for a diamond bracelet for shawdy. When we walked toward the jeweler's stand, a woman in front of us said to the dude she was with.

"Please, Crucial! Baby, I really want those boots." The name meant nothing to Ava, but it meant a lot to me.

"Shawdy, I think that's one of the niggas that bombed Big Ma's house," I whispered.

"How do you know?" she whispered back.

"Hold up." I hit Criminal ASAP. He answered on the third ring.

"What's poppin'?"

"Fam, describe that nigga, Crucial, to me again."

"Tall nigga. Sort of look like Dre 3000 from Outkast, but he's a red nigga."

"A'ight, thanks, bruh." I hung up and dropped back to a distance that wouldn't alert the couple in front of us that they were being followed. Soon, I got a real good look at the dude's face.

"Sorry, Ms. Jackson, I am for real..." I sang to myself.

From that point on, I followed Crucial to a house way out off of Jimmy Carter Boulevard. I never once let him out of my sight.

I didn't smash Crucial that night because I didn't want Ava with me when I did it. I adhered to something I read in the book written by my pop. One of the strategies my pop employed when hunting down an enemy was learning their routine. He did not follow a target for days. He just found out the place they frequented the most and then he waited on them to show up there. That's what I decided to do with Crucial. I counted on him to come back and fuck with shawdy sooner than later, and he did not let me down.

Two weeks later, I went bitch nigga hunting with my Glock .50 in my waist. I stepped out of the shadows of the walkway like the Boogie Man.

"Run, nigga, and I'll blow a hole in your coward ass back!" I snarled in Crucial's ear while digging my banger in his spine.

"I ain't gon' run, man. Please don't shoot me," he pleaded like a bitch.

"You're an arsonist, huh? You killed a grandmother and a young girl. You think that makes you a killa?"

"Man, Juwan did that. I just drove the car. I didn't even wanna do that, but I owed Zeke some money and—"

"Explain yourself to God!" I cut him off with a single shot. He dropped like dead weight, but he was still alive. I wanted him to suffer like Big Ma and Laquanda had.

Without hesitation, I doused him with gasoline until his clothes were soaked. I struck a match and dropped it on the nigga.

Three blocks away, I could still hear his cries.

The body count was approaching a new high in ATL and the year wasn't half over with yet. I had contributed to the statistics a great deal, but I was not the lone beast on the loose.

Mexicans were dropping like flies, which told me that GF was putting in stupid work. Criminal had them all turned way up! Those niggas had the dope game in a chokehold, and not one of them were relinquishing it. Young broads rocked their nigga's GF chains as a status symbol. Any nigga that got caught perpetrating— wearing fake GF chains— got dealt with.

Out of respect to Criminal, I never pressed any of his people.

"Join up with me, Trouble. I'll make you head of this shit along with me," he'd offer every time we talked. But a d-boy I was not.

"Just holla at me when you need a nigga flat lined," I told him.

I knew he didn't really need me to exterminate muthafuckas for him, because he was a killa surrounded by more killas, but my offer stood.

It was hard as hell to believe their numbers had swelled so fast. And Criminal's name was ringing loud. I wasn't on his dick, I simply respected his accomplishment. In return, he respected how I got down for mine.

A couple of weekends later, Ava and I hooked up with him and Hadiya, his new wifey who was from Miami. The four of us played Spades and got blunted.

When Ava wasn't around, Criminal always brought up Kamora's name. I hadn't seen her in months, but he obviously had. Each time he mentioned her, I would change the subject. What I wanted to talk about was whether or not he had GF homies on lock who could do a major thing for me.

"We got GF all throughout the prison system," said Criminal. "What you need done?"

I told him and he let out a slow whistle.

"I'll pay any price. Just name it," I said.

He thought about it for a minute. Then he decided. "A'ight, bruh, let me work on it. It's gonna have to be some real niggas to handle that. It can't be none of those fake niggas who got down for protection on lock."

"Okay, see what you can set up. Bruh, it means everything to me."

"I got you, fam."

I knew his word was platinum. I could hardly wait for Criminal to make it happen.

Ca$h

CHAPTER 31

"Oh, it's gonna happen no matter what I gotta do to make sure that it does. Even if I gotta get cased up myself and finagle my way to Macon State Prison where that bitch nigga is as," I promised Inez.

We were standing over the barbeque grill in her backyard discussing my plans to get at Lonnie. We kept our voices low because people were walking by and milling about.

Inez was having a cookout for Tamia and some friends of hers from school. What started out as a small thing had quickly turned into a block party. Several neighbors had wheeled their grills over to the backyard to help out. I sent one of the neighbors to the store to buy more meat.

"No pork!" said Inez, squinting her eye against the smoke rising up from the pit.

"What about beer?" the man asked.

"You might as well buy some because y'all have just taken over these children's cookout anyway," she replied, feigning an attitude.

I smiled and gave her neighbor money for beer.

"Now I'm going to have to keep a closer eye on these kids. I don't want to send any of them home drunk. Shit, I need a blunt," said Inez.

In a split second, I produced a sandwich bag of that goodness.

"When I get a chance, we'll sneak inside and blow one," she remarked, so I shoved the Kush back in my pocket.

Ava came up behind me and wrapped her arms around my waist. I caught Kamora squinting her eyes at us from across the yard. Her belly was huge. I calculated that she was just a few months from having the baby. I felt mixed emotions, but what was a nigga to do? I couldn't ask Ava not to show any affection in front of Kamora, but inside I didn't wanna hurt shawdy. We were no longer together, but I still cared about her despite how it may have seemed.

Slyly, I removed Ava's arms from around my waist, "Help Inez for a minute, let me go crank some music up."

We had rented an entire DJ hookup, and surprisingly no one had gotten the party popping yet. I went behind the makeshift DJ booth and got it crunk.

As soon as I played Swag's recent single, Tamia's friends started dancing and getting it in. Those little girls were poppin' their asses like a bunch of grown ass strippers. I looked out onto the impromptu dance floor and saw Eryka doing her thing all up on some boy. Yep, I was gonna have to kill a nigga over Hot Mama.

People were playing spades at a card table and dominoes at another.

"Muthafucka you did renege? Why do bastards always have to cheat? Damn, it's only a game," a short, fat chick screamed across the spades table at one of her opponents. Her voice boomed over the music.

Another woman chased behind a toddler in a pissy pamper while trying not to drop the paper plate full of food that was in her hands. Her skirt rode up and gave a quick peek of her ass as she kept running behind the swift toddler and reaching down to snatch him.

Meanwhile, Criminal showed up with two of his homies. He wore Rocawear Jeans, a black T-shirt, and crisp Timbs. His platinum chain with the GF medallion hung down from his neck. The diamonds in the letters sparkled right along with the diamonds in his ears. His mans were shining just as bright.

I came from behind the turntables and greeted them. "Sup, my nigga." I dapped them one by one.

"We're just fallin' through. You know my peoples Shyne and Doom, don't you?" asked Criminal, indicating his homies.

"Yeah, fam, they pulled up on me in traffic one day. I thought some beef was about to cook, but they just wanted to recruit me into y'all's thing."

Shyne, who was brown skinned and diesel, nodded in recollection. Then I recalled he had gone on that Solo thing with us. Doom's attention was on something else entirely. I followed his gaze and realized what had him stuck, better yet who.

"Don't even think about it, bruh. That's my lil' sister and she ain't legal yet." I interrupted Doom's lust.

I was gonna have to make Eryka sit her ass down somewhere. She was attracting too much attention poppin' her fourteen-year-old ass.

Doom shook his head like, "Umph, umph, umph."

I put my hand on his shoulder and warned, "It would get you killed, dawg. So, get your mind right." I softened my words with a smile.

Doom nodded.

He and Shyne went behind the turntables and turned the party up another notch. I went and snatched Eryka away from her little dance partner and roughly pulled her inside of the house.

"Do you always gotta act like your ass is on fire?" I yelled in her face. My forehead was creased.

Eryka threw her hands on her hot ass hips and shot back, "I was only dancing! And anyway, you're not my daddy."

I grabbed ahold of one of her arms and pointed my finger in her face. "Don't get breezy or I'll take that ass home."

"Humph!"

Inez came to Eryka's rescue. Seriously I was two seconds away from going there.

"Lil T, let me talk to her," said Inez gently.

I didn't say shit. I just walked out of the back door and entered the backyard. I found my other sisters, Tamia and Chante amongst a group of girls acting their age. That was a relief because Tamia could get some sizzle in her ass sometimes, too. I shook my head in exasperation, wishing I had all brothers.

Just then, Ava came up to me with a heaping plate of food. "Here you go, daddy. I know you're hungry and this food is the shit," she declared.

I accepted the plate from her, it was stacked with barbequed beef ribs, chicken, potato salad and coleslaw.

"Did they come back with the beer yet?" I asked as I bit into a beef rib.

"Yes, daddy. You want me to bring you a Heineken?"

"Yeah, and twist me up a fat stick of loud it's in my front pocket."

Ava reached in my pocket and retrieved the ounce of good-good. I felt her hand rub my dick.

"Stop being fast before I take you in the house and put a permanent hump in your back," I teased.

"Promises, promises." She stuck her tongue out at me before doing a half pirouette and going to grab my Heineken. I watched her ass as she walked away—that muthafucka was shaped like an upside-down heart. No lie.

Later, I slid up to Kamora while she was engaged in conversation with Criminal. Who seemed to prefer me with Kamora over Ava—not that he had a say in the matter, but from time to time he would plead Kamora's case.

Today, Kamora was glowing. Her face was a little fuller than normal, but her skin was radiant and she just looked pretty as hell. She wore a blue maternity top, blue pants and white and blue sandals. Her nails were long and beautifully painted and her new severely short hair style was banging.

"Let me leave y'all to talk," Criminal said before I could say a word. He winked at Kamora like they had been plotting a conspiracy to get us back together.

Criminal bopped off with half the females with their eyes on his back.

"Sup, shawdy? How you been?" I asked. "Is everything good with the baby?"

"Yes."

"That's what's up. Well do you need anything?"

"No, I'm good. Thank you."

I looked Kamora in the eyes and then took a swig from the bottle of Heineken that was in my hand. I drained the bottle and then tossed it across the fence into the yard next door. I gazed back into Kamora's eyes and asked if she was feeling some kind of way.

"As a matter of fact, I am." Her eyes narrowed and her arms folded across her chest.

"Speak your peace, shawdy," I encouraged her.

"I'm just saying, bae. You just cut a bitch off. Now you're bringing Ava around Inez and them like that's not supposed to hurt my feelings. That shit is not right. I don't care how you spin it. Let me come over here with the next nigga and you would have a real problem with it." Kamora's words spilled out like hot water that had boiled over.

Her eyes were cloudy, but I could not allow myself to be broken down by her tears. No matter what she or Criminal or Inez felt, I wasn't being cold or unfair. When a person broke their word on one thing, they'd break it on another.

"You chose this, shawdy. So, don't try to act like I cut you off for no reason. You know me better than anyone. You know how important a person's word is to me."

"I hate you!" she said and stormed off.

I stood there and measured the sincerity in which Kamora had slung those words at me. Did she really hate me? If so, how far would she go to make me feel her pain? That was something to seriously consider. Now my mood was thrown off. I went and found Ava and we said a quick and unexpected goodbye to everyone.

Heading home, I smoked a blunt and thought about what Kamora had said. Because I believed I knew her heart, and because she was carrying my seed, I decided not to kill her.

Ca$h

CHAPTER 32

"Lay down, daddy, and let me take that bitch off your mind," said Ava in a sultry tone that made the python between my legs jerk its head up. We had just stepped out of the shower and dried each other off.

I lay back on the cool, satin sheets while Ava lit vanilla scented candles and clicked on that old school slow song *Adore* by Prince.

I sparked a blunt and watched Ava go over to the stripper pole she had recently convinced me to have installed in our bedroom.

Light from the candles bounced off of the ceiling and the walls and gave a soft background to the black and gold color scheme of the bedroom.

Until the end of time/I'll be there for you. Prince crooned as Ava grabbed the pole with both arms above her head and pressed her ass up against it, staring into my eyes.

I pulled on the sticky and licked my lips in anticipation that only heightened when I noticed a lollipop in her hand.

Ava kept a big jar of them on the dresser. Ava slid her ass up and down the pole in rhythm with the song. Her firm titties gazed at me from five feet away.

She peeled the wrapper off of the lollipop and ran her tongue all around it as if it was the head of my dick. Then the lollipop disappeared into her mouth and she sucked that muthafucka so erotically I promised myself I was gonna buy a whole case of them.

She brought the lollipop out of her mouth and rubbed it down her neck, down to her perky titties, then she slowly circled her nipples with the candy— one nipple, then the other, never breaking eyes contact.

You own my heart and mind/I truly adore you.

With pretty, little hands, she trailed the lollipop down across her flat tummy and then between her thighs. She let her thighs part and bent her knees just a tad. I pulled hard on the blunt as she glided the lollipop up and down the length of her pussy, still staring into my eyes. She had my attention and that of the fat iron rod between my legs.

Ava pushed the lollipop inside of her pussy and moved it in and out while rotating her hips. A strand of hair fell over her eyes, adding even more sexy to her performance.

"Umm," she moaned as she worked that lollipop deep inside. I sat up in my king-sized bed and placed my back against the black leather and lacquered headboard. My grown man was pointed up at the ceiling.

Now the lollipop was doing its thing on Ava's clit. *"Sssss,"* she moaned, making sticky circles around that sweet sensitive button that was the key to a woman's pleasure.

"Put it in your mouth," I said.

Ava smiled at me sexy as fuck and followed my command. "Yeah, baby girl, suck your juices off that muthafucka." My voice was gruff because my dick was jumping.

I loved it when a shawdy enjoyed tasting herself.

Ava crooked a finger at me, calling me to her in a way reminiscent of that strip tease scene in New Jack City.

But my gangsta was more official that Nino Brown's. I shook my head first and then I shook nine hard inches with a mushroom top at her—and crooked my finger.

Ava walked to the bed with a glint in her eyes like she was about to devour my ass.

She crawled between my knees and whispered, "Hey daddy," speaking to what was about to stretch her jaws. He tapped against her forehead.

I sat the blunt down in an ashtray on the nightstand near the bed and took the lollipop from Ava and put it in my mouth.

"I need something to suck on," she whined and looked up at me and batted her eyes. I guided her mouth to the answer to her dilemma and she took a nigga to paradise.

Twenty minutes later, she found out that my lollipop had cream inside and she swallowed it like warm milk.

Then I laid her down and showed her how I could turn my tongue into a butterfly and make it flap its wings back and forth across her clit.

In less than ten minutes, I was smacking my lips, savoring the taste of her cream.

"Make me cum again," she pleaded, gripping my head with both hands and both knees.

I did what I do like I do it until Ava cried out, "Oh shit! Oh shit! *Ssss!"*

198

I came up and stuck my tongue in her mouth. She sucked on it like it was a cherry drop. I had to pull back before she sucked it clear out of my mouth because my fingers in her pussy had her going through some thangs.

"Dick," she uttered.

"Huh?" I was fucking with her.

"Dick, nigga!"

"Beg for it," I demanded as I continued to play in sopping wet pussy.

"Please fuck me, Trouble. Pleaassse."

"I'ma hook you up."

And my word was bond.

Ca$h

CHAPTER 33

Hadiya invited us to a birthday party she had put together for Criminal. I never liked going out to clubs, but I agreed to go, partly to show love to my nigga, but mostly because I wanted to do something with my shawdy to let her know she was my one and only.

When we stepped out, Ava was killing 'em in a Jessica McIntyre strapless satin dress decorated with zebra print and teal blue trimming. That shit was showing her thighs, which were sexy as hell, and the dress accentuated her shapely figure. She wore teal blue Prada pumps with all of the jewels I blessed her with.

I had just copped a pair of tear drop diamond earrings that blinged in her ears just as brightly as her diamond pendant.

Shawdy was indeed a *five-star* chick. Her naturally long hair was swooped up into a donut on top of her head, with her edges slicked with baby hair. My shawdy knew how to show out, fa sho!

I slapped her round ass, mainly to see how it would bounce in that dress, but also to remind her that she was all mines.

I decided to rock a pair of Evisu jeans with the matching shirt decked in grey, black and royal blue. A pair of Roc Nation gray and royal blue sneakers set my outfit, and of course, I wore my platinum chain and diamond urn. We arrived at the spot, and as I walked toward the entrance, my chain swung from side to side with every step I took.

Criminal's team was stuntin' hard up in the club, popping bottles, passing blunts and being the center of attention. Wiz Khalifa's *Black and Yellow* anthem blared through the speakers, and the GF squad put on. All I could hear was niggas yelling *Black and Yellow*, and all I could see were strips of crime scene tape being waved back and forth. Those niggas weren't just making it rain, they made it pour. They tossed stupid stacks up in the air. And shawdies were pulling out each other's weaves trying to get to that money.

In the middle of the excitement, Criminal stood and bellowed over the music, "Who put this shit together? I did! Who wiped out more Mexicans than Immigration? I did, that's who!" he clowned, mimicking Tony Montana in the movie Scarface.

His dudes went nuts.

"When niggas oppose us, what they get?" he egged them on.

"Black and Yellow, black and yellow!" the clique sang in response and waved crime scene tape over their heads.

"Muthafuckas don't pay us? What they get?"

"Black and yellow, black and yellow," everybody chanted.

"Bitch niggas snitch, they get?"

"Black and yellow, black and yellow!"

"Mob shit—beyatch!" shouted Criminal.

Two of his crewmembers wheeled a huge cake onto the stage where he stood. A voluptuous stripper popped out of the cake wearing nothing but a strip of crime scene tape.

"Black and yellow, black and yellow!" roared through the club.

The stripper put her arms around Criminal's neck and started grinding against him. He poured champagne down her cleavage and then licked her breasts.

"Hadiya is about to catch a case!" Ava whispered.

"Bruh just clowning." I defended my dude, but it did seem disrespectful. "As far as I know, Criminal keeps it funky with shawdy," I told Ava.

"I hope he's not starting to get the big head," Ava stated.

I was wondering the same thing, but I didn't speak on it. My eyes searched for Hadiya and found her with a scowl on her face like stone. I left Ava and pulled up on Hadiya.

"What's up, shawdy? Look it's all fun. You know where Criminal's heart is," I said.

She took a minute to weigh my words and then she replied, "You're right." I saw the anger disappear from her face.

When I got back to Ava, some drunk ass nigga was all over her. He wasn't simply all up in her face, he was all touchy feely and shit.

I saw that she was trying to push dude away, but dude wouldn't fall back. And being the G that I was, I stepped up in his shit aggressive as a mofo.

"Dude, what the fuck is your problem?" I shoved him hard.

The nigga took a wild swing at me and caught me in the eye. As I staggered back, I saw a GF chain dangling around from his neck. Within seconds, I was surrounded by a mob of GF niggas.

"Yo, everybody chill the fuck out!" Criminal's command saved some lives, because I was reaching for my banger.

"Sup, fam'?" he asked.

"I'm gucci. Happy Birthday, my nigga. I'm out." I grabbed Ava's hand and we headed for the exit, steam rising off of my head.

Minutes later, Criminal caught up with us in the parking lot. Somebody must've explained what went down because he had ol' boy with him.

"Apologize to my peep," he ordered.

The dude uttered a drunken apology to us.

"You good with that, fam?" Criminal asked me.

"I'ma holla later," I said. I didn't need another man to straighten my business.

I took Ava home, changed into all black and headed back to the club in a different whip.

I followed dude that disrespected us to some apartments on Cascade Road. How that drunk nigga made it home without wrecking his whip was unbelievable. They say God watches over fools and babies. But I guess dude wasn't either of the two, because his luck vanished the moment he stepped out of his car and staggered up the walkway to the building. I took aim with the yoppa and opened up his back.

"Black and yellow, black and yellow."

The next day, my phone was vibrating off of the dresser with back to back calls from Criminal. I sent him to voice mail a time or two, until it became obvious that he wasn't gonna give up.

"Fam, I asked you last night if my people's apology was good enough," he roared when I answered.

"And I didn't answer, did I?" the line went quiet.

After about thirty seconds, he said, "So you just get at my people without clearing it with me first, huh?"

I kind of laughed. "Would you have told me it was okay to smash your comrade?"

"Hell no! The nigga was drunk when he did that stupid shit last night."

"It's all good now. Maybe in his next life, he'll know better," I replied.

"It's like that? Dayum, fam, I thought we were better than that."

"That wasn't about you, bruh. But I understand if you feel obligated to ride for one of yours. I'm not saying I want beef with you, 'cause it's not like that. You know I got mad respect and love for you, and I know you do real nigga shit. To be a young general, you the best that ever done it— I tip my hat to you. But at that same time, I'm not no peon. Ya man violated the wrong nigga and he paid for it."

We debated back and forth until the verbal altercation became intense. "Yo, this ain't what you want," said Criminal.

"Fam, I'm not about to pack up and move," I declared.

The phone went dead. My battery wasn't low and the call hadn't dropped, so I understood what that meant.

Ava was wide-awake at this point.

"Trouble, can I say something without making you feel that I'm taking Criminal's side against you?"

"Ain't nothing to say."

"Now you're letting your arrogance take over. I'm calling Inez," she said in frustration.

"Shawdy, you can call President Obama if you want to. It ain't gonna change shit," I huffed.

A lesser nigga than myself might've been shook with all the beefs coming my way, but not the eldest son of Youngblood. It didn't matter to me how long or formidable my list of adversaries became. The way I saw it, we all were living on borrowed time.

Criminal was my nigga, but if he chose to take it there, I would have blood on every GF medallion in the A.

CHAPTER 34

I continued to move around the city without fear. Taxes still had to be collected and mouths still had to be fed. I ran up in a d-boy's spot and touched him for fifteen bricks and thirty bands. I did him dirty, but not filthy, leaving twenty bands in his safe for his family to bury him with. I was stacking so many bodies and creating so many enemies, paranoia began to set in. Every car that pulled up close to mine almost got sprayed with my yoppa.

Ava sensed I was a ticking time bomb. To ease the rumbling volcano threatening to erupt from within me, she hurriedly arranged a week's vacation in the Bahamas.

I sensed she was up to some slick shit, too, by the way she was acting. She was whispering to someone on the phone and pressing me very hard to take the vacation.

"What you up to, shawdy?" I questioned her.

She feigned innocence.

I guessed whatever it was, Inez was in on it, but I never would've expected the surprise that awaited me when we arrived at the resort in the Bahamas: Vacationing on the same resort where Criminal and Hadiya were.

Hadiya had duped her man, too. I saw the surprise on his face when we encountered each other at the pool. Neither of us spoke, but our shawdies' conniving asses greeted each other with a warm hug. I frowned at Ava and went back to the bungalow and began packing. Ava blocked the doorway, to prevent me from leaving out.

"Move, shawdy. I'm not bullshittin'!" I said.

"Hhmph and neither and am I! Yo ass is staying!" she shot back. Her arms were folded across her chest in defense. "The only way you're leaving is to go through me!"

I grilled her for a second or two and then I dropped my luggage on the floor and sat down on the bed. To relax my mind, I fired up one of the blunts Ava had smuggled on the plane inside a balloon that was tucked inside of her kitty.

I ignored her as she left out of the bungalow. A few minutes later, she returned with Hadiya and Criminal. The look on his face told me his girl either dragged him to our bungalow or threatened to put a padlock on the goodies if he refused to come.

"Hi, Trouble," Hadiya spoke with that sister-girl attitude. Shawdy was fine as hell, and just like my shawdy, her attitude was not to be fucked with. She stood with one hand on her hip and flung the other around as she spoke. I found it amusing.

"Me and Ava are going to leave you and this stubborn man of mines to talk like men. Whatever you all's disagreement is, it can be worked out." She turned to my girl. "Come on, Ava, let's go back to the pool." Hadiya eyeballed Criminal and then walked out of the bungalow.

Ava bent down toward my lips for a kiss. I turned my head and it landed on my cheek. "Swallow a little bit of your pride, baby. Do it for me," she whispered in my ear and then exited behind Criminal's woman.

I hit the blunt again and then offered it to bruh. He accepted it. "So where do we go from here, fam?" I spoke first, attempting to feel him out.

He sat on the silk covered chair, across from where I sat. Criminal crossed his leg over the other and made a steeple under his chin with his hands. *A young Don*, I thought to myself.

"Before I answer that, let me tell you something about the nigga you killed. He put in a lot of work for the team when we beefed with the esses. Fam really couldn't hold his liquor but when sober, he was a good nigga. My dudes wanna ride for their brother, but I won't let them. And I haven't told any of them that you killed him, but they suspect it."

"I ain't never scared," I retorted.

"Don't you think I know that? Nigga, we're cut from the same cloth. But, bruh, you was wrong. Dead ass." I saw a tear trickle down his face.

Yep gangstas do cry, I was reminded.

The raw hurt he displayed did not lessen my respect for him. The tears were for the frustration it caused him to let the murder of one of his comrades go unpunished.

"Man, you put me in a fucked up position. But my word is law with my team, and I already told them they can't come after you. I'ma just charge that one to my heart," he stated, letting out a sigh. "I'ma tell you something that only a few people know. I get my work from your people now."

"My people? Who you talkin' about?" I asked, confused and wondering what it had to do with anything.

"Swag. That's who supplies me now. I know that you're like a son to him, so that's another reason besides the hood respect I have for you, that I don't want no drama."

I smirked. "You lying! Damn, I didn't know Swag still fucked with the streets."

"You still don't know it," said Criminal. He didn't have to spell it out. My lips were sealed.

Understanding that we had another bond, we made peace between us with a gangsta hug. With the discord between Criminal and I squashed, we both were looking forward to enjoying the Islands with our girls and with each other. But the lives he and I lived seemed not to allow a moment of peace for too long .

Lounging in my hotel suite, smoking sticks of loud while Ava and Hadiya went shopping, spending bands of our blood money, I listened to Criminal tell me about his ongoing war with the esses.

"I thought they had folded their hands," I cut in.

"Nawl, bruh, those muthafuckas are like roaches— you kill ten and there's a hundred more. Madda fact, I don't feel right lamping in the Bahamas while shit is still going down back in the A."

"Understood."

"Hold up, bruh, let me hit my niggas up and make sure everything is gucci." He had been calling back checking on his crew a dozen times a day for the past two days.

"Mob shit," he said, greeting whoever answered on the other end. He held the phone to his ear and listened for about ten minutes and didn't utter another word until he said, "I'm on my way back. Y' all stand down until I get there. One."

All of a sudden Criminal hurled the cell phone against the wall. "Fuck! Fuck! Fuck!" he howled. Pain like no other was etched on his face.

"What happened, bruh?"

"Some wetbacks snatched up Doom, Shyne and Shyne's baby mama!"

I knew what that meant because esses didn't snatch muthafuckas up to talk. But I had to ask anyway. "Did they kill them?"

Criminal's head dropped. "Yeah, bruh, and they tortured them," he said in a voice that cracked.

"You know I'm on deck, if you need me."

Criminal was too distraught to reply. I knew what he was feeling. The game of money and murder was a cold ass bitch when it was time to bury one of yours.

The flight back home was somber and quiet.

CHAPTER 35

Back in the A, the temperatures was hot. And so were the streets. Criminal buried his fallen soldiers and then he made whoever got paid to ship dead Mexicans back home for burials rich. Mob shit had the city turned up. The streets said the Feds had been called in, so that quieted down everybody's guns for a minute.

With things on the hush, I spent the next few weeks kickin' it with Inez, Ava and my sisters. Inez' oldest daughter, Bianca, still hadn't returned home, but she was no longer out there headed for destruction.

Now Bianca was back living with Inez' mother who had primarily raised her anyway.

That same week, Inez and I took my sisters to see Grandma Ann at the mental facility. As soon as the nursing assistants brought her out to the picnic area where we were seated, it was apparent she was getting better. Her eyes looked clearer than they had been in a long time, and her face wasn't as swollen from the medication as it had been at the previous facility.

"Ms. Ann, your grandson and some other family members are here to see you. Here, let me help you sit down," said the plump woman who'd brought her out.

"Chile, I can sit down on my own," insisted Grandma.

The nurse continued helping Grandma Ann until she was properly seated. Then she smiled and left us alone. "Hi, Grandma, look who I brought to see you," I said.

Inez, Tamia, Chante and Eryka were standing on each side of me. She looked curiously, as if searching her memory for recognition. She must have drawn a blank because her brows furrowed.

"I'm Lil T, Grandma. Uh, Youngblood's son," I said, trying to jog her memory. "And these are his daughters, Tamia, Chante and Eryka. And this is Tamia's mother, Inez, who was your son's girlfriend."

"His girlfriend? Shan? Get her away from me!" she suddenly cried out and moaned with a pain that seemed to come from way deep down in her soul. I reached for her hand and held it in mine.

"No, Grandma, that's not Shan. That's Inez, she really loved my father," I said.

She stared at Inez while mouthing her name several times. Then something clicked, because she smiled and said to Inez, "Hi, sweetie. Where have you been? Why isn't my son with you? Is he still upset with me?" She was better, but still not well.

"No, he is not," replied Inez, fighting back tears.

"Well, you tell him to come sit with his mother for a while. You hear me?"

"Yes ma'am." Now Inez had tears streaming down her face. I could tell she tried to keep them from falling, yet they managed to slip out.

"Chile, stop that crying. And who are these pretty girls?"

I reintroduced my sisters one by one. "Oh, my! Terrence certainly has been a busy boy," she remarked.

Everybody cracked up.

"Where's Toi? Why didn't she come?" asked Grandma.

Nobody said a word.

"I want my Toi and I want Terrance. Bring my babies to me. Bring my babies to me! Bring my babies to me!" she cried.

I wrapped my arms around her and held her while she cried against my chest. I looked up and there wasn't a dry eye in our gathering, including my own.

CHAPTER 36

It took a week, a quarter pound of Kush and a half dozen boxes of Swisher Sweets to get my head back right after the heart-wrenching visit with Grandma Ann. I could see she was progressing some at the new facility, but it wasn't enough. I resigned myself to get her the best psychological care in the country, if I had to jack every hustla in Fulton County to pay for it.

I pulled on my fitted and checked my profile in the mirror. "Shawdy, hand me the Visine," I said to Ava. "Jay-Z wasn't lying when he said that stress will give a young nigga an old face."

"Boy, you don't look old, at all." She assuaged my ego. She applied the eye drops to my eyes and punctuated her tenderness with a kiss, leaving a trace of strawberry lip-gloss on my lips. I licked it off and squeezed her booty. "Don't start nothing you don't want to finish," she moaned sexily.

Shawdy was always tryna seduce a nigga when I was trying to roll out. The sultriness of her tone told me she wasn't kidding. I promised to give her a tune up when we returned from the park.

The whole hood attended a function at Grant Park to raise money to build an after-school youth center. I held my shawdy's hand as we went from booth to booth checking out what they were selling. As usual, I was strapped because I still felt uncomfortable amongst a large crowd of people, any of whom could be the enemy.

I ran into mad niggas who paid me taxes. I wasn't stressing them. Had they wanted to get at me, why choose a public place where there were hundreds of witnesses and dozens of po-po's?

Criminal and them came through stuntin' hard in Coogi gear and dumb jewels. Hadiya was not on his arm. She seldom rolled with him when his swag was on public display. He noticed Ava and me and came over to holla. His entire crew followed.

We hollered briefly and then pushed on. I caught the lingering hard stares of two or three of his comrades as they walked away. The look I returned should've let them know that they could get served, too.

At a barbeque stand, I ran into a lady who looked at me curiously and asked, "What's your daddy's name?"

"Youngblood. Why?"

"Wow! You look like he spit you out his mouth! Don't he, girl?" she asked the woman with her.

"He sure do. Your daddy was the livest muthafucka I ever met."

"Humph. And he had some good dick, too! I only got it once, but I remember it like it was yesterday. Woo, that nigga tore this cootie mama up!"

I spit out the soda I was drinking.

"Fiona, you ought to be ashamed of yourself!" exclaimed her friend.

Fiona? I tried to recall the name from my pop's book, but I drew a blank. My nigga had good taste, though. She was a fly broad and thick as hell, too. She reminded me of Lisa Raye in the face, and when she walked away, I could see she damn sure had a body like her, too.

After they left, Ava and I made our way through a throng of teenagers to the front of the stage that had been set up. Local, amateur rappers were entertaining the spectators. A few of the niggas were nice, but a chick named LaLa ate 'em up.

As the sun dimmed, a buzz floated through the crowd. Then a slow procession of SUV limos made a path through the sea of bodies all the way up to the stage. Screams filled the air when Swag and his entourage stepped out of the vehicle and climbed up on the stage.

He grabbed the mic and announced, "Anybody seen TI? When you do see Tip, tell him that I'm the muthafuckin' new King of the South!"

The spotlight that shined on Swag slowly moved to one of the tinted SUV's. The doors swung open and four big niggas stepped out. The self-proclaimed Grand Hustla himself, stepped out next and climbed up on the hood of the stretch limo.

"Nigga, it ain't but one King of the South! You tryna jack my title?" TI said into the mic he held.

The crowed went ape shit!

TI and Swag battled back and forth for an hour. It was a lyrical heavyweight fight that left both opponents spent. The crowd roared its respect for both rappers' freestyle mastery.

Then, TI, the city's prodigal son, took over the show. Swag noticed shawdy and me in the front row and sent two bodyguards to invite us on stage. I wasn't one to bask in another's nigga's glow, but I went onstage so I could tell Swag that everything was gucci with us.

Ava remained in the crowd. I climbed on stage, walked over to the side where Swag stood amongst his mans, and we embraced.

"Sup, fam'? You clowned on the mic. That shit you said about TI's girl, Tiny, stupid slick." I congratulated him. I knew it had all been in fun because TI and Swag fucked with each other.

"Yeah, I ate his ass up with that one. But Tip knows he's my nigga. Just like you are. I'll always fuck with you the long way."

"That's what's up. Just don't try to change me, unc. I'm on a mission that can't be stopped. Real talk, I been living gully ever since they stuck that needle in my pop's arm."

"It's all love," he replied. "Fuck with ya boy. Why don't you and your girl hang out with us tonight?"

"Nawl, fam', I promised shawdy some one on one time tonight. I'ma get with you next time you're in the A. I just wanted to square things away with us in case it's the last time I see you, my nigga."

"Man, what you talkin' about?"

"I'm just saying, fam— you never know. Niggas die and get cased up in these streets every day. You never when it's your time."

"Is that really all it is? Or is it something deeper? 'Cause if you got beef out here that's hot like that, I got goons who move on my command. Just say the word, nephew, and they'll ride down and dirty with you," offered Swag.

I knew he wasn't frontin', in his entourage were killas and thugs. I could do nothing but salute that. I gave him a gangsta hug and hopped off stage.

Ava and I weaved through the crowd, making our way back to the well-lit parking lot. There, we bumped into the last person I wanted to see.

"My baby!" she cried. Then she smiled, showing a bare front grill. Besides her mouth, she didn't look as tore up as I expected her to look, but her head was shaved as bald as a baby's ass and she was very thin. Some old-school nigga was with her.

Shan reached out to hug me, like we were good with each other, when we weren't. I stepped back.

"Lil T, please. I've been trying to find you so we can fix our relationship. You're all I have left now. Mama's gone, Laquanda's gone—"

"My pop is gone. Don't forget that!" I reminded her.

"I know, and I'm sorry for what I've done. If I could go back and change things, God knows I would." She sobbed over the music that thundered out to where we stood.

I felt no pity. "But you can't change shit. You can't take back the phone call you made. Because of your trife ass, this is all that's left of a good nigga!" I lifted the urn around my neck and pushed it into her face.

She wept. "Please find it in your heart to forgive me."

"What? I should spit in your face!" I blared.

"No, baby, she's still your mother! You don't have to like the things she's done, but respect her! Don't do that to her!" Ava begged me.

"Lil T, I wasn't in my right mind back then. You don't understand, I loved your father. But the more he rejected me, the more that love turned into hate."

"Miss me with that fuck shit. You fucked his partna. He should've murked ya ass. And what about Laquanda? Were you in your right mind the night you tried to prostitute her for a muthafuckin' rock? Get out of my face before I thrash your trifling ass!"

"Youngin, don't talk to your mother like that. She's already going through enough," old school said and stepped into some shit that wasn't his business.

My banger came out instantly. "Nigga, stay the fuck out of mine!" I pointed it in his face. He threw up his hands in surrender. "Step, nigga!" I slapped him in the head with the banger and he ran off in the other direction.

"Let's bounce, shawdy. I get sick every time the gutter snipe is in my presence," I said to Ava while sneering at Shan.

When we turned to walk off, Shan yelled, "Lil T, I'm dying! I have cancer and it's real bad."

I stopped in my tracks and slowly turned around to face her. "It's called Karma. And as far as I'm concerned, you've been dead." I turned and walked to the car without glancing back at her once.

Now my whole mood was thrown off. Ava said nothing as we followed traffic down Boulevard. My mind wasn't on my surroundings, and that's how I almost got caught slippin'."

"Trouble, watch out!" screamed Ava.

I glanced over to see that a car was side by side with us and a nigga was leaning out of the passenger window with a shotgun aimed at me.

Ava snatched me down just as dude let the gun blast. My driver's door window imploded into a thousand pieces of glass. The second *kaboom* peppered the door and then my assailants sped away.

I rose up and flicked the dome light. "Shawdy, you okay?" I looked over in the passenger seat. Blood covered Ava's entire upper body.

"No, I'm going to die," she moaned.

"Nawl, shawdy don't say that. You're a survivor, just hold on to my hand."

Ava gripped my hand. I raced toward the nearest hospital, which was Atlanta Medical Center.

As I glanced over at shawdy, I could see that the shotgun blast had caught her in the neck and upper chest. She was bleeding badly, and the blood was pouring out alarmingly fast. Her grip was weakening on my hand.

"Sol—dier—Boy," she groaned. He was the lick I hit through the stripper chick, Erotica, that Ava arranged that time.

"Soldier Boy?" I repeated, honking my horn to bypass traffic.

Ava nodded her head to confirm that I had heard her correctly.

"I'll get him, shawdy," I promised, but I don't think she heard me because her head went slack and her hand slipped from my grasp.

Ava was pronounced dead upon arrival at Atlanta's Medical Center. I was totally fucked up. Leaving another enemy alive had cost someone else close to me their life.

Death was a bitter pill to swallow when the enemy struck back. To prevent this from happening to yet someone else close to me, it was time to turn all the fuckin' way up.

I buried Ava a week after she died. Inez and my sisters attended the services as well as Criminal and Hadiya.

Before we laid shawdy to rest, we released twenty-two white doves. One for every year of Ava's life. The service was beautiful but heart-wrenching.

Back at the crib I had shared with Ava, memories of shawdy were in every room. I could even smell the scent of her familiar body wash in the air. I knew I could not remain living there for long. The recalls were too intense.

I smoked loud all night and thought about shawdy. In the wee hours of the morning, I strapped up. I knew where to find who I was after. I got in my whip and pushed in an old Lloyd Banks CD, programming it to my favorite track before pulling off.

Nobody here knew that they would die before they awoke/ they probably started out a few days before they were smoked/ out last night high be that murder she wrote...

Ava's absence squeezed my heart. Shawdy was gone. I was gonna miss her like crazy. I blinked back a tear and my pop came to mind.

The smell of my nigga a couple of weeks soften/ I raise hell but I speak softly/ caught in the mix...

My thoughts went from my pop to Swag and Criminal, two niggas who were proving that a few of us kept it all the way one hundred. Both had my back in different ways.

My nigga 'til the end/ fuck the bills, the freaks, the Benz/ let's toast drinks 'Til we die/ roll up the weed blow the smoke in the sky/ da da da...

I knew that with one phone call Criminal would be riding shotgun, but I could handle this on my own.

I pulled into the parking lot of the strip club where Erotica danced at now. It was closing time and customers milled out in groups. I waited until the parking lot was empty except the vehicles that belonged to the dancers and other employees.

A while later, a very familiar looking, dark colored sedan pulled into the parking lot. I strained my memory trying to quickly recall where I had seen that car. Then it hit me, it was the car I had seen screeching away the day Inez' house had gotten sprayed up while I was inside. It was also the same muthafuckin' ride that the shooters were driving when Ava was killed.

Soldier Boy got out of the car and posted up on the front hood waiting for Erotica to come outside, I concluded.

Damn, I had slumped Fat Stan for something he hadn't done. Oh well, he was a hater anyway. Fuck him.

Erotica came out of the club and walked toward Soldier Boy's car. I pounced out of my whip on some *I don't give a fuck* shit. My banger was down by my side as I crossed the street ready to take it back to the Wild, Wild West!

Soldier's Boy's street instincts were fine-tuned. He sensed danger before I could get up on him, and his hand shot to his waist as we glared at each other from about thirty feet. Just then, a police cruiser pulled into the lot. I smoothly kept my Glock hidden from the po-po's view. Soldier Boy eased his hand away from his waist, put his fingers to his lips and blew me the kiss of death.

"Another place, another time," I said.

Ca$h

CHAPTER 37

As the book was closed on one life precious to me, another began. A month after I buried Ava, Kamora gave birth to a healthy baby boy. When I arrived at the hospital, Criminal met me in the waiting room.

I was surprised he was there but he explained, "Kamora called me because your new number isn't programmed into her phone. Inez was with her during delivery."

I gave him a gangsta hug. "Thanks, bruh. You go above and beyond for a nigga and I'll never forget it."

"Don't get all mushy, nigga," he exclaimed.

A nurse pointed me to Kamora's room. I went in and found Inez at her bedside.

"Congratulations!" Inez beamed, passing me a box of Black and Mild.

"Thanks." I hugged her. "Where's my lil' nigga at?"

"The nurse will bring him back shortly. Wait 'til you see him. He looks exactly like you and your daddy."

"Does he?"

"You'll see."

I walked over to Kamora's bed. "Sup? How you feelin'?"

"I'm okay. It wasn't as bad as everyone said it would be, but I'm tired as hell now. What's going on with you?" she asked.

"You know how I do. Ain't nothin' changed but the time and date. I got a whole lot of things for you and the baby out in the car. I'll bring them over when you're released."

"That would be nice."

It felt strange holding a conversation with Kamora in this manner. The distance between us was obvious. I looked down at her and shook my head at what had become of the love we once shared. But I still felt what I felt and I knew deep inside that I was not wrong.

"What do you want me to name him?" she asked, interrupting my thoughts with a foolish question.

"C'mon Kamora, you know I'm giving my son his rightful name. Terrence Whitsmith III. And I'ma call his lil' ass Trey."

The nurse entered the room and handed my son to me. I looked at him closely and it took a nigga's breath away. He was my mirror image. I couldn't stop looking at him.

"This is some amazing shit," I remarked.

"Now, aren't you glad I didn't get an abortion?"

I looked down at Kamora with a frown. The question fucked up the moment. I didn't respond. In fact, I said nothing else to her the rest of the time I was there. I blocked her out and enjoyed the time with my son.

He smiled up at me like he knew who I was. And he gripped my finger tight with his tiny hand.

Two days later, when it was time for Kamora to be discharged, I picked her and Trey up and drove them home. Inez brought my sisters over to see the baby and they took turns holding him.

I was a proud father, despite how I had felt about Kamora's decision. I didn't have to be with her to be a good pop to my son, whom I loved instantly.

But I didn't get to spend much time with my newborn son because a week after he was born, I was on a flight to Virginia. What I was about to do had been put off long enough.

I used the same false name and ID to rent a car and register a motel as I used to purchase the airline ticket.

I used the GPS in the rental to find my way to the address on London Boulevard that was embedded in my mind so deep I could call it off in my sleep.

I had no trouble spotting Delina, that bitch had a recent photo of herself as her profile picture on Facebook.

I watched her for a whole week, getting her routine down to a science. Lying in the hotel room one evening watching CNN, I was shocked to see the top story was about the A. I turned up the volume to see what it was about.

"In the early morning hours, residents of this Atlanta community awoke to a grisly scene. A human head was stuck atop a STOP sign. Police have identified the severed head as that of Alejandro Martinez, a reported drug dealer." I recognized the name as that of the Mexican who supplied cocaine to most of the esses in the A. I shook my head in

amusement. Criminal and 'em had definitely made a statement by pumpkinizing Martinez.

I hit bruh up. "Boy, you're a beast," I said in salutation.

"Niggas better know—this shit right here ain't what they want. I'll turn everyday into Halloween. Ya heard me, fam?"

"Yeah, I heard you, dawg." I chuckled.

"Get at me later. I gotta go slap a nigga around for scratching up my paint when he washed my car this morning."

"A'ight, fool, I'll holla." I laughed.

I hung up from Criminal and dialed Inez. We talked about what had happened without mentioning Criminal's name.

In the end, Inez said, "He's not gonna last like that. Hadiya might as well get ready for those weekend trips to prison to visit him."

"Don't jinx him."

"Hmmph! He's making himself a hot boy."

Hot was definitely an understatement. I could just imagine how hard po-po was gonna come down on the hood, pressing niggas to talk. They wouldn't get much cooperation, though— not with those young GF dudes pumpkinizing muthafuckas.

I said goodbye to Inez and stood in the window of the hotel looking out over downtown Norfolk. Rain came down in sheets, drumming the window pane like a baseline. My first trip to VA wasn't for fun, so I welcomed the storm.

As I moved closer to the window in order to see through the downpour, my pop's urn clinked against the glass, reminding me what I had come to Virginia to do.

Then I heard Big Ma's voice in my head. *Vengeance is mine, said the Lord.* Wrong. I would avenge my father. It is what I had thought about every day for the past seven years. Nothing mattered more to me than that. Not even my own life.

Thunder clapped as I drove through the downtown tunnel headed back to Portsmouth. It took me all of five minutes to take the Effingham exit, make a left and then make a second left onto High Street. I saw the high school, I.C. Norcom, which I used as a landmark to find her house. It was the perfect location for me to park the rental and trek across the boulevard to Delina's.

Her house was on the corner, so it was in my peripheral view.

I parked close to the stadium and then locked the doors as I headed across the street. I didn't even feel the rain soaking my clothes—that's how focused I was as I made my way up the street and into the backyard of the house where she lived.

Having been there a few nights before, I had no trouble finding the basement window I had already broken out and taped up in preparation of what I was about to do.

I removed the tape and reached a gloved hand inside and unlatched the window lock. A minute later, I was in the basement using a pen light to find my way. I climbed some stairs that led up to the kitchen. There, I stood still for a moment and listened. I knew that Delina had a dude, but I had watched him leave for work half an hour ago. I had his routine down pat, too.

The floor squeaked with each step I took in search of the bedroom.

"Yusef, is that you?" I heard her call out. "Did you forget something, baby?" I followed the sound of her voice.

We bumped into each other in the doorway of her bedroom. Delina shrieked. I grabbed her throat and silenced her with a stern threat.

"Make another sound and I'll blow your fucking brains out!" I pushed her back into the bedroom down on the bed and stood over her.

The light from the lamp illuminated my face. She had not seen me in more than ten years, since I was a little boy, sitting in court listening to her rat my pop out, but she recognized me instantly. It was like my face was haunting her dreams.

"You're Youngblood's son," she murmured.

"And, also, his keeper, bitch!" I punched her in the eye.

She put up a fight when I duct taped her hands and mouth, but nothing compared to when I pulled out a syringe. Her eyes bulged out in horror. I sat the syringe down and tied a length of cloth around her arm. A vein popped up. She thrashed and kicked, correctly reading my intentions. I duct taped her ankles together and cracked her across the head with my banger, knocking her unconscious.

I picked the needled back up and twirled it between my thumb and forefinger, smiling manically. Inez had filled it with rat poison before I left the A.

In the hotel room, I had watched a medical instructional DVD numerous times to learn how to accurately inject someone. I did not want to kill the bitch fast. I wanted her sentenced to death by lethal injection— the same punishment her testimony helped my pop receive. I slapped her awake. She could only look up at me out of one eye because the other was swollen shut.

"Didn't you know you would have to pay one day?" I asked calmly as I skeeted a bit of rat poison up in the air to make sure the needle wasn't clogged. "You violated the code of the streets. Had my pop gotten caught first he would've never snitched on you and your rat nigga. He trusted y' all with his life and you betrayed him. For that, I sentence you to death by lethal injection."

I gripped her arm tightly and slid the tip of the needle up under her skin. Blood trickled around the syringe as I pushed it deeper inside of her vein. She fought to keep it out, but I pumped the poison into her arm and watched it slowly take effect.

Her body convulsed and her head whipped from side to side. Muffled cries escaped from around the strip of tape covering her mouth. Her eyes grew big and her chest heaved rapidly.

I felt no remorse as the poison attacked her system, and she lost control of her bowels. It was with a smile that I left the bitch stinkin'.

"For you, pop," I said touching my chain.

Back inside my room at the hotel, I celebrated by sparking a blunt and poppin' a bottle of Ace of Spade. *Pop, it's almost over. I done slumped them all except Lonnie, but I got a plan for that ass, too.*

Only death could stop me.

Ca$h

CHAPTER 38

Inez wanted a blow by blow account of Delina's body's reaction to the poison.

"You're kind of sick in the head. Did you know that?" I half-joked, sitting next to her on the living room sofa.

"No, I'm not. I hope that bitch suffered before she died because what she did was foul," Inez said.

"She suffered— take my word for it," I said.

"No, I want to hear what happened," she demanded.

So, I described every moment from the second I entered the basement window until Delina took her last breath.

Inez' eyes showed that she was pleased. "She got just what that ass deserved. Snitching ass bitch."

"Inez, you're too gangsta." I chuckled. "Now let me tell you something that I've been meaning to tell you for a few weeks."

"You and Kamora are getting back together?" she asked hopefully.

"Nah. It's something altogether different and I'm not sure how you're gonna feel once I tell you."

"Boy, will you quit blabbering and give it to me straight—no chaser."

"A'ight. Fat Stan didn't spray up your crib that day. We were both wrong about that."

"Are you sure?"

"Yep," I replied. Then I told her how I knew for certain.

The implication wasn't lost on her. She said, "I thought for sure he had done it." And just for a split-second I saw a look of regret come across her face and then just as quickly it was gone. "I have to tell you something also," she said, "but you have to promise not to say anything."

"Let me hear it first." I wasn't making any blind promises.

"No. You have to promise; otherwise, I'm not telling you."

"A'ight. I promised." I relented because the suspense was making my head hurt. Then when Inez, told me the business my head was pounding. Inez had taken Eryka to have an abortion.

"Don't you dare question her about it," Inez said.

I covered my face with both hands and fought to control my anger. "Who was she pregnant by? Just tell me the lil' nigga's name," I demanded with a scowl on my face hard enough to shatter glass.

"She won't tell me, and it really doesn't matter now."

"Where's her hot ass?"

"Upstairs asleep and you're not going up there. She already feels bad enough. Shit happens. Look, I'm going to get her on the pill because that grandmother of hers doesn't have a clue. I mean, the way she leaves those girls alone all of the time, it's a wonder both of them don't have two or three babies running around. I'm going to even ask for custody," said Inez.

Tamia and Chante came bouncing down the stairs, so we hushed.

"Hey, bruh-bruh," they both said in unison.

"Hey back. What y' all been up to?"

"Watching movies," said Tamia. She plopped down next to me and hugged my neck.

Chante sat on my lap and bit my nose.

"Oww!" I yelped and feigned a frown. But their affection brightened my mood.

"Ma, what's wrong with Eryka?" Tamia blurted out and a real frown enveloped my face.

Inez hunched her shoulders. "I don't know."

Which she and I knew was a lie.

The next day, I met Criminal at his new house out in Rockdale. The luxuriousness of his five-bedroom, three-level home spoke volumes about how well he was doing. Every room was furnished in expensively fine taste. After showing me around, Criminal led me into the den where Hadiya served us lemon pepper wings and a huge platter of potato skins along with a bowl of Kush and a bottle of Patron. Then she left us to speak privately.

"So, how do you like my spot, bruh? This is a long way from the hood, ain't it?" said Criminal.

"Yeah, it sure is. You got it poppin', fam. Then that joint you did with Swag and TI just dropped and it's raping the charts. Bruh, you gettin' ducats hand over fist."

"I told you I was gonna put the game in a choke hold. Every young nigga in the city wanna be down with GF now because they see we're not bangin', we're gettin' rich. Yet and still it's been proven that we'll escalate the city's body count if niggas wanna take it there."

"Yeah, that was some straight vicious shit y'all did to that Mexican, Martinez. That shit made the world news."

"Yep. If niggas don't bow down, we'll make them famous," boasted Criminal.

I took a second to format my words before verbalizing them. I didn't want my dude to take what I was about to say the wrong way.

"Bruh, I got nothin' but love for you. And I salute your rise to the top, but I wanna see you remain there. Shit like what y'all did to that Mexican will bring the Feds, so turn it down a notch," I advised.

"Bruh, I'm untouchable." He popped his collar, exuding tremendous arrogance.

That shocked me because Criminal had to know that no one was untouchable. In 2003, when we were both just becoming teenagers and were just two little bad ass niggas, BMF had the A on fiyah. Big Meech's name was on the tongues of everyone from middle school on up. No crew had ever done it like BMF before or since. But the Feds smashed them. They took Big Meech and them down hard.

Nobody is untouchable, I thought.

Criminal changed the subject to one that interested me the most. He had located some of his GF homies who were on lock at Macon State Prison with Lonnie. My ears perked up.

"These niggas are straight killas, and all three of them are serving fresh life sentences and won't even be considered for parole for thirty years. So, they don't give a fuck. I'm about to hit one of them up and let you talk to him," said Criminal.

"How are you gonna hit him up?" I asked without thinking.

"Bruh, everybody in the chain gang got contraband cell phones these days. Those niggas are living good in there, fuckin' country ass CO bitches and all type of shit."

"Yeah, I heard."

Criminal called up his people on lock like those niggas were out here on the streets. He spoke to his man for a minute and then passed the phone to me.

"Sup?" I said.

"Sup, bruh-bruh. Since Criminal fuck with you I know you're official. Plus, I got other homies out there who speak good about you. Check this out, that nigga who snitched on your pop was hard to find at first because he don't go by Lonnie anymore. Dude is Muslim now and they call him Hakeem. He's a real quiet dude who hardly talks to anyone. Now I know why."

"Yeah, he's afraid a big ass skeleton might fall out of his mouth."

"I know. I pulled him up on the Internet on my cell phone and found out that what you said is true. He sold your pop out. Don't worry, bruh bruh, we're gonna smash his snitchin' ass for you. The Muslims are gonna be real mad, and they're real strong at this camp, but fuck them. A rat can't hide under a kufi and a prayer rug."

I muttered in agreement.

"We're gonna dead the nigga for you. You have my word on that. Ask Criminal, my word is my bond. They call me Assassin."

"A'ight, fam, what will I need to do for y'all?" I asked because I understood that it would cost a steep price. But I was willing to pay whatever. Lonnie was the last name on the list of those who had betrayed my pop and I wanted him dead.

"Fifty stacks for me. Give it to Criminal, and he'll get it to me. My nigga Third Ward wants twenty bands, and he wants you to cop his mama an Altima. The third nigga that's gonna ride is KK. He also wants twenty bands and he wants you to smash the nigga who put his twin brother in a wheelchair. Criminal knows who the nigga is. Once you handle all of that, have Criminal holla back."

What Assassin and them were asking of me was not a problem. Ducats were no issue, at all, and neither was smashing a nigga. By now killing became second nature to me.

The next day, I brought Criminal ninety stacks. Fifty for Assassin and twenty piece for the other two. Inez took Third Ward's mama to purchase that Altima he wanted her to have. Then with Criminal's help, I went hunting the dude that paralyzed KK's twin brother.

I didn't find him right away, and meanwhile I was also still trying to find Zeke and Soldier Boy. I hadn't forgot about those bitch ass niggas. Big Ma, Laquanda and Ava had not died in vain! But they were nowhere to be found.

My gangsta had sent them into hiding and rumor was they were cliqued up together.

Months passed with no luck on finding either of my preys. I hadn't seen my son in a week because Kamora hadn't been answering my calls. So, I decided to just pop up over there unannounced.

I drove over there planning to surprise her, but the surprise was on me. As I pulled up to the curb in front of her house, she stood in the doorway locked in a deep kiss with a nigga. I scowled and took out my cell phone. I aimed it at them and snapped three pictures. They were so into the kiss they never even noticed me.

"That's why the bitch has been acting so funny style lately," I said to Inez after recounting what I saw.

"Wow!" That's the only response she could think of. "Well, I hate to be the bearer of more foul shit, but this is something that you absolutely need to know." She got up from the kitchen table where we were sitting and went upstairs. A few minutes later, she sat a small notebook-like thing down on the table in front of me.

"What's this?"

"Eryka's diary. She left it over here and curiosity got the best of me," admitted Inez.

She opened Eryka's book of secrets and flipped the pages to what she wanted me to read.

What I read floored me, but I held my cool because in an hour or so I had to go twist a nigga's shit so I needed to be on point. I checked my emotions.

"I'll deal with this soon, and that's on all I love," I said, handing the diary back to Inez. Then I stood up and hugged her goodbye.

I walked out to my truck with a face of granite and heart of stone. I drove over to what used to be Simpson Road and parked across the street from where I was told my target would be. I pushed everything else to the back of my mind and concentrated on tonight's mission. The nigga that had crippled KK's twin had been located.

An hour later, he appeared from inside of the building.

The nigga fit the description that I had been given perfectly. He was tall with a funny shaped head and he wore his hair in a short afro. He was sagging real low, as he walked to his gray Expedition. His jeans were down to his knees and his belt was pulled tight around them. With every step, he had to reach down and hold up his pants. So, there was no way that he could run when I approached him with my banger out.

"This is from KK," I informed him as I opened up his chest with six shots from my nine.

CHAPTER 39

A week later, Criminal called me out to his house. We sat in the den chopping it up. I mostly listened and let Criminal talk. My mind was preoccupied with other things.

"Sup, fam? Why you all silent and shit?" he asked.

"I'm good, bruh. I'm just thinking," I said.

"Well, I got something that'll put a smile on your face. Here, check this out. Assassin and them got that nigga, Lonnie, early this morning and they recorded it and forwarded the video to my phone. Push the play button. Those niggas handled that shit."

He handed me his Android. It was already set to the video. I pressed play and watched a real live murder of a rat.

Three dudes with torn sheets covering their faces entered a cell. One of them shook Lonnie awake. "Get up, nigga! Get the fuck up!" He dragged Lonnie out of his bunk. I could see the fright on his face.

"Asalaam alaikim!" he cried.

"Alaikim my ass. Nigga, Islam can't protect a rat!"

"Yeah, nigga, it's time to pay the piper," added another of the masked attackers.

"Youngblood's son, Lil T, sends his love," the third one taunted and shoved a long shank into Lonnie's chest. He screamed like a bitch.

"Shut up and die, snitch muthafucka!" The three of them stabbed Lonnie over and over again until blood covered the cell. They put the lense right up to his face, so I could see his mouth was slack and his pupils were dilated. He looked dead to me.

The video faded to black. I hit replay and watched Lonnie's bitch ass get smashed four more times.

"Your homies are some real niggas. Do you think they'll get away with it?" I asked as I handed him back his phone.

"It don't even matter to them, bruh. They'll probably never get out anyway. And if so, it would thirty years from now. A nigga can't see that far."

Before I bounced, I had Criminal forward the video to my phone. I planned to watch it with Inez before erasing it.

After Inez watched the video I saw that she was crying.

"Rest in peace now, baby," she said, clutching onto the big urn with my pop's ashes in it.

I hugged her and felt the same relief. I had gotten them all in revenge of my father. "I kept my promise to you, pop. No way could I have stopped until that bitch nigga was dead." I proudly touched my chain.

"What now?" asked Inez.

"I got some other things to handle. Then I'ma put Atlanta in my rearview mirror. Before I do, though, I'ma give you money for Grandma Ann's care and for yourself and my sisters. Because once I do what I gotta do, I'm out. Just remember that I love y'all."

Inez didn't try to talk me out of what she knew I had planned. She understood what principles meant to a real nigga. Because she had loved Youngblood, the realest of the real, and she had nurtured his son to be just as official.

CHAPTER 40

I still hadn't been able to hunt down Zeke and Soldier Boy. If either of them were still in the city, they had fallen all the way back.

I'd gone by the strip club where Erotica had last worked, but she too had gotten ghost. Not being able to hunt down Zeke was tormenting me. That bitch nigga had sent Big Ma and Laquanda to awful deaths— I longed to stand over him and set his body ablaze. Soldier Boy was gonna get got, too. Ava's death would not go unpunished even if it took a lifetime.

If the rumors were true that Zeke and Soldier Boy had joined forces, why were they hiding? Why not come after me with everything they got? I'm just one muthafuckin' nigga. Like Biggie said, "Let's make the beef cook!"

I guess those pussies were afraid of hard dick. Since I couldn't find those two hos, I decided to deal with something just as personal, first.

I knew that after I did this shit I would have to bounce from the A for a while, so I began falling back and spending time with my sisters and with Trey. I didn't let on to Kamora what I had peeped her doing in the doorway that night. Later for that—I had it captured and saved in my phone.

Near the end of August, Shan died from a cancerous brain tumor. "I guess the guilt from what she did to my pops was so strong in her mind that it ate her alive," I said to Inez.

"Are you going to pay for the funeral?" she asked.

"Fuck no! And I'm not attending it either."

I don't know who paid for Shan's funeral, but I suspected that Inez did out of some sense of obligation to Big Ma.

My suspicions were based on hushed phone conversations I observed Inez having over the next few days leading up to the service. I still had no desire to attend Shan's funeral, but somehow, I found myself at the viewing, staring down in the casket into my biological's mother's thin face. The cancer had eaten away at her, and in death, she looked skeletal and much darker than she had been in life.

A wig sat on her head as crooked as a tam. I reached inside the casket and straightened it. I closed my eyes and let our battles play in my mind like an urban movie. So many emotions rose up in my chest at once. Anger. Hate. Disgust. Pity. And finally sorrow.

I recalled earlier times when I was a little boy, before the thing that happened with her and my pop. Back then, I called her Mama, not Shan. Back then, there were trips to the park or a day at the circus. A dollar for ice cream or some change for candy. Kisses on my knee when I had fallen down, scraped it and ran in the house crying. And when a teacher spanked me in the first grade, the woman in the casket had come up to the school the next day and turned that classroom out.

"You had to love me back, then," I whispered to her in a voice strained by years of pain.

I had loved her, too—back then.

I could not forgive all that happened since, but I understood. Shan's anger had been guilt turned inside out and directed against me because I was my father's splitting image. I reached inside of the casket and took her cold, bony hand in mine.

"Rest in peace, Mama." I wanted to cry but a tear would not fall.

Slowly, I lifted my head, shoved my hands down in my pockets and turned and walked out.

***

"It's almost over. I'ma miss the hell out of y'all, but I'll be in touch and I'll be back when the streets calm down. It'll probably be crazy for a year or two, you know how that is," I said to Inez as we stood outside of my truck in her driveway.

Leaves from the big tree that sat in her front yard occasionally blew on us.

"We'll miss you, too. I don't know what I'm going to tell Tamia and them. I know they are going to ask a million and one questions about why you had to go away." She seemed to be on the verge of tears.

"Don't go gettin' soft on me," I kidded and a tear escaped down Inez' face. "C'mon now, it ain't like I'm never coming back, and I'll see you again tonight before I bounce."

"Okay." She dried her eyes with the back of her hands.

I reached inside of the truck and drug out a duffel bag full of money and set it at Inez' feet. "This should take care of y'all."

"Thank you. I love you, Lil T," she said and started crying again. She pulled me into her arms and gave me a motherly hug. Over Inez' shoulder I saw Tamia waving from the doorway. I waved back to her and flashed her a smile.

Inez finally released me and we said goodbye. "I'll be back later tonight, but I won't be staying long." I reminded her.

"Be careful."

"Indeed," I said.

I hopped in my truck and backed out of the driveway. The evening sun was disappearing behind the clouds, darkening the sky into a color of red or what is called *Indian Summer* in the Dirty South. But to me it looked like Heaven was on fire.

Ca$h

CHAPTER 41

As I drove away from Inez' house, Criminal hit me up. I had spoken to him earlier, but he had been in traffic and unable to chop it up long. Mob shit had the streets under its foot and Criminal's name carried the weight of God.

"Bruh, where you been?" asked Criminal as soon as I answered the phone.

"Just laying back, staying in my lane."

"I heard that good shit. But damn, homie, don't turn into no hermit. What you gon' do about Zeke and Soldier Boy? Don't let me find out you giving out passes now."

"Never. Not to them or none other. You know my get down. I just haven't been able to find those bitches."

"Nawl? Well, they're around and they're thick as thieves."

"That's all good. I'ma just put my banger on the shelf and stay out of sight until they think the streets are safe, then I'ma be on their asses like some shit from Friday the 13th."

"Yeah, that's what's up, bruh-bruh. What else is hittin'?" asked Criminal.

"I'm about to bounce out of town for a while and get my head right. You got a pound of loud on deck for me to take with me?"

"Yeah, bruh, that's nothin',"

"Can you meet me over at Kamora's with it? I'm about to go lamp over there with her and my son for a minute."

"I got you, fam'. Give me a couple hours. It's seven thirty now. I'll fall through there no later than ten."

"One," I said and then ended the call.

Kamora was looking good, as usual. Since having the baby six months ago, she had regained her shape and had gotten thicker in all the right places. Her hair was pinned up with two long bangs encasing her face.

I sat in her living room, bouncing Trey on my knee. Kamora sat next to us on the couch, smelling all lovely and shit. We talked about getting back together and about Trey and her going out of town with me.

"I would love for that to happen," she said in a voice that was full of sincerity.

"Me too."

We continued to talk about a future together, and I could tell that she wanted it more than anything. A smile was etched on my face as I listened to her go on and on about recapturing our love.

I nodded my head up and down, in agreement with her, as I kept on bouncing my son on my knee. Eventually, Trey fell asleep and I carried him back to his bedroom and gently laid him in his crib.

Kamora stood behind me with her arms around my waist. "I miss you, bae. I want you to make love to me," she said.

"Later," I promised. "Criminal will be falling through any minute now."

I took her hand and we walked back into the living room. I sat back down on the couch and Kamora took a seat on my lap. She rested her head on my shoulder and wrapped her arms around my neck.

"Bae, can things go back to the they were?" she asked.

"Is that what you want?" I had never mentioned to her what I'd seen. Could I permanently erase that image from my mind? What was up with her and that nigga now?

"Yes, Trouble, I want us to be a family. You, me and Trey. I want that more than I've ever wanted anything. If God would grant me that one blessing, I would never ask Him for anything else."

"That's something to think about," I said.

The doorbell chimed.

"That's probably Criminal," said Kamora. She got up from my lap and went to answer the door.

Criminal came right in and tossed a Ziploc freezer bag full of loud on the coffee table in front of the sofa. I stood up and dapped hands with him. "Sup, fam?"

"Nothin' but Mob shit, running the city like I'm the muthafuckin' mayor." He took his banger out of his waist and placed it on the coffee table. Then he sat down on the sofa and reached for the loud. "This that grown man," he exclaimed.

I sat down next to him and handed him some sticky paper to twist one up. Kamora took a seat in the high back chair across from us and asked Criminal about Hadiya.

"My boo is good. We just found that she's pregnant, so life is sweet."

"Yaay!" cried Kamora. "I'm happy for y'all."

"Congrats, bruh," I chimed in.

"Thanks, and I'll tell Hadiya what you said Kamora." Criminal licked the blunt and then passed it to me to spark.

I hit it once, then I passed it back. It tasted like that sho' nuff. Criminal did his thing and then offered the blunt to Kamora. She waved it off. "I don't smoke anymore," she said.

I raised an eyebrow.

"More for me," quipped Criminal.

I excused myself to go take a piss.

Five minutes later, I returned to the living room, walking behind the sofa and stopping directly behind Criminal, who was texting someone a message.

In the bathroom, I had pulled on a pair of racing gloves. In my hand, was a length of fishing line I had brought along. I wrapped the thin, sturdy cord around Criminal's throat and pulled both ends with all of my might.

His cell phone clattered to the floor, and his hands shot up to his throat. He desperately tried to dig his fingers up under the thin cord that was strangling his bitch ass.

From the chair I heard Kamora gasp loudly.

Criminal was gagging and writhing, and his feet lashed around so violently he kicked over the glass coffee table. I had that death lock on that ass. While I strangled the life out of him, I snarled.

"Bruh, you'sa snake. You fucked my sister and she ain't but fourteen years old. We were supposed to have been better than that."

"Arrggh!" Criminal grunted.

"That was a violation that can't go unpunished." Beads of sweat formed on my forehead as I went down to one knee and pulled on the line with the rage of a bull.

Criminal clawed at my hands, but I felt the fight in him weaken.

"Die, bitch ass nigga. Die!" I gritted and continued strangling him until his whole body went slack.

I stood up. The underarms of my T-shirt was soaked. The length of fishing line had cut into Criminal's throat like a razor. Blood ran down his neck. I walked around the couch and stared at him. His body was slouched and his eyes bulged. His tongue hung out of the side of his mouth in a grotesque fashion. The smell of shit and piss overtook the smell of the loud that lingered in the room.

Oblivious to everything else but Criminal, until now, I turned and looked at Kamora. Her hand was over her mouth, stifling a scream. Her eyes were wide with utter surprise.

"Why?" The question seeped right through her fingers.

"That bitch nigga fucked Eryka and got her pregnant. And it wasn't enough for him to fuck my little fourteen-year-old sister. Nawl, that slimey ass nigga fucked my bitch, too."

Her other hand went over her mouth and she stood up and started to back away.

"Yeah, bitch, I know."

My Glock was in my hand now, aimed between her eyes. Kamora backed into the wall. I placed the banger against her forehead and retrieved my cell phone from my pocket. It was already turned on and the picture I had taken that night of Kamora and Criminal kissing in her doorway was set as my screensaver. It covered the full screen on the phone.

I held it up inches from her face.

Kamora stared at the screen for a minute and then she closed her eyes.

"It—only—happened—once," she claimed as tears of guilt poured down her face. "You were running around with Ava on your arm, treating her like she was a queen—"

"So, fuckin' what, bitch! Ava wasn't your friend. Criminal was my nigga. Wasn't you the one who told me that you would never violate me like my mother did my pop? Didn't you say that real bitches don't fuck their niggas' friends? So, that makes you fake."

Kamora cried out, "What about all of the real shit I did? Doesn't that count for anything? I'm sorry, bae, I truly am."

"Tell it to God."

Boc!

Kamora's head split open like a piñata. Her body slid down the wall leaving a smear of blood. I aimed the banger down at her. "Disloyalty is unforgivable."

Boc! Boc!

I walked back over to Criminal and put two in his head. "The same goes for you," I spat.

I dropped the banger on the floor next to his body. Then I went to get Trey.

Ca$h

CHAPTER 42

"It's over," I told Inez, keeping my voice low so as not to awaken Tamia.

"Both of them?" asked Inez.

"Yep. Now they can be together for eternity."

Inez held Trey across her shoulder. She shook her head.

"Where will you go?" she asked.

"I don't even know yet. I'm a just get in my truck, turn on the music, and let it lead me to wherever." I paused as another thought came to mind. I put a loving hand on her shoulder. "You know the po-po is gonna question you."

"I don't know shit. I was asked by Kamora to babysit. Criminal had enemies. Any one of them could have caught him at Kamora's house and killed them. Don't worry about me, I'm tried, tested and proven."

"I know you are."

Trey stirred and I held out my hand for him. Inez handed him to me and I held him to my chest. "My little nigga," I said. "Never be slimey." I kissed him and gave him back to Inez.

No sense in dragging the goodbyes out. I removed the chain from around my neck and placed it around Trey's.

"Like father, like son." I anointed my seed.

I saw that Inez was about to get all foggy eyed again, and I couldn't deal with all those emotions at the moment. This was why I had chosen to leave without telling my sisters. I just couldn't handle all those tears.

"Take care of my sisters, my seed and yourself, too," I told Inez. "I love you."

"I love you more," she replied.

I stepped out into the moonless night, bopping toward my truck with the weight of so many sins on my back— some justified and some not. On one hand, I had avenged my pop. On the other hand, I had killed callously, and some of my victims had been innocent. What felt like a pang of remorse shot through my chest. I wondered if Big Ma was behind those pearly gates pleading with God to put his hands on me and soften my heart.

Then the rustling movement brought real life back into focus.

Out of the shadows stepped a dark figure. From behind the huge tree appeared another. Zeke and Soldier Boy held shotguns on me. There was no sense in me reaching for my waist because for the first time in years, I was not strapped. I imagined this is how many of my victims had felt.

Helpless.

My heart thumped.

"I told you that I bury little, reckless niggas like you," Zeke bragged. His shotgun was aimed square at my chest.

"It's Judgement Day, youngin'," said Soldier Boy with a wicked grin on his face.

He was right about that, but if these niggas expected to hear me beg for my life, they had the game fucked up. Even unstrapped, I still had the artillery, which was my father's blood, running through my veins. It wasn't that I was not afraid, but courage was being able to stare fear in the face and not back down. The same way my pop faced lethal injection.

I looked from Zeke to Soldier Boy, then back to Zeke. Then I said, "What? Y'all bitch niggas must want an autograph."

I hawked a gob of spit in Zeke's face.

Boom!

My chest filled with buck shots and I slammed into the side of my truck.

Kaboom!

Soldier Boy blasted me in the gut. I slid down the side off of my truck and was twisted on the ground. I faintly heard a scream come from the vicinity of the porch. My mouth quickly filled with blood as more blood leaked out of my body and onto the cold pavement.

"That's—all—y'all—niggas—got?" I mocked my executioners.

Boom!

Everything went dark.

THE END

244

Stay Connected with Us!

Text **LOCKDOWN** to 22828 to stay up-to-date with new releases, sneak peaks, contests and more…

Coming Soon from Lock Down Publications/Ca$h Presents

TORN BETWEEN TWO

By **Coffee**

LAY IT DOWN **III**

By **Jamaica**

BLOOD OF A BOSS **IV**

By **Askari**

BRIDE OF A HUSTLA **III**

By **Destiny Skai**

WHEN A GOOD GIRL GOES BAD **II**

By **Adrienne**

LOVE & CHASIN' PAPER

By **Qay Crockett**

I STILL RIDE FOR MY HITTA

By **Misty Holt**

THE HEART OF A GANGSTA **II**

By **Jerry Jackson**

Available Now

RESTRAING ORDER **I & II**

By **CA$H & Coffee**

LOVE KNOWS NO BOUNDARIES **I, II & III**

By **Coffee**

LAY IT DOWN **I & II**

By **Jamaica**

GANGSTA SHYT **I, II & III**

By **CATO**

PUSH IT TO THE LIMIT

By **Bre' Hayes**

BLOOD OF A BOSS **I, II & III**

By **Askari**

THE STREETS BLEED MURDER **I, II & III**

By **Jerry Jackson**

CUM FOR ME

An **LDP Erotica Collaboration**

BRIDE OF A HUSTLA **I & II**

By **Destiny Skai**

WHEN A GOOD GIRL GOES BAD

By **Adrienne**

A GANGSTER'S REVENGE **I II III & IV**

A SAVAGE LOVE **I & II**

By **Aryanna**

WHAT ABOUT US **I & II**

NEVER LOVE AGAIN

THUG ADDICTION

By **Kim Kaye**

THE KING CARTEL **I, II & III**

By **Frank Gresham**

THESE NIGGAS AIN'T LOYAL **I, II & III**

By **Nikki Tee**

THE ULTIMATE BETRAYAL

By **Phoenix**

DON'T FU#K WITH MY HEART **I & II**

By **Linnea**

BOSS'N UP **I & II**

By **Royal Nicole**

I LOVE YOU TO DEATH

By Destiny J

I RIDE FOR MY HITTA

By **Misty Holt**

BOOKS BY LDP'S CEO, CA$H

TRUST NO MAN

TRUST NO MAN 2

TRUST NO MAN 3

BONDED BY BLOOD

SHORTY GOT A THUG

A DIRTY SOUTH LOVE

THUGS CRY

THUGS CRY 2

TRUST NO BITCH

TRUST NO BITCH 2

TRUST NO BITCH 3

TIL MY CASKET DROPS

RESTRAINING ORDER

RESTRAINING ORDER 2

Coming Soon

THUGS CRY 3

BONDED BY BLOOD 2

BOW DOWN TO MY GANGSTA

TRUST NO BITCH (KIAM & EYEZ' STORY)

Ca$h

CPSIA information can be obtained
at www.ICGtesting.com
Printed in the USA
FSHW021808130221
78479FS